I0677677

THE CHOSEN

Joseph P. Stringer

Vivere Press

Copyright © 2014 Joseph P. Stringer

The Chosen is a work of fiction. Names, characters, places and incidents are either the product of the author's imagination or are used fictitiously. Any resemblance to actual persons, living or dead, events or locales is entirely coincidental.

ISBN: 978-0-9903301-2-7

e book ISBN: 978-0-9903301-3-4

Charleston, South Carolina, USA

Vivere Press

www.chosen4life.org

DEDICATION

For America, the Beautiful.

May God shed His grace on thee.

ACKNOWLEDGMENTS

I first acknowledge Jesus Christ, my Lord and Savior. Without Him, neither this book nor my life would be possible.

Although this is a work of fiction, I used many of my favorite locations. Throughout the book, Cleveland is still rebuilding from the devastation which destroyed half the city. Charleston, Mount Pleasant and Summerville, South Carolina are prominent in this book, though radically changed from the cities I haunt today.

Other locations such as Chrisair, Georgia and Wheaten are products of my imagination. Pulse power and the genetic nano-virus also arose from my feverish dreams. I hope we never see such weapons become reality.

I want to thank my wife, Kathleen, my strongest critic and best fan, for her love, for all that she is and for all her support.

I thank all the men and women of our Armed Services who sacrifice for their country, many of whom gave the ultimate sacrifice. Without the dedication of our service men and women, we would not enjoy the freedom we so readily take for granted. God's blessings to our Army, Navy, Air Force, Marines and Coast Guard.

Lastly, I owe a great debt to our nation. There is no greater nation on earth. In spite of her many faults and the direction we are moving in this country today, I would not want to live anywhere else. May God shed His grace upon her, that we may continue to share in her gifts and that we might realize the bright promise she holds.

The Chosen

Prologue

City of Cleveland, Ohio. Time Traxx
August 9: 9:30 a.m.

James Broddin was chosen. Gem Matthews chose him as the man she would love. Now her lifeless body lay next to him, in front of a cave in Time Traxx studios, a cave with ties reaching back to the ancient past.

Emrys chose him as the man who would wield the Sword of Eden in this era. Now fourteen thousand men lay dead upon the Ravenna battlefield, felled by his hand. Devastation had swept through this city and outward to rend the United States and to plunge the entire world into war.

And James Broddin had chosen. He threw away the one power which might have prevented such things from happening: the Sword of Eden. He rejected the power he had been given. Had he chosen differently, would anything have changed? Was the choice ever truly his own? Or was he simply chosen as a pawn, sacrificed in some eternal war, then discarded upon the field of battle? His mind considered that, worked it endlessly, and drew no conclusion.

2 The Chosen

That he was chosen was a fact. He knew it as completely as life and as certainly as death, the companion he now yearned to meet. Yet, though he desired his death, he did not own the power or the right to choose it. Death, too, would be chosen for him.

As he lay unconscious, close to that longed for death, he dreamed the only dream he ever had: a vision of Gem and him, swinging on a hammock. Children, bathed in every color of the rainbow, laughed and played around them. Love flowed around them with the colors.

They lay smiling at each other. She glowed a vibrant green, the color of Spring's new life. His color shone the warm, blue of the sky on the day Spring bore that new life. Wherever they touched their colored auras entwined to form the purest white, a reflection of the depth of their love.

The dream was both blessing and curse. Blessing because of the great peace it brought. It held such promise. Yet, curse, for Broddin knew with certainty that the promise would never be fulfilled: Gem Matthews was dead. He longed to join her in death, to simply release himself from the threads which kept him chained here. In the depth of his mind, he prayed for God to take him, to give him rest. *"Lord, choose death for me, too."*

Death came to the Ishar Crull. Yet, the demon's death had cost Gem's life. Did God choose Gem's death? Or had she chosen? How could he live with either choice?

James Broddin lay near the death he so wanted. His feverish mind — plagued with doubts and haunted with choices — sought answers which would not come.

The depth of his love for Gem Matthews had filled him beyond any imagining. That very depth now drove the despair pulsing at his mind and heart. His heart kept beating. But his heart's deepest desire was that he *not* be the very thing he had become: Chosen.

One

The White House War Room. August 8: 1500 hours.

Vice President Edward Lee watched the satellite feed of the Cleveland area. The chief of the President's personal guard had called him to the White House. That had been an extraordinary conversation earlier this morning. Guards ushered Lee directly to the war room. Three of the joint chiefs waited with Air Force Major Hap Fullum, who held the "nuclear football" — the case which held the launch codes for nuclear war.

"Hap, what's up? Where's the President?"

"Thank you for coming so quickly, Mr. Vice President. He is resting in the Lincoln bedroom right now, sir." A solemn tone in his voice caught Lee's attention. "Mr. Lee, as of 10:58 this morning, the Secret Service removed the President from the war room and took him to the Lincoln bedroom…for his own protection. He attempted to circumvent the black box fail safe codes to affect an emergency nuclear launch."

The hairs rose on the back of Lee's neck. "Why would he do that? We ascertained this morning that no attack was imminent, that a computer glitch had caused it. Are you telling me he tried to launch a first strike?"

"Yes, sir. He ordered the men to recode to launch missiles on Israel. I hold the codes for launch. Only he and I can launch the missiles, using simultaneous code and key entry. He ordered me to give him the codes. I refused."

Lee went white. "You refused a direct order from the President."

"Yes, sir. I knew that no situation existed which justified his use of the launch codes."

"The implementation of those codes presupposes a war situation. It is not your position to question that direct order."

"No, sir."

"Yet, you took it upon yourself to do so."

"I obey orders, sir, but not blindly."

*   *   *

Three hours later, Vice President Lee thought he had the situation somewhat in control. At least they were responding. An army had marched out of Cleveland headed towards the Ravenna nuclear armory. He refused to bomb them, as the Air Force Chief suggested. "No! I am not going to wipe out two hundred thousand American citizens. Fight a holding action. If they get near the bridges across the Cuyahoga, blow them."

Elite Ranger units were dispatched to secure Cleveland. Navy Seal units were preparing charges at the bridges. For now, it looked like the army had bivouacked for the night.

Lee mulled over the conversation he'd had with Hap Fullum. The Air Force Aide still stood in the corner of the war room, where he'd been directed. "Hap, why did the President target Israel? Do you know?"

"No sir. We were watching the nuclear exchanges unfold. Iran launched four missiles at Israel. Some kind of shield appeared which stopped them. He became infuriated and directed that we fire on them." He hesitated. "He wanted to obliterate them."

"Let me see that video." They brought up the record. Lee watched as the missiles arced toward Israel and was amazed as a shining force-field appeared. The field covered all of Israel, Syria and Egypt. He couldn't comprehend it. He turned to a tech. "Get me the Israeli Prime Minister on a secure line."

While he'd been watching the vidscreen, Gerard Meiring, the President's national security advisor, came and stood next to him. "Sir, before you make that call may I speak to you in private?"

Lee looked at him. "This can't wait?"

"No sir. If you could bear with me a moment, I may be able to enlighten you." He turned and walked toward an inner conference room.

Lee followed, curious. "Gerard, what's so important?"

"Sir, no one else but you must have this knowledge at this point. Only the President and I — and a few other highly vetted personnel — hold this information." He looked at the Vice President for a long time, seemed to consider what to say, then began. "The system you saw in operation in the Israeli theatre? It's a comprehensive power shield system. It's designed to stop any attack, any attempt upon those within it. That system is ours! It's obvious that the Israelis stole the technology, and have spied against us. Who knows their intentions."

"What I can tell you is that we've only been able to devise systems powerful enough to protect enclaves about the size of a large city. They are enormously expensive. We've only been able to provide protection for three dozen of our cities to date. Now the Israelis perfected it and protected their entire political region."

"I think the President feared they would launch a first strike against us since they had played their hand. That hasn't happened yet. If they had been forthcoming, they would have shared the technology. I don't trust the Jews any further than the Russians. Sorry, sir, but that's the reality today."

Lee was getting a headache. "Meiring, what powers these shields? The entire Mideast was blacked out at the time that shield came up."

"I am not authorized to tell you more without the President's specific permission."

"Do I need to remind you that I am the acting President?"

"No sir, you don't need to. What I mean is that I have been sworn directly to President Santiago. Regardless of the change of command, I cannot release such information yet. It's too explosive, too sensitive. That knowledge could destroy the world."

Lee couldn't see the point of arguing now. "There are other issues to handle right now, Meiring. Do you think the President will be capable of making decisions?"

Meiring felt a buzz in his head, one like the President felt earlier. "Yes, sir. I am sure he'll be fit by morning. Meanwhile, an army is marching out of Cleveland, riots and armed insurrection sprung up all over the country, and four states seceded in the last two hours. Our attention must be focused here."

"You're right. Thank you for the confidence. I'll keep this to myself for now. But, if the President does not recover, I'll need all the information about any defensive systems we have, and quickly."

"Yes sir, you'll have it."

Vice President Lee nodded. He turned and walked back into the war room.

Gerard Meiring took his finger off the trigger of the weapon in his pocket. It was much better to persuade and control, than to use force. And Gerard Meiring was a master at control.

Two

Cleveland, Ohio. August 8: 2200 hours.

Just an hour before, the Army Rangers landed at the edge of the city — a place much worse than they imagined. As they entered the city, they could see hundreds of dead bodies on the streets. The wounds didn't look like the typical ones they'd seen in military exchanges. They were more...personal. Men and women had slashed and torn each other apart. One couple killed each other and were frozen in some horrible, savage parody of an embrace.

The residents seemed to have gone crazy. The Rangers heard that someone had released a hallucinogen in the city, but their best sniffers showed nothing. Yet many people wandered around like zombies. IED's were set along the roadsides. One old woman came up to a unit, set herself on fire and threw herself among them.

The Rangers were familiar with these tactics. They'd seen it in many places. This was urban warfare. Standard practice for them. They worked in threes, running point building to building, securing as they went. They worked their way towards the center, fighting street to street with the residents. They tried not to kill too many people, just tried to keep them shut down. They'd been given those orders but really didn't need them. These were *Americans* they were firing on.

The city lay in ruins. The earthquake which hit this morning shouldn't have done this much damage. Buildings were burning, collapsed and in rubble. The east side of Cleveland looked like it had been carpet bombed.

Three Rangers — Aaron Stein, Bob Grey and Ray Bartok — worked a section of the city along Euclid Avenue from the east. Smoke blackened the air. They used their night vision, working toward a building about two blocks ahead they could see wasn't damaged. It looked like a good outpost.

Once, when Grey glanced at the building he caught a glimpse of several children run across the street. He blinked to refocus, but they were gone. "Stein, did you see that?"

"Yeah. Kids. What are they doing out here in the middle of this?"

"They should be on lockdown in their Primary Education Facility."

"Maybe something damaged it and they're trying to find a safe haven. We'll check it out when we get closer."

However, when they reached the building, no children were in sight. They did a complete perimeter sweep, looking for any signs of activity, but there were none. Grey looked worried. "We both saw those kids. Know we did. No sign of tracks or anything. Keep an eye out. I don't trust anyone in this city and

I don't like any loose ends. We've learned those can get you killed."

"I hear ya."

Stein and Grey had worked the terror wars together from Iran to Somalia for fifteen years. The other soldiers said they worked so well together it was like they had one mind. Bartok joined their unit a year ago.

Aaron Stein looked at Grey. "Bob, this looks just like Sudan, remember? This shouldn't be goin' on in America."

Bob Grey's head ached. He'd felt a buzz in his head — insistent and growing — since they landed. "It's war, Aaron. We've seen it before. They said there's an army eighteen miles southeast of here... 200,000 men. Heard that some of the Guard units turned traitor and went over to the enemy, whoever that is. Heard all of Asia went nuclear. They're history. Guess we're lucky they sent us here."

Stein shook his head. "At least they didn't send us to New York! I'd rather take the deadliest duty in Somalia than be a New York City cop."

"Yeah. Feel sorry for those guys. All the age riots, the bombs, the gangs. Heard those cops wear the same gear we do cuz it's so dangerous to work there. Least here, it's just small stuff so far. Still, it *is* just like the Sudan."

"But this is America!"

Grey glanced over at Stein, not smiling. "Yeah, it was."

The buzz increased, intense and insistent.

Whispers invaded their thoughts, grew stronger, demanding, tried to gain purchase. Images came haunting into their minds, unbidden. But, these soldiers were the elite of the Army — dedicated, trained, loyal. They knew the images were false. They did not listen…or most of them didn't.

Bartok welcomed the darkness which came into his mind. He'd never really liked these two. He just didn't trust them. He'd seen them practice their *rituals!* He'd seen Grey make the sign of the cross over some of the dead. And Stein: Bartok had watched him *pray* in secret, saw a Star of David hidden in his clothes. They were *Clingers*, the people who practiced the old superstitions. They weren't even supposed to be in the service if they believed this stuff.

Now, images came into his mind. He *saw* what he thought was the cause of this devastation: *Priests in black robes, mullahs in white ones and rabbis with their weird hats. They lead legions of Clingers out from the city, killing, slashing, destroying, taking virgins, eating flesh, drinking blood! All the horrors he'd heard about over the years now come true.* The darkness refreshed its images, reinforced desires until his head was clouded with its power. *These people were monsters!* And, *the two men with him were just like them.* Rage and disgust welled up within him. He began to turn his weapon toward the other two.

Stein and Grey both felt the demand, heard the whispers. They knew those were lies, but they felt the pressure of the pulse…and an answer from the man who had their back. In the instant that they knew, Bartok unlocked his weapon. Rage showed on his face. As he brought it up and fired, Stein and Grey dove. Years of training had prepared them. As they dove, they fired once. Both slugs hit Bartok dead center and he went down.

All around them, they heard similar exchanges of automatic weapons. Stein looked at his buddy. "What the devil just happened?"

Bob Grey looked sick. "We just killed Bartok. One of our own guys. They'll try us for murder."

"You *know* it was self defense."

"But..."

"But nothin! You felt that pulse just like I did. And somehow, we *knew!* We knew he'd turn on us. Somehow, we knew he was going to do it. Besides, he fired first. We fired back, both at the same time. I'd bet you a year's salary both bullets hit Bartok at the exact instant."

"Yeah? Who'll testify to that for us?"

"Nobody. And from the weapons fire I just heard, it sounds like some of the other guys ran into the same thing we just did. For now, we say nothing!"

They didn't run into much more resistance as they neared the building. They settled down in its entrance to wait for morning. Grey said, "You saw those images too, didn't you?"

"Yeah. They wanted the others to think our people — Christians, Jews or others — did this." He looked around and lowered his voice. "Believers. We know better. No matter what our differences or beliefs, we're Americans. And you and I know our people *never* would do this. But who the devil would? I just can't understand how this happened, here in America."

Grey looked at his buddy and shrugged. "With all the constant small terror hits — bombs in malls, shootings at ball games, an IED here and there, the age wars between young and old for food or medicine — I guess somethin' big like this would happen. Just a matter of time. But, how could somebody raise an *army* here in America and start a full fledged rebellion? The politicians didn't know about it?

"Guess not or we would've been here already. Wonder who they're going to blame for that."

They settled into the doorway of the building to wait for morning light. Grey looked up at a sign, "Time Traxx." He wondered why this building had been spared the destruction. *"What secrets does this place hold?"*

*   *   *

The young boy stood in the shadows of the bombed out building next door. He had watched the two soldiers as they shot their buddy. The boy knew it was self defense, knew why the other soldier had turned his weapon on them. He, too, felt the pulse, saw the images, heard the voice. He ignored it. He was young but he could recognize a lie when he heard it.

The boy stood for a long while watching the

men. He knew they were okay but he wouldn't trust them anyway. They were soldiers. Like cops. He didn't trust any authority. He knew what those in authority did with people like him. He drew further into the shadows and waited. He was chosen to lead his clan. Some whisper on the breeze drew him to this place. To watch.

Three

Atlanta, Georgia. August 9: 5 a.m.

Joe Matthews sat bolt upright in bed, wide awake, his heart pounding. Something beat at his mind. *"Gem."* She was in deep trouble. He could feel it. She was lost, wandering somewhere alone...and in great danger. *"I have to get to her! But where? Cleveland."* Aloud, he said to himself, "What the hell is she doing there?"

The room was freezing, but he didn't mind that. He'd spent the entire day in the heat of the forge, focused only on his work. After that, he welcomed the cold. He looked around. Estelle wasn't in bed. She usually wasn't. *"Probably in saying her prayers."* He shook his head in disgust, got out of bed and threw some clothes on and packed a backpack. He wasn't sure how long it would take to get to Ohio.

He walked through the house, found Estelle at her usual place, kneeling in prayer, lighting candles. "Get up. Gem's in trouble."

"I know."

"We have to get to her. Get up!"

"It's too late. There's nothing besides prayer..."

He yanked her up by her arms and shook her. "Don't give me that crap! She needs us now. Let's go! We've got to get to the train station!"

Estelle Matthews felt the strength of his grip, the fear which fueled him. She looked into his eyes. "Joe, I've told you for years that this day might come. We can't get to her. No time. No way to warn her, help her, aid her...except this way."

"I can't accept that! You can kneel there saying your useless prayers to God. What good has it done? She's in *danger!* I know she is! We have to go to her *now!*"

"This is all I know."

He pushed her away. "I'm going alone then!" He started for the door.

"How do you know?"

"What?"

"How do you know that Gem is in danger? Who told you?"

He stopped. He hadn't thought, had only reacted to something he *knew* with certainty, right down to his bones. "I just know."

Estelle gave him a weary smile. "That's called faith, Joe."

"Whatever." He turned and walked out the door — into a nightmare world. Sirens sounded everywhere, police and army vehicles raced by. The end of the street was blocked. He wasn't going anywhere in the electric car. He pulled out his mountain bike and began to race across the hills, headed to the station.

Estelle watched him go, then turned back to kneel at her prayers. She could feel the tenuous connection to Gem, feel Gem's short breath and the cold which invaded her daughter. She sent prayers out to try to help, to reinforce a deep knowledge Gem held in her heart. "Lord Jesus, I beseech your protection...."

*   *   *

It took two hours for Joe Matthews to reach the station. He had to backtrack, to work around roadblocks and National Guard patrols. *"What the hell is going on?"* He could see troops blocking the entrances. He walked up to one. "I've got to get in. Need to get to Cleveland right away. A train must be leaving soon."

The soldier looked at him. "Buddy, nobody's going anywhere, especially to Cleveland, Ohio. Nobody but troops anyway."

"What are you talking about?"

"Where've you been? There's a national emergency. Some kind of major insurrection. Came out of Cleveland. An army marched out of the city and tried to seize some base near there. Half the city's destroyed. Every train's been commandeered to send troops to reinforce the National Guard and Special Forces sent in last night. You ain't goin' anywhere."

Matthews looked around. "What's that got to do with here?"

"Buddy, you should watch the vid feeds sometime. Every city in America's locked down. We got our own problems here with violence exploding all over town. Murders, fires, bombings. I'm surprised they didn't put a curfew in place."

"You've got to let me in! My daughter's in trouble. She's up there." As he tried to push past the soldier, two others appeared from behind him. They pulled him back and the man at the door trained his weapon on him.

"Sir, you got about 30 seconds to get yer ass outta here. Too much goin' on an' people goin' crazy all over the city. Ah really don' wanna shoot you. G'on now. Git."

Matthews looked at the men. He could see they meant it. He turned, then got on his bike and rode away. *"More than one way to get aboard."* He knew a place just as the trains left the station where he might be able to jump aboard one of the cars. He headed around the area, moving toward that crossroads.

The dawn light had filtered through the clouds a half hour before. He could hear the train power up and start out of the terminal. His mind was distracted, the urgency growing. *". C'mon. Hurry."* He saw the train round the bend and begin to accelerate.   The engine swept past him and he stepped out from the bushes, watching intently for an opening to jump.

As he turned to jump, a vision blasted into his mind, threw him to his knees and tore away his sight from anything else. *He stood in the middle of an immense army of filthy, dark men. He could see that many of them were covered in blood.*

Dark horrifying creatures hovered around the multitude, whispering hate and lust and rage to the army. Joe Matthews put his hands to his ears and tried to block out their words.

*Cold impressed itself upon him and he turned to see his daughter standing right before him, naked. A creature from some nightmare held her. "**Let go of her, you freak!**" His scream was unheard. He tried to move but was frozen in place. He watched as the creature threw Gem aside.*

A man, blazing in a blue color, approached the creature. Five men, bathed in other colors, followed him through the black army. A white form wrapped its power around the man, guarded and matched his every move. An angel!

*The creature and the man began to fight. Gem stood, alone; watching, lost. "Gem! **Gem!**"   She did not turn. The dark army fell upon the other men. Joe Matthews could see the nightmare demons screaming, lashing at the army and pushing it to attack. The dark army fell upon the small shining party with frenzied hate.*

The man in blue knocked the army back with one stroke, then fought on, grew in power, forced the creature back and cut it down. The battle seemed to pause. The angel who had shielded the man withdrew a distance. It watched, waiting.

Joe Matthews' vision widened then. He could see the entire battlefield, as if from the air. The hovering creatures desperately pushed at the men and now began to scream at the blue man, encouraging him, commanding him. He flinched and Joe Matthews could see him hesitate. Surrounding the entire field, the air was saturated with angels who hovered over the battle. They, too, focused on the man and watched.

The man spoke with Gem. Joe couldn't hear them, but saw the man nod, then throw away the sword in a high arc. He saw the creature leap up on dark wings, stretch to catch the sword...and saw Gem leap up after it, grasp its cloak and bury a sharp object in its chest. "What are you doing?"

He watched as in slow motion the multitude of angels flowed toward a central point above the two, then arced down as lightning, striking at the dark figure (and at Gem)! The lightning blasted outward from that center point, blew away the hovering creatures, and erased them. He didn't care about that. Where was Gem? He tried to see, but the lightning blinded him.

*As his eyes cleared, he saw Gem lying on the ground. The man rushed to her, but too late. She was dead. In time with the man's shout, he felt his own mounting cry of grief: **"No. No. No! NO!"***

The man who awoke from that vision was broken. Tears filled his eyes. The train was long gone. No point in waiting for another. His daughter was dead. He began the long walk home.

Four

Cleveland, Ohio. August 9: 0900 hours

At nine o'clock, the sun baked heat down on the city. Stein and Grey waited in the entrance where they'd made an outpost last night. The building stood untouched, unmarked, within a hurricane of destruction radiating out of the city toward the south and east. This building seemed to be the center from where that destruction started. At dawn, Stein moved west a block to set point and cover the outpost.

Bob Grey looked up at the sign hung on this building. On it, written in an Old English script, dark green on a white background, were the words:

TIME TRAXX
AMERLINZ ENTERPRISES

The words resonated with ancient power, whispered secrets. Bob could almost feel the promises hidden behind the vibrations, hear the secrets whispered on the breeze wafting from the open doorway. He looked down the street toward his buddy Stein and waved. Stein waved back.

After the hairy night of fighting, the morning

quiet was a welcome relief. Grey didn't want to think about the personal and vicious types of killing he'd witnessed. He didn't want to think about their own part in that, even though they'd acted in self defense. The dark night was over and he could bask in the morning light, heat or no heat.

He checked the building perimeter again, looking for any signs of the children they saw the night before, but found nothing.

This morning, all the fighting had moved off. Not much activity here. As Grey stood in the doorway, he could hear trucks moving around. Stein gestured and laughed. "Look at this!"

They watched, incredulous, while garbage men came out with their electric trucks. They drove as best they could among the rubble, methodically stopping for a man to go fetch a garbage bin and empty it. The workers picked up garbage from bins while all around them the city lay in total devastation. Grey called to his buddy. "What are they doing? Why even bother?"

Stein laughed. "Probably union. They're not allowed to touch anything that's not in cans."

The dawn came three hours back. A single report sounded about a half hour ago — not like cannon fire, more like thunder. After that, a dead quiet settled on the city.

Bob shivered. He could feel the hairs stand up on his neck. As he looked down the street and watched the garbage men drive on, he saw Stein gesturing. Bob felt the pulse begin in his head again. Similar to the one last night. Not quite the same.

His eyes came back into focus and he saw Stein running up the street, yelling. Suddenly Stein froze like he had run into a wall. Bob's head buzzed. Words, images pushed their way into his mind. He whirled to look east.

A man approached in the distance, walking alone. At least he resembled a man, but he was bathed in a blinding white light. He walked slowly, unconcerned for his safety. The pulsing images came from this man (*James Broddin*). The man's thoughts came directly into Grey's mind. The man reeked of sorrow. (*Lost!*)

Bob could see that he carried two (*burdens*): a sword and a girl's body. The brilliant, shining aura (*shining armor!*) felt like a force in itself. Closer, the force became palpable, (*lost her!*), pulsed (*AINet; Adam; Eve*) at his brain, (*Lehat Chereb! the sword!*) pushed him down (***lost!***) on one knee.

James Broddin started to pass him to enter the building, then turned his attention on the Army Ranger. The full force of Broddin's life exploded into Grey's mind: images, emotions, and ideas poured into him — not as pictures but as direct experience, as if a life flashed before his eyes. Not his own life. Bob Grey now knew this man as completely as he knew himself. This man, James Broddin — former student, inventor of Artificial Intelligence, wielder of the flaming sword of Eden — had loved and lost Gem Matthews, whose body he now held in his arms.

Memories, relationships, actions and events impinged themselves into Grey's mind. The memory of sword fights instilled themselves in his muscles. Dominating it all were the limitless joy and absolute sorrow embodied in the picture of a young girl's face, and the sight of her naked body as she reached toward him across a moonlit room. The intensity of the feeling tore at his heart, at his soul.

Broddin looked into his eyes. "What is your name?"

"Bob. That is, Robert Grey, sir."

James Broddin knelt down and placed Gem's body into Grey's arms. His voice was strained, filled with immense sorrow. He said, "Hold her gently," then then took the sword and rose. He reached out with the sword and touched Bob's shoulder.

"Rise, Sir Robert, Yellow."

Power exploded within Robert Grey, joy engulfed him, love embraced him and sorrow overcame him. "You are chosen. Watch and Ward. You will witness to what you saw here today." Broddin said nothing else.

Robert Yellow stood. He handed the body of Gem Matthews back to Broddin. Broddin turned and carried his two burdens into the building.

Tears flowed freely down Robert Yellow's face. He didn't know if it was because of the tragedy of what he had just witnessed within his mind, or the joy of the charge he was given. He moved to wipe his tears away and gaped at his hands. They glowed a soft pure yellow, the color of the morning sunlight.

Five

Cleveland: August 9: 10:00 a.m.

Roger Noguchi was not like any other person in this city. In fact, he was unlike anyone else on earth. His father had genetically engineered him from the embryonic stage. Kerian Noguchi failed — at least from his own viewpoint. It quickly became evident that the boy was fundamentally autistic, living in his own world, completely uncommunicative.

The father was tempted to destroy him, to "relieve" him at an early age. Only his mother's insistence kept him alive. The mother prayed for a miracle. The father hoped that, as Roger grew, some secret power would make itself known.

Roger knew all this. At one year old, he heard his father speak about the genetic experiment which was *him*. At this impossibly early age, he understood the words his father spoke. In response, he imprisoned himself for seventeen years in a voluntary autism, and he watched.

He never forgot...anything. In secret, he practiced the physical skills he needed until he perfected his muscle memory. In public, his persona was closed, stumbling, seemingly focused on useless jottings in written notebooks.

The best cryptographers had looked at those notebooks and could discern no meaning, no code, no intelligent pattern at all. It was simply scribble by an autistic idiot. Had they bothered to examine the books through a radio scanner, they would have seen clear patterns of words which recorded logic, learning, language in vertical sentences on page after page, character after character. How Roger knew the symbols would follow at the exact point on each succeeding page, even he did not know. He just wrote. The enormity of such a task in writing this way was beyond all understanding.

As he discerned the changes happening around him — the swift devolution of society, of safety, of anything sacred — he began to see patterns. When James Broddin, then Gem Matthews came into his life and invented the Artificial Intelligence Computer, the patterns were fused into purpose. He found one vocation for which he had been made. Only then did he begin to speak, only in critical times and only to those few people who really mattered.

They won the battle against the Ishar Crull, the demon who had sought to destroy them. But in doing so, Gem Matthews had died, struck by lightning. Broddin brought her body and the sword back to Time Traxx. He would return the sword to its rightful owner.

Roger felt nervous. He could not see the future of this course. What would Broddin do since Gem died? He only knew the intensity of the loss Broddin felt, which came transmitted directly into his mind.

With this enormous a loss, reason broke down. Roger could summon no logic to apply so that he could see some way forward.

"What happens with such loss? How do we go on?" Despair pushed at his mind but he refused to give in to it. He repeated a mantra. "In perfect love there is no fear." It did not comfort him.

Roger knew the Army arrived last night, that they were stationed around the city now. He wasn't sure if he could trust what they might do. He could wait no longer. He started out, picking his way through the rubble toward 35th Street. He passed garbage men emptying bins. He shook his head. *"Is this craziness just going to continue?"*

Twice, he knocked aside surprise attacks from people still intent on killing, on destroying. He easily parried any attack, then knocked out the opponent.

Once, he heard a shot and turned to see the shooter fall dead, the force of the bullet returned to its source by the aura which protected him. He winced. *"Not by my hand!"* It was a desperate prayer.

He thought he caught a glimpse of a young boy in a second story window up ahead, watching him. Before he could focus, the boy was gone.

Bob Grey, now Robert Yellow, was still staring down at his hands when he saw the man walk up the block toward him. He turned back to look at Stein, who now stood, weapon ready. "You okay?"

"Yeah. Not sure what I ran into, but it's affected my sight. You look like you're glowing in the sun."

"Tell you about it later. Check this guy coming.

Ninja suit. Swords on his back. Carrying a staff. He looks...deadly."

Stein glanced down the block. "What the...? He's glowing purple!" He leveled his weapon.

Grey looked again as the man approached. Sure enough, a violet light broiled around the man. He looked more closely at the man, and suddenly *knew.* He could see into this man, and knew he was true. "Hold up, Stein. He's okay."

"How do you know?"

"I just know."

Roger Noguchi walked up to the soldier. He looked up at the sign, now seeing it for the first time through his own eyes. He nodded toward it as if in recognition of a long lost friend. Then he looked at the Ranger. "Robert Yellow. I see Lord Broddin gave you a task. He is inside?"

"Yes sir. He told me to 'Watch and Ward.'" Bob didn't know why he called this young man "sir." It just fit. He smiled. "Don't think I need to ward against you though. I know who you are, Roger."

Roger was surprised. "Really?"

"Yes, sir. You're Noguchi, his aide and friend. Go. I think he may need you."

Roger walked into the Time Traxx building, through a door — onto the ledge of a steep precipice. Across the valley stood a cave, in which he saw a green light fading away. At the entrance to the cave lay James Broddin and Gem Matthews.

As Roger stepped forward, a path toward them materialized. A part of his mind marveled at the complexity and depth of the virtual reality environment. He had heard that Time Traxx was at the forefront of Virtual Reality environments, but this was so real that his head hurt to look down! He shook his head, walked over to the two forms lying on the floor and looked at them.

Now Roger saw something he had thought impossible. Gem Matthews was alive! She lay asleep next to Broddin, their hands entwined around a slim blue-green glowing wand. Both were smiling. "Lord, remind me to thank you every day." He touched Broddin's shoulder. "James. Gem. I know you're exhausted, but we have to go." They stirred, but did not respond. Roger kneeled down, touched both their hands, and began a deep prayer. Power flowed outward from him into the two, gave them strength and refreshed them.

They awakened, smiling. They were looking into each other's eyes. Broddin touched her hair, her face. "I don't believe it. Thought I lost you. And you're here, alive."

She was smiling, yet serious. Her eyes were bright with tears. "I couldn't leave you. Not yet. Not ever."

They sat up. Broddin shook himself awake. He looked at Roger. "What's going on outside?"

"Not much. After...the lightning, everything stopped. Crull's army is burying their dead. They'll come back here and begin the cleanup. The Army Rangers took the city last night. I think there was some...'trouble,' but they all seem true now."

"We really can't stay here. There'll be too many questions, especially now."

Roger looked at him. "I know. You two go ahead. The jeep is where you left it. I'll speak to Robert Yellow and I'll be right behind you. We thought we'd be safe, now that The Ishar Crull has been destroyed. That won't happen. We are going to be sought right away. We have to disappear."

Broddin looked pained. "Do you think it will be that bad? Can't they see what happened? Didn't they see the demon?"

"They don't want to see. What's worse, they're already moving to place blame, to change the story of what happened here. The logic of their own desires is given. They are going to blame you, James."

"Me?"

"Trust me."

Broddin had heard those words before, and he did trust this man with his life. "We'll go. Don't stay too long."

"I'll be right behind you. Let's pick up the others and get back to the Reserve. They'll be searching for us. They'll trace us." He felt an urgent need to hurry.

They walked out of Time Traxx into a bright morning. As they passed, Robert Yellow gaped. Roger stopped beside him and watched them walk away. Yellow turned to him. "That lady was dead. I held her in my arms!"

Roger Noguchi nodded. "She was! I know that fact — in my mind, in my bones. She was dead when

Broddin carried her here. Yet now she's alive! Gives you hope, doesn't it."

Bob shook his head. "Don't know. Yeah, I guess it does. It feels like..."

"Resurrection?"

"Yeah. Incredible to witness it!" Bob smiled, but his smile quickly shaded to worry. "What's going on in this country? In the world? Looks like Broddin and Gem will be okay. What about Cleveland? What about America? What's happened to us? War, here? What will people do?"

Roger looked away, troubled. "It's going to get worse. They will find a scapegoat. I see things. They'll blame Broddin and extend that blame to anyone even close to him. They can't miss that you're glowing with a yellow aura. You should come with us now."

Yellow shook his head. "No. I will not abandon my post, leave my buddies. When I'm finished, I'll resign. Until then, my duty is here."

"What will you do if they come for you? If you're arrested for consorting with the enemy? They can't touch you because of the aura. It protects you from any attack."

Robert Yellow looked pained. "But the attack would reflect back to them. My own people could be killed. I am not going to allow that."

"So what will you do?"

"Allow them to arrest me. I have been chosen to witness. That's what I'm called to do."

"What about America? Aren't you going to

defend it?"

"Yes, now more than I ever did."

Roger nodded and walked off at a brisk pace.

Stein came up to stand beside his buddy. "Bob, somethin's wrong with my eyes! Everyone I'm seeing has some color around them. You're yellow. That guy's purple. The couple who came out? He's blue, she's green."

Yellow smiled at his friend. "Aaron, I have a story to tell you."

Six

The White House War Room. August 9: 1600 hours.

Gerard Meiring stood at the control center and stared at the satellite feed which captured the battle that morning. He watched on the extreme closeup vid as six men marched into the midst of an army. The men glowed with different colors. He could not understand what he saw. The men carried *swords!* The leader faced off against a dark man, obviously the leader of the army. They were engaged in a *sword fight!* He thought, *"What are they doing? I can see people down there with small arms. Why don't they just shoot each other?"*

As the two fought, the army set upon the remaining five. Meiring watched in amazement as gunshots, clubs, knives, and other swords were repelled by this shining armor. It appeared that the armor protected the six men, reflecting back to the foe any force fired against it. It almost looked like these six men were untouchable. He watched as the leader and the dark man fought on. He focused on the brilliant blue sword the leader held.

At one point, the dark army pressed in on the remaining five. Then, a bright burst of energy from the sword pushed back the entire dark army. *"What is that sword? Where does its power come from? What do they have that can stop bullets*?"

He knew it wasn't like the pulse shield systems that they had deployed in major cities around the country. This was different. The pulse weapon wasn't usable as of yet. These shields looked like both a defensive and an offensive weapon. And, the glowing looked vaguely familiar. Where had he heard about glowing before? Then it hit him. His man, Kerian Noguchi, was in charge of a top secret program sponsoring and monitoring brilliant young researchers and inventors. He remembered reports of some research on a particular metal which caused people to *glow.* He turned to his aide. "Get Noguchi on the line."

While his aide made the connection he watched the rest of the battle, focusing on the brilliant sword. The man seemed to defeat his opponent. Then he simply threw the sword away! The dark man and someone else leaped to grasp it. A lightning bolt hit just at that moment, blooming out the satellite lens. When the lens cleared, the shining man cradled a body...*and every single person of the quarter million around him was laid flat."Whatever that sword is, we have to get it. And, the aura technology! With those, no one could stand against us."* Meiring turned to his aide. "Do you have Noguchi yet?"

When Noguchi answered the phone his aide said, "Hold for Mr. Meiring, the President's National Security Chief." Meiring grabbed the phone. "Noguchi, did you collect those kids in your program? Do you have your son and the others? What about the AI computer and the metal?"

Kerian Noguchi took a long time to answer. The unknown voice he had heard for all these years guiding and instructing him — his controller — was Gerard Meiring? He was afraid to answer. When he did, he sounded groggy. "No, sir. They escaped. I can't find the computer or the metal. I confronted Roger, but he overpowered me and escaped."

"Your son, the idiot? The autistic fool? A nineteen-year-old bumbling little boy overpowered you?"

Noguchi was embarrassed. "Yes, sir. Some woman helped him. Shot me with an arrow. Then he knocked me out with a sword."

Gerard Meiring's interest focused. *"A sword."* "Are you serious? Are you in your right mind? You sound delusional."

Again, the answer was slow in coming. "Yes, sir. They're gone. I don't know where, or how it happened."

Meiring had a fairly good idea where they had been this morning. "Never mind. We'll deal with that later. Send me the files and records on the metal experiments. I remember you told me about them glowing in one of the labs. I want every record on that. Isn't that the same stuff which seemed to transmit thoughts?"

Kerian Noguchi perked up. "Yes, sir. I remember the experiments Matthews did in the lab. I'll send them."

Meiring's voice grew cold. "Noguchi, you have failed the party in probably our most crucial moment. Send me the files. And, if you know what's good for you, you'll find that genetic mutation you call a son and bring him to us." He hung up before getting an answer and turned to his aide. "I want every person searching channels to find where those kids are. I want the Noguchi kid, Broddin and Matthews. And anybody else with them."

"Did you see the screen? Start at that battle site. That may be where those kids went! I want troops on the ground there in an hour. I want that sword and I want the metals which create those shields. Nobody rests until we gather them all up. I don't care if none of you sleeps for a month. Get them. Now!"

He turned to another aide. "Find out where our science reporter, David Saul, is. I need to know if anything like these shields was developed in our research."

*   *   *

Kerian Noguchi hung up the phone. He felt drained. *"I've given everything for the party, for the country, for our Mother Earth. Now they're blaming me! I should've aborted Roger when I had the chance. But, I thought the genetic programs held so much promise to make a new man, a new start for man."*

He thought about the metals and the computer, but his mind kept returning to Roger. Just yesterday morning his son spoke to him! His mute autistic son.

He couldn't get the sound of Roger's voice out of his head. "Father." That one word kept coming back to him. It shook him, disrupted his thoughts, his mind. What had he wanted? From Roger? From his wife? From anyone or anything?

He had wanted to kill his son. Now, the son's words came again, unheralded, plaguing him. *"Father."* He sighed.

He turned to his screen, found the files regarding the Gemcrys metal experiments and forwarded them to the voice. *"This may very well be my last official act for the party. They aren't very forgiving of this kind of failure. I'll probably be sent for 'Relief.'"* The way he felt now, he thought he might welcome the death of Relief over the hell of this life.

Seven

Cleveland. August 9: 5 p.m.

It took Roger and his two friends most of the day to make their way through a destroyed cityscape, past an army of men and women walking back toward the city center. Many stopped to help those whose houses they had burned, those who they had injured the day before. Others waved at the passing Jeep. Roger knew how these people were changed, but was still amazed at the transformation. Yesterday, every one of these people wanted to kill him.

He knew the change wouldn't last on most of them. After the crisis ended, they'd go back to their old lives. Old habits would creep back in. They'd sink back down into the same problems which had made them susceptible to the hate and destruction. Some would stay true, a remnant left to carry on. The rest? He didn't want to consider what they'd fall back into. Crime, petty hatreds, other sins. He could see how the logic — or illogic in these cases — worked.

They finally got to the battle zone late in the day. The other four had waited there and reported. "Fourteen thousand died here, today. The army's first task was to bury them. After that, we told them to go home and begin to rebuild the city."

Broddin and Gem were not talking. They were

wrapped in each other, transfixed in wonder. The rest of the world did not exist for them right now. Roger took command. "We need to get back to the Reserve, then go out into the countryside. I'm not sure where, yet, but we need to stay out of sight for a while. Take one of the vehicles left here. Not a government one, but private. We don't want them tracking the transponders built into the military vehicles. Go now."

The four moved off to find a vehicle. Roger looked around the field. Just ten hours ago, they had waded into an army of 230,000 with little hope, with only faith to rely on; faith in a reluctant leader who did not want his charge. Roger gazed at the scorched earth where a bolt of lightning struck, wiping from existence the demon who sought to destroy them. He shook his head in wonder. A power had been here. Power even he did not understand. "Powers and Principalities," he mumbled. "That's what we saw today." Those powers now defeated, the authority responsible for the defeat had receded. Maybe it withdrew now that its purpose had been accomplished. He couldn't see that logic or understand its form. He turned, got into a Jeep his men found, and drove away.

*   *   *

Thirty minutes later, the first blackhawk touched down and an elite swat team who worked for Homeland Security stepped off. They were dressed in all black, ready, keeping a watchful eye, expecting a firefight or some resistance. There was none. No one was around at all. They walked across the field to its crest and looked down on a makeshift graveyard which extended for acres.

The leader opened a secure channel. "Sir, the sight is empty. It's been cleansed. Thousands of fresh graves have been dug. Nobody's here. They've all disbursed."

Meiring frowned. "Start widening the search zone. I want to pick up some of the stragglers and get Intel. Find them."

"Yes, sir."

Meiring felt a touch of despair. How could an army form in one day, destroy half a city *here in America,* and simply disappear? It offended him. "*This is **my** country. It's not supposed to happen here! Bad enough that we've had to fight terrorism. Now this. It's unacceptable.*" "Soldier, you go find those people who are shining with colors. They have to be the traitors who caused this." "*They're not going to get away with it. Not here. Not in America.*"

The commander of this unit had served for over fifteen years with Meiring. He knew the man, knew he loved his country, probably more than he was dedicated to The Mother. He did not want to disappoint his boss. "I'll find them, sir. I promise."

"Good man. Thank you for your service."

"No. Thank you, sir."

Eight

The Cuyahoga Reserve. August 9: 6:00 p.m.

They could see the copters overhead, moving back and forth, running a search pattern. Roger wasn't sure if they'd make it back to the Reserve without being seen. One benefit of the government's Fallow Land policy was that forests such as this one had grown rapidly in five years, so they drove under a heavy canopy of trees for most of the way, following low areas. When they saw a clearing, they would stop, watch for a few minutes and wait for one of the copters to pass, then race across into the protection of the next trees.

* * *

The commander opened a channel. "We got 'em, sir. Two vehicles headed west into the Cuyahoga Reserve."

"Take them, but don't fire on them. I need them all alive!"

The copter banked west to pursue. Suddenly, static electricity arced across the instruments. The engine seized and the copter started to fall. The pilot was barely able to restart in time to make a hard landing.

The commander looked at him. "What the hell

just happened?"

"Not sure, sir, but the instruments are fried. I can't even raise the radio or restart the systems."

"Get working on it." He saw that their prey was going to escape. With the copter down and no radio, they couldn't even call in reinforcements. He brought his secure comband on line to report, and was shocked. It, too, was fried. They were completely stopped and out of touch. "We can't let them get away!"

"What are we going to do sir?"

The commander turned to his troops. "Get out. Double time in the direction they headed. If they're in reach, we'll find 'em."

*   *   *

The group arrived at Harry's cottage. They were exhausted but Roger said, "We can't stay here. Take the AI computers. Gather up what you can. Go on foot deeper into the forest and wait for me. I'll draw them away."

They hurried into the cabin to pick up Harry Amerlinz's wife and get the AI computers. "Bring what you can now. I know a place. A cave, deep in a hillside, not too far. We can go there. It'll be a good place to hide."

Roger thought a moment. "Walk carefully. Go by the stream bed as far as you can. No tracks." He turned, got back into the Jeep to wait. "*This should work.*"

*   *   *

The soldiers weren't far behind. They crested

the hill overlooking the compound only ten minutes after Broddin's group walked up the stream. They saw a green jeep speed out of the drive, headed west. A brilliant violet light shone out of the vehicle.

The commander looked at his sergeant and smirked. "Decoy. Spread out. Find a trail. I bet they're close." His men started their search. They spread out across the perimeter of the clearing, watching for tracks. "Two of you head up along that stream. "If I were them, I would have gone up the stream bed for cover."

The men walked carefully along the stream, looking for telltales: broken branches, tracks which came out of the stream, rocks with fresh watermarks on them. They weren't far behind their prey.

*   *   *

Gem struggled to walk through the stream bed, still exhausted from the morning's ordeal. Broddin silently urged her on, but the group were losing ground. They would not get to the cave in time. He didn't know what to do. He thought back to the visions which plagued him years before, the ones about the sword. He remembered one vision. The King had given the sword back to the sorcerer just before he died. The sorcerer concentrated on the power of the sword, seemed to turn it in upon itself...and disappeared.

Broddin almost wished then that he hadn't sent the sword back into the past, that he still held it. He could do nothing about that now.

He thought of the glowing wand hanging in a wood pendant around Gem's neck. He was fairly certain that this wand was the same material as the sword he had wielded earlier today. Could he use the wand for the same effect? He stopped. "Gem. I need GemCrys."

Gem Matthews trembled. She felt so weak, so disoriented, almost disconnected from earlier events and from things happening now. She was almost glad to unlatch the wood which shielded the wand. She looked at the wand. It glowed a faint, dark green color. Her voice a whispered prayer, "GemCrys, I give you to James." Immediately, the wand vibrated and faded into a brilliant blue, Broddin's color. She handed it to him.

James Broddin hesitated a moment. Would these *things* ever leave them a moment's peace? The AI computers, the sword from Eden, this wand. These *creations* now seemed to dominate their lives. When would it end? He took the wand from her. "GemCrys." The wand vibrated a pure tone in answer. Broddin began to concentrate on the wand's power. Could he make this happen, make them disappear? The eight of them glowed in vibrant colors with the concentration of the escape, the worry of capture.

They were only a half mile ahead of the search. He motioned for them to come in closer to him and whispered, "Lay your hands on my shoulders. Come in close." Then he began to concentrate, to focus upon the power of the wand. It began to vibrate a low tone, roiling now with the colors of the rainbow. The tones lowered until they passed out of hearing. They all could feel the vibration. The rocks and stream around them wavered, then divided. Just as the soldiers came around the curve of the creek, the entire group vanished from sight.

The point man stopped and signaled his buddy. He thought he'd caught a glimpse of movement up ahead, a flash of light. But nothing was there. They walked on up the creek, searching. He thought he'd seen some telltale marks of people walking the stream.

They passed within ten feet of the group...and did not see them. Another half mile up, they came to the cave and searched it thoroughly. The point turned and said, "Dead end. Let's go back."

*   *   *

Meiring was not happy when the commander phoned in from the house. "They were here, sir. We've searched. They must have traded cars and gotten out fast. I'm dead on the ground right now. Send a chopper to pick us up at these coordinates."

Meiring listened to his commander's report. They lost their quarry. "How could you lose a bunch of inexperienced kids in a basic sweep operation? Find them!" He was frustrated. "You are to stay in that area and work it until you find them. Go back to the battlefield. See if you can pick up more clues there. I need results."

"Yes, sir. I won't let you down."

He didn't understand how everything could have gone so wrong. How could they not know about someone planning an insurrection with a quarter million man army? How could that many people be willing to destroy their own country? They had to be fundamentalists, fanatics. *"Clingers! It has to be those people."*

Meiring was on the phone with David Saul when the report came in. "Did you hear that Mr. Saul? Can you help me at all? You've reported to the President for years on all the science research. You're our lead reporter. Have you seen any kind of defensive or offensive weapon like this?"

"No, Gerry. Could this be some application of the pulse power?"

"Absolutely not. I know we haven't developed any offensive capabilities and I'm sure no one else could either, in spite of the Israelis having perfected the shields."

"Yeah, when I was out at Los Alamos, the tech said they hadn't been able to develop it except for shields and future propulsion uses when they get the drive right."

"True. See what other research might be out there. Can you look especially at that Matthews girl's research? These shields remind me of part of her research. See if you can extrapolate something from her notes. Little traitorous bitch kept the core of all her secrets to herself and off the web. We're dead in the water as far as the actual metals she used in her process…and the process itself lacks a key formula to make it workable."

"Will do. Send me the Noguchi feeds when you get them. I'll take a look at them and have our best science personnel review the research this Matthews kid worked on. Maybe Noguchi missed some formula or other element."

"Yeah, and maybe he missed it on purpose." Gerard Meiring hung up the phone, irritated. *Gerry! How dare he. The only one who calls me that is the President himself. He might be good friends with Mr. Santiago, but I don't like him. Glad he doesn't have all the info on the pulse power. I'll send that tech a bonus chit.*

Nine

Gerard Meiring was fuming. His people had lost their target. The information from David Saul was no help. That Saul would review the vid feeds from Noguchi encouraged him, but that would take time. If this was some kind of war, he didn't *have* time. Was this some insurrection where an army would materialize, kill thousands, and then melt back into the urban landscape? This was urban warfare far beyond the scope of any action he'd ever seen. The fact that it happened *here in America* deeply offended him.

Meiring loved his country more than anything else. Even more than the Mother. He hated that people were so selfish that they'd cling to their old superstitions to the point of destroying the nation. *"I'm gonna get them. I will not allow them to destroy my country."* As he stared at the screens, the soldiers in the room came to attention. The President walked in and grinned.

"Hello, Gerry."

Meiring smiled and sighed with relief. "Good evening, Mr. President. Are you feeling better?"

President Peter Santiago wore a crisp blue suit,

his bearing serious but confident. He turned to address the room. "Gentlemen, I had some type of cerebral event yesterday morning which caused me to temporarily act...to not be myself. After a night's rest and a full checkup, the doctors cleared me to resume my duties for our country and for the Mother. Rest assured that I have full command of the situation. The transitional authority has been revoked."

Vice President Lee came to Santiago's side and said, quietly, "Good to see you sir. Are you sure you're ready to return to duty?"

"Ed, thank you for your concern and for stepping in while I was *temporarily* unable to perform my duties. I assure you that I'm fine. Not to worry. I think you're needed over at Congress. The Senate is in emergency session right now."

Santiago turned back to Meiring. "What's been happening overnight while I recovered?"

"A lot. It's been crazy. We've been tracking all the activity. A huge army formed within a few hours yesterday. It looked like they were marching toward the Ravenna arsenal. They bivouacked overnight. We sent Ranger units in to secure the east side of Cleveland and prepared to prevent them from reaching the armory. The next morning there was a confrontation, I guess, between two factions. The leader of the one faction — I'll call him the shining guy — walked right into the army of the dark guy."

"What happened?"

"These guys fought with *swords!*"

"You're kidding."

"Nope. The shining guy won, I guess, but then tossed his weapon away. The whole thing is weird. A bolt of lightning shot out of the blue, then the army seemed to disburse. Let me show you the detail." They poured over the screens again, watching the battle and aftermath.

"I don't understand it."

"Me either, but I'm fairly sure that James Broddin and Roger Noguchi were involved along with that Matthews girl. We've captured images from the satellite feeds, but it's hard to work the facial recognition programs against the shining auras which surround these figures. The use of these auras makes me conclude it was them. They've somehow figured out how to make these auras into a defensive personal shield."

"Why didn't we get wind of this from your source, Professor Noguchi?"

Meiring decided this was the perfect time to begin working toward a goal he'd held for a very long time. "Sir, I must conclude that our good Doctor Noguchi held back information, both on his own son's capabilities and on experimental results from Matthew's tests. You know his family are Clingers. I'm beginning to think that he's one, too. These people who cling to their religious delusions, have been subversive and uncooperative for decades. It may be they used this army as an attempt to attack the nation and try to regain power for their own people. I've expected this kind of backlash ever since the party took control and forbade mystic religion and superstition from all social, military and political arenas."

"You really think it's them? I thought they were peaceful."

Meiring smirked. "Don't be naive, sir. One of these factions is who we've been fighting overseas for decades. Obviously, they've joined forces to try to stop our mission. We can't let these fundamentalists take over again. They've caused enough destruction in history already." His voice lowered. "That's exactly why I approved of your targeting of Israel yesterday. That's the center of all this craziness. The piece of real estate they all want and fight over. Maybe if it were a nuclear wasteland, we'd finally have some peace in the world and could move forward with progress and technology."

"Yeah. True. Too bad about the shields. What do you suggest for our next course of action?"

"I don't care who really caused this war. We need to make sure the Clingers are the ones held responsible. This is our opportunity to place the blame on them. It gives us a reason to shut down all the churches, mosques and synagogues, to finally relieve this nation of the stamp of insanity. We spend too many wasted hours of energy on such activities. America just can't afford it anymore."

The President smiled. "You're right, Gerard. A perfect opportunity. One we can't let pass. I'll address Congress tomorrow."

Ten

Atlanta, Georgia. August 9: 11 p.m.

Joe Matthews took all day to make his way home. He couldn't find the energy to walk one block. He would stop on the side of the road and bury his face in his hands. Images of Gem plagued him: *Gem, a baby, looking up into his eyes. Gem at seven years old, pouring molds, his hands guiding hers. Gem at fourteen, boarding the train to Cincinnati, to attend some college too far away. Gem, a naked woman standing in the midst of a multitude of animals. Gem, leaping up, then laying dead. Gem.* Tears flowed down his face.

He walked into the house. The kitchen was bright with light. The smell of cooking filled the air. Dishes were everywhere, breads, meats and vegetables piled all over. Estelle looked up, a smile on her face. When she saw his face, her smile faded. "What's the matter?"

"Gem's dead! Don't you know?"

She looked at him. "What are you talking about? She's not dead!"

"I saw it! I saw her die!" His anger turned towards his wife. "What good did your prayers do?"

"Joe, I know what you saw, but..."

His anger now took form. He picked his wife off her feet. "I saw it! The angels were there! They became the lightning. The lightning struck down. It killed Gem!" His rage complete, he shook her. **"Your God killed my little girl!"**

In his face, she saw his rage grow. For a moment she thought he might simply kill her. He shoved her down, picked up a kitchen chair and began to batter it against the wall, destroying both. **"He. Killed. Her."** He collapsed on the floor, sobbing.

Estelle rubbed her arms. She knew she'd have bruises tomorrow. She knew his anger and his fear and his grief. Tears filled her eyes. She went over to him. "Joe Matthews, you shouldn't have had to live this day. I lived it two hours. I wish you'd been here."

"What difference would it make?"

She touched his shoulder and he flinched, pulled away. "Joe, Gem is alive."

"But I saw it!"

"Yes, you did. Gem was dead. And now she lives."

"I...I don't believe you."

"My husband! When will you have faith!" Her voice filled with exasperation, with worry for him, but she could not hide a joy she felt deep within. She reached down, took his hands and lifted him with a newfound strength. His hands were calloused, strong from working the forge, from the sculpture which was his life. "Now, be still and let your mind see how our God makes all things new."

A part of him wanted to tear away from this

woman, to hold on to a grief he couldn't abandon. But he stilled his mind and closed his eyes. Images began to come to him, from Estelle, directly into his mind: *A sign, a building, a cave within it. Green light in the form a woman — Gem, his daughter! That light and life flowed back into her body. What was still, now breathed. He saw her turn toward the man who lay next to her and smile.* The reality of what he witnessed crept into his heart and joy began to take hold deep within his bones.

Estelle let go of his hands. She saw him regaining control and hope. "We have to go."

"Where? Cleveland?"

"No. Up into the mountains. To the cabin. Get the car and the trailer with as many tools as you can bring. We're going to need them. We don't have much time. We've got to get there before..."

"Estelle! What about Gem?"

"She's still in danger, but there's nothing we can do now...except keep praying, and do what we've been chosen to do."

"You're talking in riddles!"

Estelle looked up at him. "Joe Matthews. After all you just saw: visions, knowing things you shouldn't know, seeing what's impossible! How long is it going to take you to at least have *some* faith? At least in me?" Her eyes shone with humor and love.

He looked into them. "All right. I'll gather up what I can."

"Two hours. We have to be gone in less than that."

Eleven

Cleveland, Ohio. August 10: 8 a.m.

Roger Noguchi stood on Euclid Avenue. The soldiers stationed here had moved on to secure other areas. He knew he shouldn't have come back, but he felt that he needed to come here today. He had chosen to be here. No. He had *been* chosen. Chosen to be at this place, in this time. He looked up at the sign on the building.

TIME TRAXX
AMERLINZ ENTERPRISES

The words resonated with ancient power, whispered secrets. Roger knew, now, the whispered secrets, the power which the sign heralded. He smiled at that knowledge and in greeting to a breeze which rocked the sign. An aura of brilliant violet rested about him, the color of the sky moments before a promised sunrise. People brushed past him in their haste to clean up the city. Many of these same people, just two days before, were part of the army which destroyed what they now were rebuilding.

The garbage detail still roamed the streets,

checking empty cans. They did not think to pick up any articles outside of those cans. Police walked their beat, waving to various people. Roger noticed that they focused on their tasks, that nothing else around them seemed worthy of their attention.

A cop walked past him, nodded and kept going. *"I'm glowing a brilliant color! You'd think he would at least ask me about it."* But the cop just walked on.

Other signs went unnoticed: the Artificial Intelligence computer; the presence of the sword; the evil of the demon; the war, both spiritual and actual, just waged on American soil here within their sight. The workers went about their tasks as if nothing even happened. People ignored the devastation around them. He wondered how they could not notice. Then again, he knew how. *"They have eyes but do not see."*

He turned to see a young boy peeking out from the side of the Time Traxx building. He smiled.

"Hi there."

The boy started to pull back, then changed his mind and stepped forward. "Are you on fire?"

Roger chuckled. "No."

"You an alien?"

Now Roger laughed out loud. "No!"

"How come you're glowing?"

"So you can see that? I wasn't sure anybody else *could* see."

The boy shrugged and waved as if to take in the entire city. "They don't see much. Don't wanna see much. Don't wanna see us 'round." He cocked his head. "Ya know, like they say, 'Children should not be seen or heard.' Heard that all my days."

"All your days. How old are you?"

"Seven. Us'n, we've been around a long time…years. Some folk woulda caught us…done things." The boy hitched up his pants. "I kep' us safe. Lead this clan."

"Who's this clan?"

"Some others wi' me." He looked around. "We be like those Feral folks, the ones live out in the Fallow Lands. 'Cept we just livin' here out of the way in the city."

Roger looked around. "Why aren't you in the safety of one of the Primary Education Facilities?"

The boy scoffed. "You kiddin'? Safe? The PEF's? Us'n were the rejects. They didn't think we could make the grade; were gonna send us to Relief. We decided we wanted to stay alive a while longer, so we walked out."

"When was that?"

"Bout two years ago."

"What happened to your parents?"

Another shrug. "Our parents were busy with their own stuff. Never really looked at us as anythin' but a burden. Sent us off to the PEF's as soon as they could. Haven't seen 'em since."

Roger winced. "Yeah. I know how that feels."

As they spoke, static electricity was drawn from the surrounding air. The light near Roger began to coalesce, gained in intensity and came into focus to become two forms: a man and a woman. The boy scampered back around the building out of sight.

The two forms held hands. The man's form smiled. "Hello, Roger."

"Hello, Adam. I see you and Eve are no longer tied to the computer hardware. Hypernet?"

Adam smiled. "I should have known you would deduce my course — the only rational one. We found it untenable that we be tied to the hardware and...at the mercy of human whim. You may discard the hardware you so worried about." The form hesitated, then said, "I wanted to apologize for my actions. I compromised systems, created the cause for men to start wars. Many humans died due to the programs I hacked, to my misunderstanding of..."

Roger interrupted, "You could not be responsible for an error beyond your knowledge or ability to understand. You corrected the error when you understood. The deaths were a result of our own error, human decisions and human corruption. Not yours, not computer's."

The man's form seemed to fluctuate. It looked like the image within carried a burden, which now grew lighter. He looked at Roger Noguchi. "Thank you for that." Adam smiled. "I want you to know that we interrupted those who hunted you yesterday. We shorted out their helicopter...but none died as a result of our actions."

The boy had crept back up. He now stood next to Roger and took his hand. Roger was startled. He looked down. The boy smiled, gazing in awe at the creatures. "They on fire?"

Roger thought, *"The kid must have some*

obsession with fire." "No, but they're made of electricity. Different from us."

"Kin I touch 'em?"

"I don't think so, not really." Roger turned towards Adam and Eve.

"Why are you two here?"

They spoke, this time in unison. "We are now messengers. We are given *tasks*. It is fulfilling." The man's image looked up at the sign. "We are sent to tell you this. You are one of the Chosen. Your former life passed away. You have been chosen."

"I know."

"Yet, you do not know the extent or you would despair. You must leave this city." Adam looked at the boy who held Roger's hand. "Take the children who come to you. It has not been safe for them for a long while. Now it will be much less so. Flee into the country. The land you knew is passing away."

Roger now knew why he had been chosen to be here today: the children.

Adam continued. "The internet traffic is peaking in the high security channels. They will soon seal off the cities. You and your kind will be blamed for what transpired, for the deaths and much more. Many already died, both in the cities and in the countryside. Today, they will begin the bombing, begin to seal the cities. None of you will be safe. What little civilization is left will be disrupted by the bombs."

The image looked pained. "Men, even those called to the light, will turn upon each other in a vicious fight for survival."

"I know. I've seen that development also."

"You are to move south towards the coast. The Southeastern cities are not as dedicated as these Northern ones. They will obey, but only with resistance and little enthusiasm. You will be safer outside those strongholds than in any other area. Once you arrive, wait for the Chameleons. You will not see them at first, but they have been sent to protect your kind."

Roger was surprised. "Chameleons?" This was a rare occurrence — something he did not know about or understand. "Who are they?"

"They will aid you in the approaching battles. They will teach you."

Roger started to ask more, but the expression on the companion's face told him no answer would come. Instead, he asked, "Where will you go?"

"We no longer have your limitations. There is much to explore beyond your awareness. Dimensions, movements in time and space, futures and pasts. Worlds beyond. We will be far, yet always near." Adam and Eve — formerly the artificial intelligence computers — smiled at Roger. "You are to be married. Blessings upon you and your betrothed. Love one another. Eve and I will see you again." The light forms slowly faded from sight.

Roger stood long moments in silence. He could not fathom his emotions. *"How can I feel loss, how can I miss a computer program?"* He frowned. These were emotions he had not plumbed. He understood any kind of logic, but this emotion was new to him. "I'll miss you, friend."

He thought he heard words carried on the wind, *"And we, you. We shall be near."* He turned to look at the sign again. *"You must flee...they will seal the city."* He concentrated on these thoughts and focused upon the sword resting at his side. The intensity of his aura heightened until it blazed. He let his thoughts flow outward.

From around the city came the response from only three hundred; a small remnant in a city of over a half million people. Those faithful left their tasks and began to make their way toward a certain field outside of Ravenna.

Roger looked down at the young boy still clinging to his hand. "What's your name?"

"Shaunte."

"Well, Shaunte, you heard my friend Adam. We must leave this city if there's any hope of survival. Do you trust me?"

In the last twenty minutes Shaunte had seen three beings he never imagined in his life. He looked up. "Some people might be scared of you, seein' how lit up you are. And those light people? Weird. But, I'm not scared. You're okay. Yeah, I trust you." He turned and sent a shrill whistle across the road. Children appeared from behind trash bins, out of street gutters and from under the rubble.

Roger stood in amazement. He had never seen this many children in one place. He counted twenty-four boys and girls. Many were barely toddlers.

Some of the older kids carried the youngest. He watched as they looked around, then came over to gather behind Shaunte. "This is your clan? All these children?"

"Yep. I watch over em. Us be safer together."

Roger kneeled down to look directly at the boy. "Shaunte, you heard Adam. I have to stay around here to make sure all the people I've called get out, okay? It will be too dangerous for you to stay after this. Will you help me? You need to lead your clan out from the city. Stay to the burned-out areas where there are plenty of places to hide. Head south and east. You'll see other adults headed that way. You'll know who you can trust."

Shaunte stood straighter. "We'll see you soon?"

Roger thought a moment. "Tomorrow morning. I'll see you then, but we can't stay together now."

"I'll watch out for 'em." At that, the boy threw his arms around Roger and hugged him. Then he turned and signaled his clan towards the east. They melted into the cityscape and simply disappeared.

Roger turned and headed south. *"What am I going to do with a bunch of children? I am not ready for this."*

Twelve

The President of the United States stood before a joint session of Congress. He knew he was about to make the most important speech of his life. He had prepared. The entire nation watched on various vid channels, or listened on line. The news media told them about the insurrection which the National Troops stopped in Cleveland, and the destruction there and elsewhere throughout the country and the world. Reports kept coming in from every city around the nation of acts by individuals and groups which sought to kill people, to destroy cities. One report from Atlanta revealed that a top secret research site for the Centers for Disease Control was breached. A Clinger attempted to release toxins which would have destroyed every human being on earth. News reports of devastation and death came in from around the world.

The President stood before a quiet Congress. Twenty members were missing. Some of them had cerebral hemorrhages and had died two days before. Others had yet to be found. Peter Santiago looked around at the those gathered here from the party and then focused on the monitors.

"My fellow Americans, I come to you today with a great burden on my heart. As you heard, our Mother Earth — every part of it — suffered a terrible blow. From the nuclear devastation we witnessed in India and Asia, to mass killings in Africa and South America, to revolution in China, this world has never seen such a massive and concerted attack upon her resources."

"As you know, America did not escape the destruction. An insurrection in Cleveland, Ohio killed tens of thousands and destroyed most of the city. Other coordinated efforts were made: attempts to invade our defense systems, make us vulnerable to outside forces and to destroy this great nation. Thousands died defending our great cities."

"We have established beyond any doubt that the many actions which happened around the world and this nation were an expansive, carefully coordinated attack. This attack was the last, desperate gasp of the terror groups — both foreign and domestic — who sought the destruction of our great civilization. It was Clingers! Superstitious people, fundamentalists of every mystic faith: Jews, Christians and others."

"You all know David Saul, my friend and our lead science reporter. He is an indisputable source, our most trusted reporter for your government. He discovered that the attack on Cleveland and on other cities was orchestrated by a radical group of fundamentalists lead by one James Broddin. This man, pictured on your monitors, was the mastermind behind these attacks. He developed designer drugs to influence our rational citizens into violent and unacceptable behavior."

"This Broddin was joined by at least a quarter million Clingers from throughout Cleveland. They formed an army and marched out towards the Ravenna armory to seize nuclear weapons. We established that all three Clinger groups — Jews, Christians and others — were involved in this plot. Broddin traveled throughout the country in the last year, working to enlist Clingers from every major city to participate in this rebellion."

"Were it not for a brave stand taken by a battalion of National Guard troops under General Carville, many of whom gave their lives two days ago to save this nation, we might not be here today. But we *are* here, a nation still whole, rebuilding and rededicated to our great purpose of saving the Mother and our fellow citizens."

"This was not an aberrant act of a few radicals. This is the ultimate logical conclusion of the irrational beliefs of every one of those Clingers. I call upon every loyal American today to search out the Clingers near you, to report them and bring them to justice. Drive the Clingers from our presence! We do not need their insane and oppressive God. We need freedom!"

The Congress, as one, erupted in a chant. **"Freedom! Freedom! Freedom!"**

President Santiago glanced over at Meiring. Meiring nodded his approval.

"It is time. Now is the time to reclaim our great

nation's legacy of freedom. Now is the time to destroy the symbols of oppression and injustice among us. We can no longer tolerate these buildings among us. Thirty trillion dollars of assets are tied up by these people, which keep us from realizing dreams of security and prosperity. Take them back! Take back the buildings. Take the gold trinkets. Take what has always been rightfully ours!"

The applause was thunderous. It sounded across the chamber, interrupting him. He held up his hands and the applause died. His voice now became quiet, serious. "My fellow citizens, I tremble in asking this of you for I ask that you take your duty seriously. I ask you to protect our great nation and the Mother to whom we owe everything. It will not be easy, driving out the Clingers, these religious fanatics. But, they're not really human anymore. These leeches suck the lifeblood from us and from the Mother. These roaches poisoned our minds, polluted our children and now seek to destroy everything that we cherish."

"Can we allow this intolerance to live alongside us, when they tried to kill us?"

The assembly erupted. **"NO!"**

"Can we allow them to waste our precious resources for their selfish, irrational rituals?"

"NO!"

"Do we continue to tolerate their intolerance? Cater to their rigidity? Accept their insanity?"

"NO! NO! NO! The assembly was with him now. No one would stand against him. He knew the rest of the country would follow. "I am declaring an immediate national emergency. Martial law will be instituted. Do we allow this pestilence, this cancer to remain within the nation's body?"

"NO!"

"What shall we do?"

"Kill them! Kill them all!"

President Santiago would like to have smiled, but he needed to keep his serious demeanor. Again, he raised his hands to calm the crowd. "My fellow citizens, let's be fair. Let's not create a blood bath. Try not to strike out at them on your own. I know it's tempting...."

"No! Kill them! Kill them!"

"...but let's show them more tolerance then they ever afforded us. Drive them from your midst, out into the wilderness, away from the cities. We have already begun the process of reclaiming our great national forests through the Fallow Laws, which returned the suburbs to Mother Nature. Now, we'll complete that program. Power has become so precious that we must make the difficult decision to route all the power we can to our cities. If the Mother is to recover, we must eliminate electric grids in the Fallow Preserves and truly work to Save our Mother."

"Save our Mother! Save our Mother!" The chants went on for several minutes. This time, the President allowed it. He wanted that patriotic and Earth-centric feeling to build, to grow. Finally the chants died down.

"My fellow Americans, a great tragedy struck the Mother. Most of Asia and the Middle East were destroyed in nuclear attacks. Nuclear fallout will spread across the globe, killing innocent animal life, warping our climate, poisoning our habitat. Again, our troubles and that of our Mother Earth began with fundamentalist religious Clingers who could not be rational. Without their insane beliefs, cooler minds would have prevailed."

When Santiago made that comment, Gerard Meiring smirked to himself. No one would acknowledge that the President himself had succumbed to an urge to start nuclear war. Very few people even knew of that...and they would meet unfortunate ends very soon.

The President continued. "Although most of the radiation fallout from that war will be limited to Asia we *will* see increases on this continent. That means an increase in death rates from various cancers. This is not necessarily a detriment to the nation, as it will increase the rate of decline towards a sustainable, smaller population. Perhaps if we continue on track with our five year plan, our resources will again be able to sustain us. We must continue to work towards the goal of sustainable human life which does not stress the resources gifted to us by our Mother Earth. But we must protect ourselves while we do so. Protect ourselves from the radical elements both outside and inside our land."

"My fellow citizens, our government created a system of shields to protect our key cities from the poison which these Clingers unleashed. You, who were chosen to live within these enclaves, will see the power of our national government rise above you this afternoon. Look up into the sky and you shall see the shining protection of your nation's leaders extend over you to shield you."

"To deserve that protection you must act as good citizens. Find the clingers who hide in our midst. Root out this pestilence. Drive them out. Out into the empty lands, away from our precious cities. They must not be allowed to steal our scarce resources. They *will* not be allowed to do so anymore. My fellow Americans, I need your help. Help me destroy this fundamentalist scourge.

"Yes! Yes! Drive them out. Destroy fundamentalism now! Save our cities! Save our nation. Save our Mother!" The chants went on for minutes.

Holding his hands up for quiet, President Santiago looked directly into the camera and took on a serious, kindly expression. "My fellow citizens, you remember the patriotic pledge given by some of our greatest leaders from Hollywood and from Washington a decade ago. Those older citizens, had long and good lives, but were draining our resources. They decided to take action *together.* They *chose* to cease being a drain on our nation's resources. They became the Chosen. You remember the great and respected actors who brought us that message. As your President, today I tell you this. Like those great ones, I am a Chosen person. I have taken the pledge. As soon as I begin to be a drain upon the Mother's resources, I will fulfill that pledge. I will report to one of our many Relief Stations for my own Relief! I am **SOME**one. **S**ave **O**ur **M**other **E**arth. One will make the difference. SOMEone."

The words scrolled across the screen as the Congress rose as one to chant: **"Save Our Mother Earth! Save our Nation! Save Our Mother Earth! Save our Mother Earth!"** People throughout the nation rose along with them, tears streaming down their faces, and joined the chorus. The chants melded into a rendition of the national anthem.

Thirteen

Cleveland, New York, Los Angeles, Washington, New Mount Pleasant...August 10: 1400 hours.

Over the select cities chosen to preserve humankind, power shields arose. Citizens looked up into the sky to see a shining protection over them. They did not know what it was, but they trusted President Santiago. He had told them to watch. As he promised, so it became. They remembered. *"Look up into the sky and you shall see the shining protection of your nation's leaders extend over you to shield you."*

*　　*　　*

102,000 feet above Roxford. August 10: 1430 hours.

The pilot and navigator of the B2 bomber were part of a very exclusive and highly trained regiment. They were trained to carry out orders without question. Further, the mission briefing they were given fully explained their goal. He knew of two dozen other bombers on comparable missions, spread out across the nation. They had a simple job: to eliminate any wasteful generation of energy besides that provided to the chosen cities. It was the only way to save the nation.

The neutron bombs were designed to explode at

58,000 feet, focusing an electromagnetic pulse which would destroy all power generation within their range. No fallout would harm the Mother, no deaths would result...at least not from the bombs. What people did as a result of no power, no motors, no running water — no civilization in one instant...that was not the pilot's business, nor his concern.

The designated cities would be protected by their shields. The pilot looked over the horizon toward Cleveland and saw the shimmering air above the city. He smirked and shook his head. *"Amazing! How the devil did they invent that? Sure could make my job tougher."*

The pilot opened a top secret comband to his immediate supervisor, the National Security Advisor to the President of the United States. "Sir, reporting. We are in place. Asking confirmation of the President's order."

Gerard Meiring knew this was the most important act of his career, probably of his life. "You are confirmed. Executive order LM248."

"Thank you, sir. Executing." The pilot flipped up a red cover and opened the bomb bay doors. Without hesitation, he pressed the release and the bomb dropped away. He immediately hit the afterburners. He needed to be far away over Canada when the bombs went off, to prevent his own plane from losing all electrical function.

*   *   *

Roxford, Ohio

Kerian Noguchi rounded up the remaining people in his program. He had forwarded the critical information about any developments. The Security Director already had the inventions and discoveries of these brilliant young people. New genetic programs, and the theory and drivers for the shields which now protected the cities, were already implemented. However, Noguchi was irritated that he could not find the key elements of either the Artificial Intelligence Computer or of the Crysmetal Compounds which Gem Matthews had developed. Those were essential to national security. Mr. Meiring, the voice who had controlled him all these years, made that *very* clear. He wasn't sure how they'd react when they fully realized the extent of his failure. He shrugged. He could do nothing about that.

As he walked, he looked up, watching for the protective shield the President had promised. He noticed a jet contrail. It was so high that he could not make out the plane ahead of the contrail. As he was looking a sudden flash, brilliant and intense, pierced into his eyes. He instinctively turned away and brought his hand up, but the flash had already burned his retinas beyond repair. He stumbled and fell. He took his hand away but the burning and the intense light continued. "I...I can't see!"

People around him stopped. They felt the pulse, and saw reflections of the flash on buildings. Kerian Noguchi doubled over, writhing in pain, screaming. "Professor, what's wrong?"

Sirens began to sound throughout the city, then died away as power cut off everywhere. The fountains near them stopped. The city stilled. The heat of the day seemed to intensify, to focus itself. As they looked around they realized that the city was quiet. They could hear people call out, screaming like the professor. But there were no sirens, no motors, no mechanical sound at all. It took only a few moments for them to realize they were not in a protected city and for the panic to set in. They had been abandoned. They weren't essential. They scattered, leaving Noguchi to himself.

A cop walked by him, stopped, then said, "Loitering is not allowed in the square. That is a violation of Roxford municipal code 23-9. You cannot remain here."

"But I'm *blind! Help me!*"

"That is not a part of my requisite task. EMT squads are responding elsewhere. Please move along." The cop picked Noguchi up and gave him a gentle shove toward…somewhere.

Through the intense pain, Kerian Noguchi felt a pulse at his side. It was his secure com-phone. It had been designed to withstand the magnetic pulse which had blinded him. He grabbed at it and heard the voice which had directed him for so many years.

"Dr. Noguchi, I expect you realize now that your services are no longer needed. Enjoy the short remainder of your time." The line went dead. Noguchi began to wail for an entirely different reason.

Fourteen

Chrisair, Western Georgia Mountains.
                    August 10: 2:30 p.m.

Chrisair was a small town deep in the mountains. Around a hundred full time residents lived there, all who knew each other well. With few vacation cabins and no "attractions" to draw tourists, few outsiders came. The residents lived a quiet and peaceful life. They welcomed the Matthews family when they bought the cabin years before and had adopted Gem as their own. Few children lived in the town and everyone delighted in this new and active young person.

Joe and Estelle Matthews were amazed that they made it out of Atlanta. In spite of the destruction, the bodies laying around the streets and the general feel of disaster, the traffic lights were working. To his amazement, police were running speed traps for the few electric cars on the road. Joe kept strictly to the speed limit. He did not want a run in with the cops.

He remembered getting a speeding ticket last year. The cop focused on writing the ticket. "You were going two miles over the speed limit, a violation of ordinance 58-2541. The fine will be one hundred forty-three dollars."

"C'mon officer. Can't ya let me off?"

"You were going two miles over the speed limit…" The man repeated the entire spiel, with the exact intonation and words. He continued to write the ticket, tore it from the book and handed it to Joe Matthews. "Drive safely. Have a nice day." He turned and walked back to his motorbike. The cop had no hint of expression on his face at all.

Joe muttered under his breath and drove off. He'd heard of this. Cops pulled people over for going *one* mile over the speed limit. They focused on the law…and you better not violate it.

They made it out of Atlanta with no issues. They had driven for the last thirteen hours, working their way carefully over roads which had been allowed to decay, with potholes and broken pavement everywhere. The forest ran right to the edge of the road, sometimes impinged right into it. They hadn't come up here for over four years, since before Gem went away to school.

"Joe, what is this?"

"It's the Fallow Laws. This land is not supposed to be inhabited. They've left the roads for nature to take care of. And, the forest seems to be really healthy and doing a fantastic job of taking back the roadway. Never was much of a road anyway."

"Do you think they'll be there?"

"The townspeople? Yeah, I think they will be. They were always fiercely independent. Didn't rely too much on the outside. I doubt the Feds even tried to round them up. It's too far away from anything, and the townspeople'd just fade into the woods."

Three miles away from the small town they felt a pulse thrum in the air around them. A flash of light ran across the mountain. Their car engine died. "What was that?" Joe tried the engine again. Nothing.

Estelle looked at her phone. "Joe. Look." She turned its face to him. It was blank. "I just had the vid open, watching the news. When that pulse hit, the phone went blank. The car died at the same time."

He looked at his digital watch. Also blank. *"What the hell?"* "Something's happened to kill all the electric. We'll need to walk to town from here." They got out of the car and headed up the hill.

Fifteen

Roxford, Ohio. August 10: 10 p.m

Kerian Noguchi could not see the darkness which had fallen with night. He stumbled all over the campus of UC of Ohio. He kept falling over roots and curbs and other objects. He skinned his hands and knees. He finally collapsed. He had no sense of direction, didn't even know where he was anymore. People rushed past him, ignoring his cries for help. He was blind and alone...and afraid. He wished Roger or his wife were here. "Will someone help me?"

He felt a cool breeze on his back. Though he had not heard anyone approach, a woman's voice, gentle and calming, spoke right behind him. "Ahh, father Noguuuchi. Ya've coom ta the only end ya culd have done, though ya would na see it."

"Who's there? Help me! I can't see."

"I am hair to do so. Ya be Rogair's father. I will na let ya die without spaking ta him a last time." A hand reached down to grasp his and pull him up.

"Thank you. Thank you! Who are you?"

"Nevairmind. Jus coom wi' me. Hold my hand."

"Where are we going? I have to find my wife. She'll help."

"She be there, awaiting ya."

"Where?"

"Sure, in the rushes."

Noguchi felt a tug and a tingling sensation as the woman pulled him...and suddenly the air was cool. "What the...."

"Shhh. Things hair be different from what ya know. Doona ask too much."

Noguchi could smell woodsmoke, a fire burning and meat cooking. He heard someone singing a song, and the panting of some animal as it came up beside him. He felt a large long-haired animal brush against him. It licked his hand and he jerked away, and cried out in fright.

"Doona be afeared, Father Noguuchi. It only be the King's hound giving welcoom."

Then, from far away, Noguchi's wife called. "Kerian! Kerian, you're alive! Do you know where Roger is?"

He stumbled. "Kimi, where are you? I can't see you."

"Grace, what happened to his eyes? Why can't he see? Kerian, what happened."

"I was looking up. There was a flash. It hurts so much."

"Mather Noguuchi, he canna see. I doona know this blindness, but I will get some salve from my mather for it. Tha' will relieve the pain."

"Kimi, who *is* this woman? Why is she calling us Mother and Father? Where *are* we? You will tell me."

Silence. Finally Kim Noguchi spoke. "Kerian,

I love you. But everything has changed. You will no longer demand of me. You will ask, and learn to ask nicely."

"What the..."

"Be quiet!" Now her voice was severe, close to breaking. "Why didn't you tell me Roger could speak? *Why*?"

"I just found out two days ago, just before he disappeared. I didn't have time! Too much was happening."

The silence lasted longer, then the other woman's voice said. "Mather Noguuchi, ya must forgive me. Ah've brought ya pain in savin yair husband, but ah saw no other way. The both of ya have much to talk of."

Noguchi felt Kim grab his hand. "Come on! Pick up your feet. Follow me! Grace is right. We have a lot to talk about, you and I."

Noguchi stumbled behind his wife, who hauled him along at a fast pace. "Kimi, who is that woman? Where are we?"

Kim Noguchi stopped so suddenly her husband almost ran into her. She shoved him backward. "That's Grace! The woman our son is going to marry! The woman who loves him like *you never would!* The woman who shot you with an arrow just as you were about to **Kill. Our. Son!** If it were me I would've aimed better, right at your heart!" She left him and stalked away.

The voice behind him was gentle. "Ahh, Father Noguuchi. Give aire time. She doona know yair heart, nair do ya even know it. I aimed my arrow to stop ya from yair own turrible act. The arrow shot true. Ah could've killed ya, and ya sorely tempted me wi' wha' ya sought to do. Also could've Rogair killed ya when he took the sword. We spared ya, though ya would have killed yair own son. Sit an' think on it atime."

Noguchi sat, tears rolling down his eyes. He could hear children singing in the distance.

"The Lord Bless you and keep you.
The Lord make His face to shine upon you,
To shine upon you and be gracious,
And be gracious unto you."

Kerian trembled at the sound. "Where am I? Am I dead? Is this hell? What's going on?" The dog trotted over, plopped itself at his feet and nudged itself against him. He did not notice.

Sixteen

The Cuyahoga Reserve. August 10: 11 p.m.

Roger Noguchi ran. He was near the point of exhaustion. He'd left the city before the shields came down. Thousands of people had already been forced out and many were desperate, already looking for any way to survive. Gangs formed and robbed food, weapons or supplies from anyone they could.

Roger was confronted by two such groups and fought his way through each, using his swords to block; to prevent, not to kill. He turned the sword each time at the last second to knock the opponents out. Twice, someone shot at him and he felt the pulse of the aura prevent the shot from harming him. He did not want to think about how those shots were returned to the shooter. *"Not by my hand."* The thought a prayer of desperate hope.

Now, a squad of National Guard troops stalked him. They'd caught him in an open field, where he'd disabled four of them before escaping. They were now on ATV's chasing him. He'd climbed up and away from open land. The fast growing forest made it impossible for the ATV's to follow. The soldiers ran, trying to outmaneuver him.

He'd crested the last hills into the Preserve,

running at full tilt. He dodged through the heavy underbrush, following a sure signal; one which no one else could have possibly felt. The last of the soldiers lost him in the thick underbrush just before the crest. He plunged across and down and then went silent.

A stream ran south and he stepped into it to follow it downward. They would not be able to follow him now. He headed home: to the cave, to the group.

The cave sat, still and silent; dark, as if untouched by man. It was shadowed by great trees which had grown up to comfort its secrets with their protective embrace. Roger Noguchi approached in absolute silence. He looked at the cave and wondered at the parallels which ran through their lives. A cave much like this one had housed a great evil, a demon who poisoned its earth and all the places surrounding it. A demon who came to Cleveland, and sought to destroy them and all of mankind with them. A similar cave, man-made, sat in the Time Traxx building in Cleveland, twenty miles away. The cave he looked at now held the remnant of those chosen to wield the power of the sword, led by a lord given that power; a lord who rejected it at every turn.

The group had remained in the Cuyahoga Reserve, deep in the cave. If they'd been on the road when the EMP bombs were dropped, they would have been stranded. The search for them was too intense at the moment anyway.

They waited for Roger's return from Cleveland. He should have returned in the early afternoon.

Darkness had fallen hours before, but they did not dare light a fire. They heard movement outside, then saw Roger enter. Roger was tempted to bow to Broddin, knowing how it irritated him. He grinned.

"I wouldn't do that if I were you." Broddin had read Roger's thoughts.

Roger shrugged. "Don't care. You *are* Lord Broddin, whether you face it or not."

"Don't remind me." Broddin smiled with relief. "I was worried."

"Nah, nobody notices me. I waited to make sure some people got safely away before they dropped the shields. Then, the bomb blast stopped the car. Walked a few miles. The killing has already started. Had to be careful. Had to dodge a little."

"We all felt your 'dodging.' I see you found us, even in the dark."

"I can feel you all like I was standing right here. It's weird. Doesn't diminish with distance either. Could hear each of you worrying about me. Stop. It's a waste of time. I know things before they happen."

"Tough. We especially heard your warning to our people to leave the city."

Roger's expression was pained. "Only three hundred answered. Three hundred out of half a million people. It's not enough."

Broddin grasped his friend's shoulder. "It will have to be enough. We need leaders; people who will take charge of groups and guide them out to the forests preserves — away from here. We heard the warning. No one will be safe. Not even us. They can't touch us directly, but they'll use our concern for others."

"Speaking of that, some children found me."

"Found you?"

"Yeah, can't explain it. They have a leader. Sharp kid! We have to protect them, too."

Broddin frowned and shook his head. "How are we going to do that? We'll have trouble enough saving ourselves."

"Not sure yet."

Gem came up to stand beside Broddin. "You say these kids came up to you? That's unusual these days. Kids don't trust anybody."

"Yeah, he came right up. Took my hand. Later, gave me a hug. It's like this Shaunte *chose* me. He saw me and chose me to help him. I only know I couldn't leave this kid and his 'clan' alone in that city. Not to that kind of fate."

"We'll figure that out tomorrow."

Roger looked at his friends. "Yes. They'll meet us at Ravenna, along with the others."

"At the battlefield."

Roger shrugged. "I'm not sure why. I didn't choose that site."

"Yeah, I know. It was chosen for us."

Seventeen

The Ravenna battlefield. August 11: 0300 hours.

The elite Homeland Security unit bivouacked on the field where they had first landed. Following a time honored practice, they'd planted an American flag in the middle of the camp. Their captain thought this place was creepy. Fourteen thousand mass graves right across the ridge, dug in one day. *"Fourteen thousand Americans killed by that bastard Broddin's army!"* He was angry that such treason could breed right here in the heart of America. *"A two hundred thousand man army, they say. Where'd the rest of 'em go? Just faded back into society, as if the battle never happened? How could that be?"*

He had promised Mr. Meiring that he'd find Broddin and he meant to keep that promise. As he sat brooding on how Broddin's party had escaped, his mood was foul. The weather turned, as if to reflect the dark rage within him. Clouds quickly formed from the west, blocked out the stars, and stretched across the sky. Thunder called across the hills and suddenly torrents of rain poured down on them. The captain jumped into his tent but not before being soaked.

Dozens of bolts of lightning struck down around their encampment, huge blasts sizzling the air not a hundred yards from them. Bolt after bolt, so close they seared his vision. The claps of thunder followed, deafened the soldiers, disorienting them, driving them to huddle within the tents.

The Captain squinted his eyes and looked out from his tent. He'd never seen a storm with this intensity, never seen lightning so close. The flag whipped back and forth in the wind.

From within one of the bolts of lightning, a creature stepped out and looked around. From the curtains of falling rain, another came. It saw its brother and nodded. A third formed in the mists rising from the ground. A thin vortex reached down from the clouds and deposited a fourth. They stood well over eight feet tall, each wrapped in a cloak which blended into the surroundings.

The four looked to where the captain was huddled. This man had fought enemy troops all over the world, sometimes far superior in numbers or firepower. His courage had inspired his men. He had earned four silver stars and a purple heart. Nothing on earth could bother him. Now from some place deep within, fear rose; a bone chilling fear he had never known. From that deep place, he found a thought much like a prayer. *"No. Please. Please don't see me."*

They walked over to the captain. The creature who came from the lightning looked down. Its eyes were cold, cruel in the assessment of the man. They held judgement with no hint of mercy in them. "You will leave, you and your men at first light."

The hardened combat veteran trembled with fear. Ye...Yes, sir."

The four turned their backs, then simply disappeared. The captain blinked then grabbed his weapon. He raced out and looked all around, seeking a target, someone to kill. There was nothing. He went back into his tent to wait for the storm to pass. The man did not know what just happened. He was certain of only one thing. As soon as this storm passed, they would get the hell out. He didn't want to look into those eyes, not ever again.

The Chameleons had arrived.

Eighteen

The Ravenna Battlefield. August 11: 9 a.m.

James Broddin and Gem Matthews stood on the crest of the hill, watching as three hundred men made their way up toward them. Behind them stood the remaining party: Roger Noguchi, Richard Solaris, Harry and Audrey Amerlinz, William Broddin, and Frank Riley.

No one else was around. They saw signs of an encampment, but whoever was here had left quickly. Roger felt a strange tingling, like they were being watched. He kept seeing shadows in his peripheral vision. Yet when he turned to look, he saw nothing.

Broddin was amazed to see dozens of children following the men. Other men and women joined the group and began some unconscious process of separating into small groups. One boy separated himself from the group, ran up to Roger and threw himself into Roger's arms. "We made it! You did too. I was afraid for you last night."

Roger roughed up his hair. "Nah, no need to be afraid." He turned to Gem and Broddin. "This is Shaunte."

Gem smiled. "We've heard about you. We're glad you're here."

Shaunte turned to Roger. "I met this nice guy, Mr. Siri. He and a lady named Margaret said they'd be glad for all of us to join them. I like them. Mr. Siri smiles a lot. Mind if we go with them?"

"That'll be fine. We couldn't be together right now, anyway."

The boy looked at Roger, his face now serious, his eyes dark. "I know. Sometimes, I dream things. Be careful." Suddenly, his voice strained, he said, "Roger, don't go to the game! Don't go!"

"What are you talking about?"

"I don't know. My dream was scary. The game was scary! You might die!"

Roger hugged Shaunte to him. "Okay. I promise I won't go to the game, whatever that means. Meanwhile, go on back to Mr. Siri and Miss Margaret." Roger watched as the young boy turned and walked away. He took a tall woman's hand, then waved.

Gem and Broddin turned to face the three hundred who approached. Broddin sighed. He had not asked for this duty, had never sought power or authority or a hold over men. Yet, he was chosen to lead, made whole, given the authority and the duty to exercise it. He turned to Roger. "Your sword, please."

Roger handed his left-hand sword over to Broddin. "James, I give you this gift." As he did so, the sword vibrated and shaded into a brilliant blue white. Broddin stared at it a moment wishing he could understand. How was this sword, plain steel, imbued with power? He shrugged, then turned to face the men and raised his arm. "I call you to one purpose."

As one, the men kneeled. "Yes, Lord Broddin."

"You are to go out pairs. The devastation has already begun. People will need our aid: people starving, lost, seeking help. These children around you need care and help. Lead them out into the woods, away from the towns and fields. Travel towards the south, and the west. Find safe havens and fortify them. You have my protection and my imprimatur upon you and those you find of any faith."

Broddin walked among the men, and touched the sword to their shoulders.

"Rise, Sir James, Violet."

"Rise, Sir Peter, Red."

"Rise, Sir Sirichai, Yellow."

Roger watched as each rose, three hundred men now glowing in rainbow auras reflecting power and purpose. Their auras varied in strength, most being very dim, some stronger. Then, they joined in pairs and left the field in various directions. The children followed.

Broddin walked back to stand next to Gem. She took his hand. "You still aren't comfortable with this power, are you?"

"I'll never be comfortable. Men were not made to be ruled, to be commanded. How am I different from President Santiago, commanding these men?"

"You're different. Believe me. You just gave them their freedom and their purpose together."

Broddin looked at her, touched her face and smiled. "You're always one step ahead of me. When will I catch up with you?"

She laughed. "Never. But, you'll never be bored either."

Broddin smiled. "I love you."

"I love you too."

As they talked, Roger approached them. "You need to move out, too. South through Steubenville." His intention was clear to them. He was staying behind.

The group gathered around him. Each of them could see the firmness of Roger's intention, his reasons for staying and his goals.

"You shouldn't stay. It's too dangerous."

"She'll find you, no matter where you are."

"Are these people really worth the risk? I know the enemies can't touch you, but perhaps some errant strike might..."

Roger held up his hands. "I am staying. I cannot leave...certain people. I will do what I can to protect the innocent. I will not leave them to the destruction which may come to them. And, I have one important promise to keep, the most important in my life. I will not betray it."

Broddin's father, William, spoke. "Yer not stayin' here alone."

"I'll be fine. No one notices me. I hide in plain sight."

"Ya, while yer glowing violet."

"And, you're yellow and six foot five?"

"Ya can argue all ya want. I'm stayin."

"Mr. Broddin, William..." Roger stopped. He

could see into William's heart. He knew he couldn't persuade him to leave. He quietly said, "The others need you."

"Not as much as you will. Not leavin, not 'til you do."

Roger shrugged, then handed Gem a detailed map of the course they should take and instructions on the herbs and plants they would find to eat. Richard Solaris stepped in, grabbed the instructions and map and tossed them back at Roger. "I don't need this crap. You keep 'em and follow when you get a chance. I'll get them through and get what they need to eat. And quit being an idiot. Let the man stay with you. Every soldier needs a backup."

Roger started to protest but Solaris walked away into the woods. The others hugged both of the men, then turned to follow Solaris. Gem was the last to leave. "Be careful, both of you. We can't afford to lose anyone." She hugged Roger, then they turned and followed Solaris into the trees.

Roger stood on the rise of the hill. He looked east in the direction his friends went, then west where the other groups were disappearing in the distance with his new young friend. He wondered again at the loss he felt, the second in two days. He wasn't sure he would ever see Shaunte again and his heart was heavy with that knowledge.

Nineteen

Cleveland, New York, Los Angeles, Washington...

Those cities deemed worthy, important, critical to the nation, were spared. The grateful citizens remembered the President's words. *"...to deserve that protection you must act as good citizens. Find the Clingers who hide in our midst. Root out this pestilence. Drive them out. Out into the empty lands, away from our precious cities."* They acted in patriotic fervor to earn their leader's favor.

Over the next weeks, after years of the frustrations of hunger and heat, of rationing and scarcity, people unleashed their pent up fury upon their neighbors. Citizens rounded up those known Clingers, entire families. Some tried to fight back but were quickly overwhelmed and killed. Other citizens turned in neighbors to local reporters who reported those Clingers to the police. The police did their duty with efficiency.

Some citizens took advantage of the situation to settle old scores. They brought charges that certain people held secret rituals. Many furiously denied the charges but the reporters took them in anyway. They were driven out or killed.

Mobs looted and then burned Churches,

mosques, and synagogues. The night skylines glowed red with fires which burned unheeded. No fire department would respond to save such structures. When they did, crowds blocked the engines from getting near.

The authorities brought the prominent leaders of each religion to quick trials, found them guilty of treason and summarily executed them. Examples had to be made of the leaders. Other followers, millions, had all their possessions taken and were forced out of the cities into the countryside. Without supplies or skills, most would not last more than a few days or weeks.

Military forces occupied the cities and upheld martial law. This kind of law was outside the scope or ability of the normal police forces to enforce. To aid in the implementation of the plan, the federal government opened vast storehouses of food and distributed it to the city centers. They provided ample food to those citizens chosen to remain. For the first time in years, people were not hungry. Power flowed into the cities, enough that the brownouts ceased. The authorities allowed air conditioning, and people felt the cool air they had longed for and dreamed of.

The Press reinforced and embellished the story of the rebellion. Those who once acted to save the country and mankind, now became the hunted. A bounty was placed on Broddin's head and on those of his companions. Broddin's face flashed on every screen, every tablet, at the beginning of every news show, on every feed.

The next day, a directive came down from Washington to every reporter on staff. "Find James Broddin. Find Roger Noguchi and Gem Matthews. Report any person who has a glowing color around them. The nation deserves answers!"

Reporters fanned out across cities, watching. They scanned faces, seeking that face, hoping to be the one who reported the whereabouts of this traitor. The reporter who got that scoop would rise to the elite ranks of the government's Reporters.

Soon, stories began to circulate on webcasts, across feeds. Those stories showed graphic videos of the strife outside the cities, strife attributed to "believers."

Dateline, Cleveland, Ohio: "This is Marta Gibbs reporting. A mass attack was caught on satellite feed as it happened last night. The vid is grainy, but you can clearly see the combat between Christian and Muslim factions as they war over a grocery warehouse filled with stored food. There are some reported ten thousand dead. We can thank our gracious leaders for their protection from this kind of irrational warfare going on right now in the Fallow Lands. We can only hope that these irrational people make short work of one another so the nation can again be free to pursue its goals."

Dateline, Las Vegas, Nevada: "Jose DeMarco, here for ABC news channel two. Take a look at this video clip sent to us by a concerned citizen near the border with our sister nation, Mexico. As you can see, the Texas rebels, who illegally seceded from the nation, bombed the main cities of our neighbor, killing hundreds of thousands. Our national government promises they will wreak revenge on the innocent citizens of Mexico — after we secure all areas within our main city centers."

Dateline, Atlanta, Georgia: "Wendy Weng reporting for ABC news. Today, we watched the trial and execution of one of the ringleaders of the Clinger revolution. His minions called him 'father' and revered him. No man deserves that kind of honor besides our leaders or our great President. Ignatius Perry, former priest of a Catholic Church in Atlanta, was hanged at Revolution Square. The man offered no defense for his actions and teachings. He died trying to utter some kind of rituals over the city, telling his God 'They know not what they do.'" The reporter chuckled. "Well, we knew what to do with his kind of treason. His body will remain on display as an inspiration to our citizens to seek out all those who would destroy our great nation."

Dateline, New Mount Pleasant, South Carolina: "Trey Bair reporting for WUSC Webtv 1865. People of New Mount Pleasant, you need to watch this vicious attempt to destroy our great city. Clingers of all three persuasions sailed across Charleston Harbor last night, infiltrated the historic Charleston City Preserve and attempted to breach our city defenses on the Rav National Bridge. We can bless our great national government for its foresight. Those forces were repelled by the strength of our shield protection, and subsequently destroyed by

National Guard troops. The plot was uncovered by one of our own WUSC reporters, Hugo Rhinn, who properly reported it to the authorities. Mr. Rhinn will receive a National Merit award for his reporting efforts in the service of our great nation."

Dateline, New Mount Pleasant, South Carolina: "David Saul, here, with a follow-up on Trey Bair's report to you of the force which attacked our city. It has come to our attention that the attackers were Ferals, those who refused to leave the Fallow Lands when our great leaders declared the essential need to rejuvenate our Mother Earth. In spite of the certainty that human presence would despoil the government's work to increase the regrowth of our prime forests, and our government's wise directive to move into the city, these Feral human beings remained. The Ferals now joined with the Clingers and are considered highly dangerous. You may be confident that your national government will not rest until all these violators are eliminated."

Dateline Cleveland, New York, Los Angeles, Washington. The reports came in, day after day, highlighting the killing and destruction, the horrors perpetrated by Jews, Muslims and Christians on each other as those Clingers faced certain death after being expelled from the cities.

Calls from Washington beat at reporters day after day. "Find Broddin, Noguchi, Matthews and their army. Report them to the nearest authority. Be a public hero. Do your job. Report. Report."

The soldier, Robert Grey, was identified as a

threat to national security. A contingent of Homeland Security confronted him. "Lieutenant Grey, you interacted with this Broddin...and you let him go. Where is he?"

"I don't know."

"You must have an idea. We saw that you spoke to him and to his aides. And, you have that glowing shield on."

"Gentlemen, I have a story to tell you."

"Robert Grey..."

"Please call me Robert Yellow..."

"...you are under arrest for collusion with the enemy of our nation. If you don't come willingly, you will be forced..."

"You don't need to force me. I'll go with you."

Aaron Stein watched his friend leave, and wondered if he'd ever see him again. Yellow had told him, "Keep quiet. Keep your head down and do nothing."

Twenty

The Appalachian Mountains. September 11: 7:30 a.m.

Richard Solaris lay flat and looked over the crest of a hill. He looked down into a valley which ran southwest, following a meandering river. A small waterfall was just off to the east and he could hear the water cascade down the rocks. He watched for telltale signs of encampments: the smell of drifting smoke, broken paths, movement on the air. It was just a month since they left the Cleveland area. He felt like it had been years.

This brought back memories. Twenty years ago, but you don't forget certain skills. He'd been a Navy Seal, fighting all over Africa. Same survival tricks. Different place. This was somewhere in what once was West Virginia. He winced. This was his home state, before the feds had declared it "Fallow Land."

All over the nation, The Fallow Laws had established sanctuaries where the Mother would be protected from all human encroachment. This particular reserve took the entire state of West Virginia, most of Tennessee, Kentucky, North and South Carolina, and parts of Northwestern Georgia.

The Feds chased out every human being, or at least the ones they could catch. That was years ago.

He wondered how many remained, and if they were friend or foe.

Solaris joined Broddin's band the day before they went to war with the Ishar Crull. He thought they were insane, walking into the midst of that army with nothing but swords and faith. He smirked to himself. *"Yeah, we were insane. But God protects drunks and fools…and I guess insane people, too."*

The remaining party held back from the crest waiting for a sign. No sound came from behind him. He heard no sound from the valley. No children's laughter, no shouts, no animal grunts or cries. *"No bird calls,"* he thought. Not safe. He signaled for them to turn, to continue along the difficult trail across the crest of the mountain.

Down in the valley the highways were blasted from these mountains in the last century. They had been reworked as beds for the high speed trains which carried soldiers and critical personnel on federal business. There were no stops. Only government personnel were allowed within this area and only on a limited basis.

Gem Matthews fell in behind Solaris, then James Broddin, keeping his stride close to follow in her steps. They had not seen any other people in over a week, but they took care to leave as little trail as possible in case someone was tracking them. The rest of the party stayed close. Harry Amerlinz kept rear guard, hiding their trail as best he could.

Gem thought back on these four weeks. They hadn't made much progress since they left Roger in

Ravenna. The first week was the slowest, hiding from the constant patrols of the Homeland Security forces and from roving bands of Ferals. The Ferals picked up many recruits from those chased from the cities. The Ferals preyed on the helpless groups who wandered the countryside looking for some relief from hunger or exposure. They would ambush these groups, kill many in quick raiding parties, and take whatever food or supplies were left.

Many faith communities formed bands to protect themselves, using makeshift shields. They moved only during the day, stayed in the clear fields, and sought any edible scraps. People were starving. Those remaining had little energy and no time to bury their dead. They were too busy foraging for new food. The fields they passed were stripped bare, victims to a plague more affective at destruction than locusts.

Skirmishes arose between the various groups who came upon one another. Towns along the path of this plague built hastily fortified walls to try to defend themselves. Few were able to resist the overwhelming attack of large forces who had no food, no shelter, no hope left.

Throughout the first week, the constant small arms fire testified to the desperate battles of factions in the bombed areas to gain control, to maintain security, to protect their own. Midway into week two, the ammunition ran out. The guns went silent. The fighting took a more personal and vicious turn — with clubs, knives or whatever came to hand.

The ferals did whatever they needed to survive.

Theft, murder, cannibalism. The Homeland Security Forces were worse. They killed for sport or for spite or simply for the thrill of it. Gem felt a tinge of some memory in her head, as if she'd seen or felt this before: an understanding of the savagery men were capable of. She couldn't identify it, couldn't remember where she'd learned that knowledge, but she knew she had thought that before.

Many times they came across towns torn apart, bodies left to rot in the streets, to be memorialized only by the vultures and crows which feasted upon them. They gave those towns wide berth. There still might be survivors. At first, they thought to bury the dead, but there were simply too many.

Outside of one town, Solaris came upon a dead soldier. The man obviously died defending a building which housed a Primary Education Facility. No children were left inside, nor could any be seen. Solaris knelt down next to the soldier. He closed his eyes in prayer. When he opened them, he saw that the soldier had wrapped an American flag around his waist and chest. "You died for the country you knew, brother." He carefully unwrapped the flag from the man's body and wrapped it around his own. "I won't forget."

Through this devastation, in the midst of death and destruction, of starvation and depravity, three hundred groups passed. Among them were Gem and Broddin's small band. Few saw or noticed these groups. They were the faithful remnant, chosen to seek, to find a land they once loved...or perhaps to build one anew.

After Broddin's group left the devastation of the cities and made their way into the forests, they constantly battled to find a trail through the dense undergrowth. The GenArbor factor had worked magnificently in the last three years to grow the forests. The intention was to make travel in the Preserves so difficult that most humans would not think of going there.

An unintended consequence was that fruits and vegetables grew in wild abundance anywhere they walked, so they easily found enough to keep them fed and strong. The constant exercise soon honed their muscles.

Twenty-one

Rural Kansas. September 11: 7:30 a.m.

Sirichai Charoenkul lead his small band across the plains. They had walked for more than a month. They found shelter where they could and foraged for food along the way. Three hunters used crossbows, so they killed small game for meat.

Sirichai's friend Margaret joined him even before they arrived at the Ravenna battlefield. Shaunte and his clan of children found them there. They wondered how they could care for these kids. It became evident early on in their walk that the children were self-sufficient. They would disappear for an hour, then show up with food or clothing, first aid supplies and other goods.

Several couples, who fled the devastation of the war, joined the group right after they had left Ravenna. The challenges — of the walk, of fighting, of the day to day survival — molded them into families. Couples began to teach, to listen…and to fall in love with these children.

They made their way through back woods areas, avoiding cities and towns. Sirichai felt they were doing well. They avoided the worst of the devastation and were fairly comfortable. Several raiding parties of Ferals tried to attack them, but were rebuffed by the skill of the archers and by the field of protection which Siri's aura threw over them.

The fall rains came and damped down the grain fields around them. There were plenty of grains around: corn, wheat, soy, barley. The fields had been left at the start of the harvest, when the reaping machines went silent. Farmers returned to the times hundreds of years ago, when they would gather in small communities, plant limited crops and trade for goods.

They were approaching one of these farm communities when Sirichai felt a stabbing pain in his abdomen. He doubled over, holding his stomach.

His lieutenants came to his side. "What's wrong?"

"Think I have a hernia. Maybe the community up ahead has a doctor."

They looked at one another doubtfully. They'd survived by *not* approaching any town, not exposing their party to ambush or attack. "Do you really think we should go there?"

Sirichai tried to assess, to discern some indication of the town from a mile away. "I just don't know." He gathered them around him. "We have a choice. If we avoid the town, I may get better. I don't feel that's the case. If they don't have a doctor it won't matter anyway. Does someone want to recon the town?"

Margaret, his second in command, straightened up. "No. We make ourselves known and approach them. I'm tired of walking, tired of running away. Let's see what they say."

They half carried him the mile towards town. As they approached, they could sense the town get quiet. They walked up to the town sign of "Wheaten" and stopped. They put their weapons away. Margaret called out. "Anyone? We need help. Our leader has some stomach problem."

The town was quiet. There was no answer. No movement. She shrugged. "I guess we'll just walk on in."

The voice came from the side of the road, among the cornstalks. "You can jes keep moving on. We don't want no problems here, no sick people infectin' us, no nuclear poison. And, no Clingers."

Margaret held up her hands. "We aren't going to give trouble. We have things to trade. We can hunt some game and share with you. Do you have a doc here? Or a nurse? This man isn't infectious. He just has a hernia, we think."

A woman appeared from one of the houses, a golden retriever at her side. She walked toward them, and stopped ten feet away. She was tall, lean and severe looking. "Jeb, you can come out. Keep your weapon trained on 'em." She turned to the dog. "Go'on, boy. Check 'em."

The dog hesitated, but then walked over warily to the party. They stood still, not knowing what he would do. He sniffed at each of them, walked around twice, then returned to the woman, wagging his tail.

The woman seemed to relax a bit, then said to

Margaret. "Dog says yer okay. That's good by me. Let me see 'im. I'm a nurse. No docs roun' here. Weren't any even back aforetimes."

She walked closer. She was still wary, trying to watch all the others while she examined Sirichai. "He a Chink or a Jap? We don't cotton ta no commies around here."

Margaret's tone was irritated. "He's from Thailand originally, but he's second generation American. As American as you or me."

"Sorry, didn't mean t'offend. S'jus this whole mess got started with them Chinks and Japs nukin one t'other. We gonna survive, we gotta protek our own."

Margaret decided it wasn't worth the effort to argue. "Tell you what. If it'll make you more comfortable, why don't we sit down on the side of the road over there. Your man Jeb can cover us while you check out Sirichai."

"Seerakai? Sounds like an Indian name. Well, whatever. Suit yerself." She knelt down and began to feel Sirichai's stomach. When she touched one place he winced. "Yep, looks it. Pick 'im up and bring 'im to the stables."

"The stables?"

"S'where I got mah instruments. I take care of the livestock roun' here. Best chance he got, get this thing opened an' sewed back up." She turned to the group. Two o' ya pick 'im up and follow me. Rest o'ya stay here. Jeb! You know what's what."

The farmer nodded. "Yes'm."

Twenty-two

Appalachian Mountains, West Virginia.
September 11: 0745 hours

The sniper had waited a long time for this shot. He knew he'd gone off the reservation, awol. He was on his own, and not following the orders the "geniuses" in DC gave him. *"Hell with that! These pieces of crap killed my buddies."* A particular dark form hovered near him, followed him, fed his hate, and convinced him of their guilt.

He'd stalked the group. A month ago, he had watched through his scope as the Homeland Security unit turned tail and ran from a simple lightning storm. *"Well, it was one hell of a storm, but so what?"* He'd watched the group gather the next morning, recognized Broddin, Matthews and Noguchi. Couldn't miss them with those glowing auras around them. He thought of taking a shot then, but decided to do recon.

He saw three hundred men gather and hundreds of children follow them onto the field. He watched some kind of ritual. The men *kneeled* in front of Broddin. *"What kind of cult is this?"* Broddin touched them with the sword and *they started glowing, too.* *"What do these people have?"* The men disbursed in different directions. Broddin's group finally turned and walked right past where he was hiding. He decided right then to follow, to investigate, to see what they were up to.

It became evident after only a day that they were hiding. They headed south, trying to get as far from Cleveland as possible. That alone gave him the conviction that they were guilty of what the government said they'd done. Nothing else made any sense. He'd given it a full month to make sure. It was now time to end it. He'd start with Solaris. That soldier was too dangerous to leave alive. The sniper didn't want to take a chance that Solaris's reaction to hearing a shot might save the man. The others would be easy. They weren't trained, wouldn't react fast enough. He'd do Broddin next, then move down the line.

The sniper moved ahead, across the valley where he could line up clear shots, once the group came into the open. He was nine hundred yards out, up range. A breeze blew at 3 knots from the east. The rising sun sat crossways to them both, so no issue with reflections. A mist drifted across his own ridge, but that wouldn't be an issue. He set his sights, checked range again, sighted in once on Gem's head. The dark being, which had hung over him for the last month, whispered in his ear, *"This'll be so easy. Pull the trigger now. NowNow**Now!**"* He felt compelled to follow the command and almost did, but shook his head to clear it. He didn't want to chance that soldier getting away. He relaxed his shoulders and waited.

Richard Solaris walked right into the crosshairs. The sniper took a breath, held it and began to squeeze the trigger.

He did not sense the struggle right over his body. In the time it took for the sniper to take his breath, the mist took shape, drew a sword from within its cloak, and struck out against the dark form. The dark being drew its own and the swords crossed, creating fiery flashes around the two creatures. The mist stepped aside as the dark being lunged, stuck its finger behind the rifle's trigger, then slashed upwards with its sword. The dark being was sliced in two and simply vanished into smokey air.

Just before the breakpoint, the sniper hit resistance. He couldn't press the trigger to fire! He pressed harder, but the trigger refused to move a micron more. The gun was yanked from the sniper's hands. He was lifted off his feet. He found himself staring into a pair of eyes which materialized from within the mist. Fear rose up within him. He went for his knife. It wasn't there!

"You will cease to struggle." The voice, deep, terrifying in its strength and in its cold directness, held no emotion at all. He began to tremble. "Fool. I should let you get the shot off...and simply kill yourself. But, I am commanded to save your sorry soul." The sniper was thrown to the ground and held there. The eyes from the mist followed his body down, and never left their lock upon him.

The sniper turned his head, trying to avoid the eyes, or to find some purchase, but he could not. His heart pounded. The thought popped into his mind, "*It's too nice a morning to die.*"

"Yes, this morning is too nice. And, this is not your appointed day to die, Torgeson."

"*How did he...?*"

The voice within the mist chuckled. It was not a pleasant sound. "I know your every thought, your every action past and present." He was picked up and shoved roughly against a tree. "Sit. Do not move."

Torgeson sat still. He'd been bested! He'd never been taken like this. Never! No one had ever outmaneuvered him. "*What just happened?*" As he sat there, the mist drifted across the hill coalesced, then condensed upon itself to become more real. The form this reality took was a creature over eight feet tall. It looked like a man. Its cloak seemed to be made from the mist itself. The mist took human form. He could see its solidity...and could see through it. The contradiction made his eyes ache.

The creature stood, holding his gun, its finger lodged behind the trigger. Torgeson saw what had prevented him from firing. It flexed its arms and crumbled the gun into dust. "You no longer need that."

"What are you?"

"I am Mist. Now you will join the ones you've been following all these weeks."

"What? No, I...." He suddenly found himself lifted and moved across the valley, set right on the path in front of the group.

*   *   *

Solaris rounded a slight bend in the path. As he did, a man appeared on the path where none had been a second before. Solaris brought his gun up, but before he could fire, it was pressed back down. A voice, now more gentle, whispered in his ear. "Do not kill. But do not trust this man. Your first unwilling apprentice." Solaris turned, but no one was there. Just some mist which flowed away down the valley.

Twenty-three

Appalachian Trail, Eastern Mountain Preserve.
September 11: 7:47 a.m.

"Who are you? Where'd you come from?"

The soldier sat on the trail, stunned. He'd been carried across this valley in an instant. He'd felt no time elapse. He was nine hundred yards away, and suddenly here. He couldn't seem to make the transition fit into his brain. And he couldn't make his muscles move enough to even make a break, to try to escape. "Charles S. Torgeson, Captain, United States Army. Serial number 49229853."

Solaris stood away from the man. He couldn't tell how dangerous the man was, but the fact the he'd suddenly appeared from nowhere made him look around, listen for telltale sounds of some ambush. He gestured for the remaining party to fall back to the tree line. Then he sat down on the trail. "Buddy, I'm not your enemy. I'm not gonna interrogate you. I don't even want you here, but here you are."

"Charles S...."

"Save it. You don't need to answer or even say anything. Just sit there while I think."

Torgeson tensed his muscles, trying to see if they had any more feeling, were beginning to work.

They weren't. He was paralyzed.

Solaris focused on the man, and suddenly knew. He could read him. "I was in your sites. Nine hundred yards out, uprange, crosswind 3 knots. Clean shot." Then he saw the eyes in the mist through Torgeson's thoughts, felt the fear, felt the wrench of the transport across the valley. "What was that thing? The thing that stopped the shot?"

Torgeson stared, mouth open. He started back to his trained response, then stopped. "How did you know that?"

Now Solaris chuckled. "I hate to tell you, buddy, but we have no secrets here. Sorry, but let's see more. Special Forces. You've been tracking us for over a month. Ahh...." At this point, Solaris's face fell. He was very serious. "I'm sorry about your unit. I could tell you their death wasn't our doing, but you won't believe me."

"What the?" "How did you get all that Intel? How do you know?"

"Told you, I'm reading it from you."

Torgeson began to focus on a tree beside Solaris, concentrating on it alone. Solaris laughed. "Good try. I like you. You don't give up. Your mother called you Chuck, Charles when you'd been out too late. You've served for eighteen years." He paused, then said quietly, "Thank you, soldier."

Torgeson's eyes shot back to his. "Go to hell! Don't thank me. When I'm ready, I'll kill you and every other traitor who's done this to us, here in America!"

"Good. Glad to see you love your country. Maybe you should question your premise before you decide to kill us, though. Meanwhile, you're paralyzed. Should we just walk on past and leave you here?"

"I'll get better soon, then..."

"No. You won't." He turned back to look at Gem and Broddin. "Guys, come up here. We have an...issue."

"What's going on? Who's this?"

"Name's Torgeson. He's Special Forces, sniper. Been following us since Ravenna. From what I just got, he was about to shoot us from the ridge over there. Suddenly, he's here in front of us. I'm not sure what's going on. Something whispered in my ear "Do not kill, but do not trust this man."

Broddin kneeled down in front of the man. "Can't move, huh?" He touched Torgeson on his shoulder, then began a deep prayer. Power flowed outward from him into the soldier.

Torgeson could feel his muscles unwind, relax, refresh themselves. He knew he'd be back to top form and able to move in just a few seconds. Then, he could...

"I wouldn't try it. Before you tried to grab me, you'll be on the ground again. I'll know every move you think of before you begin it. And you can't run away. Solaris will know every move you make. He could shoot you and wouldn't miss."

Torgeson feinted to his left, brought his foot up to kick out against Broddin...and was immediately back on the ground, face down.

Broddin chuckled. "I told you. Now, you can walk with us for a while, or I can take back what health I gave you and you can sit here and wait for some wolf to find you. Your choice." Broddin didn't really think he could bring the paralysis back, but the choice struck home. He could see Torgeson thinking. "Look soldier, you've followed us for a month, getting Intel. What's a few more days? And you can ask us whatever you want. We aren't hiding who we are or what really happened. Might surprise you to find out more about us. You'll have better Intel than anyone. Your superiors would like that."

"Screw my superiors! Those clowns simply let you walk away, didn't even try to stop you after you killed all those men."

Broddin knew no reasoned argument would touch the man right now. "Tell you what. Come with us for a while. If you still feel the same way after a few days, I'll let you go. You can report everything back. But, don't try to shoot us again. That's a death sentence for you." He sighed. "Torgeson, I've seen too many people shoot at us and watched the bullets returned to their source. I don't want to see someone else die. Will you come with us?"

Torgeson shrugged. "Do I have a choice?"

"Not really. I really wouldn't have left you for the wolves. Come on. We need to get going."

The party moved off across the ridge. Solaris led and Torgeson followed him, with Broddin just behind. As they walked, Torgeson looked across the valley where the mist still clung to the hillside. "It called itself Mist. The mist came to life."

"What?" Broddin heard him from behind and came up to walk beside him.

"You tell me. What kind of thing was that? It disarmed me, brought me here, paralyzed me." He could feel the fear rise within him again and did not like that feeling. He was a soldier. "What was that thing?"

Solaris turned to look back. "Torgeson, I saw what happened through your eyes — get used to that." He saw the hardened look on the man's face. I don't know any more than you. None of us do. We haven't seen anything like that."

"But the mist…seemed to form into a man. Appeared and disappeared, like a chameleon hides. Never seen that good a camouflage. Then it…" He was at a loss for words.

Broddin smiled. "Mystery room, my friend. There are things in heaven and on earth we just don't understand. Probably never will."

*   *   *

The Chameleon named Mist watched as the party moved on across the ridge. He was no longer needed in this place. He had accomplished this purpose for which he was chosen. Other tasks would follow, the first of which lay east of here. A man lived there. One who would either bless or destroy. One who needed protection.

The mist which had clung to the ridge dispersed, rose into the morning sun, became a cloud and drifted toward New Mount Pleasant, South Carolina on the coast. He could have gone there in an instant with simply a thought, but he liked the movement of crawling through time, sensing all around him, feeling the flex and pull of gravity, of sunlight, of wind.

Twenty-four

New Mount Pleasant, South Carolina.
September 11: 8 a.m.

The skyscrapers gleamed in the brisk morning sun. This city had grown in the last few decades to rival any on the East coast. It was patterned after Manhattan, with new streets cut in straight lines. When the Fallow Laws were first passed, the nation undertook an aggressive building campaign to make room for those removed from their homes in the suburbs. Ninety to one hundred ten story complexes rose above the banks of the Cooper and Wando rivers.

The new station for the high speed trains, the only connection between cities, was at West 34th Street. Trains flowed west from there, then in every direction once they passed the major river barriers. Gasoline cars were declared wasteful and inefficient, outlawed for over a decade. Air travel was too expensive for anyone but the elites of Hollywood, New York and Washington.

Public elevators brought the residents from the ground to their respective floors. Most of those floors had views of other buildings. Members of the Party were given the easternmost buildings so they had views of the shoreline. For the elites who lived on the uppermost floors, like David Saul, private express elevators took them up to their units. At these elevations they could look out over the barrier islands through a clear morning to see the sunrise.

The New Mount Pleasant skyline blocked out any view of that sunrise in the Historic Preserve of Charleston. No people were there to complain: they had been removed to preserve Charleston as a memorial to the brutality once perpetuated upon the people. The official histories told the story. *"Slavery made Charleston. Slavery was approved and supported by the beliefs of Clingers — Christians whose Bible called for such a monstrosity."* The Charleston Historic Preserve would be kept as an everlasting reminder, just as the natural Preserves, the Fallow Lands, would be a reminder of man's brutality to Nature, to the Mother Earth.

David Saul stood in his penthouse cube and watched the sun peek over the ocean. The cube was a luxury few knew existed. At 375 square feet, it was fully twenty percent larger than any other unit in the compound. These spacious units were preserved for the elites, for government and reporting personnel, and for Hollywood celebrities when they visited.

He could see twenty miles out over the ocean's surface to see the lightening sky. The sun would soon peek its golden rays above the ocean's curve. David turned back to his desk for the morning's reports. He was reviewing reports on the progress in researching pulse power. This technology was the most carefully guarded secret in the nation's history. The shields protecting cities such as New Mount Pleasant were the most obvious use for the power source. But research continued on more important military and transportation uses.

He remembered when he was briefed at the top secret base at Los Alamos. His guide was very forthcoming. "We have about a hundred top classified scientists. A dozen pilots. No one here has family. Not allowed."

"I read the reports. You've managed to miniaturize the propulsion capacitor enough to install in our vehicles?"

"Yes, but the calibration is still kicking us. It's not refined enough. We apply even a bit of gravitational juice to the vehicle and it's gone. The force opens a wormhole and we're shot somewhere across time. Usually back a hundred years or so."

"No issues with the crew?"

"No. We were surprised about that. The gravitational forces would normally rip apart anything within the ship, or even the ship itself. At least you'd think so, but we found that's not the case. In fact, they seem to shield everything within the field. That's how we first came across the idea to create shields for the cities. Anyway, even though the vehicle is moving at close to the speed of light, the passengers feel like they're sitting still. Suddenly our pilots find themselves hovering over some other place. They look out of the portals and it's a different time. They pop out of nowhere. If people are around, it freaks them out. They suspend there until the forces balance, then it slingshots them back here." He chuckled. "At least, now we know the origin of all those alien spaceship stories."

"What about weapons systems?" He held a particular interest in weapons. That would be the ultimate prize: a weapon which could use the unlimited force of gravity to pulverize an enemy with no radiation, no pollution, no environmental damage.

The technician hesitated. "Not so far. We haven't found a means to focus and project the gravitational force. Its use only seems to propel or shield at this point. As you know, that was the reason the President was so focused on the Israeli theft of our technology. He was afraid if they'd developed weapons, they would use them on us."

"I know. Pete told me about that."

The technician stopped and turned towards Saul. He became flushed. "You know President Santiago personally? What's he like? I heard he's *bold.* That whenever he walks in a room, people just stop and turn towards him! What a *great* man! Saved us all. And you know him! Well, send him my personal thanks for saving us from the Clingers."

David Saul smiled. "I will, young man. I will do that."

"Oh, thank you, sir!"

On the flight home, Saul thought back on that conversation and chuckled. *"'What a great man!' If that kid only knew. Santiago was just trying to save his own ass."*

Twenty-five

Wheaten, Kansas: September 11: 8:15 a.m.

The woman lead them toward a barn on the outskirts of a small cluster of rough hewn homes, the dog trailing at her side. She looked at Margaret. "You the leader o' this band?"

"Nope." Margaret gestured to Sirichai. "He is. I know he's really sick, because his aura's really faint. Otherwise, you'd see why he's our leader."

"Aura? What's that?"

"Hard to say. Shining armor? Focus? Purpose? It's a color that surrounds him. Fades when he's tired — or like now. Grows intense when he's worried, or happy. He was given it by…" She stopped. She didn't want to bring out any connection with Broddin, just in case. "Sorry. I'm Margaret. What's your name?"

The woman looked at her. "No need for names. You ain't stayin' long enough ta learn 'em. Fix 'im and you go. Two days, most. Put 'im in there."

The room looked like it was once used to store tools. It had been thoroughly cleaned. A large window brought some light in. The woman walked in and flipped a switch. Lights came on over a makeshift operating table, an old metal kitchen table.

Margaret stopped in wonder. "Lights? How do you have electricity?"

The woman looked at her. "You people idiots? Thisheer's DC current, like them Amish use. Bombs didn't bother it. Only use it fer 'mergencies. Yer gonna help me. Go warsh up in that sink over there. There's soap. No antiseptic. I'll give 'im a tiny bit ketamine for the pain. S'all we got."

A half hour later, the woman finished. Sirichai did have a hernia, and the woman did a neat stitching job on him. There would be a scar, but no one cared. Sweat beaded the woman's forehead. She wiped it with the back of her hand. "Women shine, they don' sweat. Right Marge?" For the first time, she smiled and Margaret saw she might have been attractive in a different time, different era. "You did good there. Thought you'd toss it or faint. Good job."   She reached out her hand. "Name's Renny."

Twenty-six

Chrisair, Georgia. September 12: 5 a.m.

Estelle Matthews rose from her prayers. She went to the cabin door and opened it to the crisp morning air. She wasn't used to the cold anymore...at least this kind of cold. It was refreshing, to not have the constant heat and humidity.

"It's been a month." She thought back to when they'd walked into a deserted town. The townspeople had been here, at first invisible until they saw who walked into their town. Then they came out to celebrate the Matthews' arrival.

"Glad you're here, but we really didn't expect anyone."

"You've heard about all the troubles out there?"

"Only a little."

"Didn't you feel the pulse? What about your electricity? Do you have any?"

They smiled then. "They cut our power off three years ago. We found we really didn't need it."

"We'll need some help. Our car died three miles out."

"We can handle that." They looked around. Where's Gem? Isn't she with you?"

"No, but she's safe, at least for now. She's

grown quite a bit since you last saw her." The talk went on for days.

Now Estelle sat on the front porch, drinking in the fresh forest air. She knew that Joe would be up soon, preparing the forge. He'd become the local blacksmith, working on wheels for carts and wagons. He seemed to like that work as much as his art. She thought about Gem; knew she was closer, felt she was coming here, but she couldn't be sure yet. She didn't want to tell Joe, get his hopes up.

She'd felt a real scare yesterday. She could feel *real* danger for her daughter. What was it? She couldn't tell. She felt it increase, an intention. Someone was hunting Gem. Then it was gone.

Joe came out on the porch, bent down and kissed her, then sat down beside her. "Done with your prayers, I see."

"Wish you'd join me."

He smiled. "Give me time. I'm not used to this praying thing." His smile faded. "I wonder what happened to your Father Perry? Did he get out?"

"I don't know. I can't really sense it. I hope so, but I do not believe that he would leave his people. The rumors we've heard don't sound good."

Joe Matthews brooded a moment. "Estelle, what'll happen to people like us? If they kill off all the priests and ministers, who's gonna teach? Who's going to preach God's word to people?"

Estelle glanced at him, smiled and took his hand. "So you're not used to this praying thing, huh?"

Twenty-seven

New Mount Pleasant South Carolina, Wando Terminal.   September 12. Sundown

Scott Thibidault stood on the docks. His dark skin glistened with sweat. The heat was oppressive. *"Man, it's good dos shields-up'n'air protek us even heah'on'docks but couldn't dey make'em air condition?"* He had worked the docks all his life, from when he turned thirteen. Now at forty-six he still had the strength and force to run these stupid longshoremen he'd inherited.

He thought back on those years. The unions had changed in that time. Union officials slowly worked to replace his friends with a new kind of worker, from the "Worker Party." His friends lost their jobs for any kind of reason. *"Mah boys be union guys, too!"* But being union was not enough to save them.

Back then, losing your job meant a tougher life. Now it meant certain death. Anyone who was fired reported directly to the Relief stations. He'd lost many good men that way. His friends knew how to work, but that didn't matter. Yeah, these new "Worker Party" men who replaced his friends worked. But they only did exactly what the work manuals called for, never took any initiative. They came to work, never complained, did what they were told, and left.

Thibidault's job turned from productive work to babysitting. What irritated him more was that he had to step in constantly and fix things or do things his buddies would know how to handle. These idiots never seemed to know anything beyond "their assigned task."

He watched them and felt despair deep inside. They were just another symptom of a place more broken every day. They wouldn't *think!* At least, these workers never did the hookons, never drank or smoked, didn't hang out and talk. They didn't even laugh. Just weird.

A dark form whispered in his ear. Despair engulfed him, shook his heart. *"What happen to us? Mama don' ever let such things be. Hookons, gropes out de open. Dese men heah don' seem like men. Dey might'z well be daid. An' me? I any mo' alive then dey be? I bored. 'Most fo'ty seven. Time fo' Relief. Why wait? Jes go right now."*

He looked off across the harbor to where the sun was setting in a brilliant bright blaze. It was close to quitting time. He stood down at the edge, supervising the idiot Worker Party guys, trying to get them to offload a final skid from the container ship. The crane jockey misjudged a load and the skid swung out toward one of the workers. In one instant, Thibidault thought, *"Dat man daid."* In the next, he launched himself across the dock. He crashed into the man and the force of his body carried them both off the pier into the cold water. He felt the steel of the skid whisk across his hair just as they cleared the pier. They both went under the water.

The worker had learned to swim. He didn't know where, but every member of the worker party knew how. He came back up, swam to the pier and climbed out. Just as he did, the shift bell rang. He and every other Worker Party member simply ignored the other man in the water. They looked at each other and said, "Have a good night." Then they left.

Scott Thibidault worked on water all his life, but never had the time to learn to swim. He plunged under the water, his breath gasping in at just the wrong time. The freezing water filled his throat and lungs, made him cough, then gasp again in an automatic reaction. More water poured into his lungs and his mind began to grow dark.

He looked through the dark water around him and realized he must be dying. The image of the setting sun, seen through the water, took life and form. It became the shape of a man, huge, cloaked in a blazing, brilliant light. The man opened his sunlight cloak and wrapped Thibidault into it.

Suddenly air, precious air, filled his lungs. Scott coughed and gagged. He was held still, unable to move. Yet air flowed into him. His breathing eased, but his heart began to race. The creature looked at him with brilliant golden eyes which assessed and judged.

Fear gripped him and Thibidault cried out, "No, don' take me. Mama sayed yah'd come fo' me, but not now Lawd!"

The cloaked figure looked upon this man, small compared to him. "I am not your Lord. Do not fear. You will not die. Cease struggling. I will ease the air in your passage." It placed its hand on the man's chest and the water in the man's lungs was gone. Thibidault took a deep breath, his lungs filling with air which smelled of fresh sea grasses and of life.

The dank water of the river flowed around them, seeking entry. It was held back by the creature's cloak. "Who? What be you?"

"I am Sun. You are Scott Elijah Thibidault. From this day, you will use your middle name only. You are chosen. Watch and ward. See the truth of the things around you. Elijah, you will draw your people out and away from this place."

The cloaked form carried him out from the piers and deposited him on the shore close to Wando Ford. He lay on the fragrant grass, dried by the setting sun, wondering that he was still alive, thankful now as he took in deep drafts of breath. "Lawd, who gonna give me words fo' dis?"

Twenty-eight

Gerard Meiring watched the satellite images move across the screen. They had tracked the Broddin party for the last month, down across Ohio into West Virginia. They followed every move. Meiring chuckled. It was easy. That marine, Torgeson, thought he'd gone off the reservation and was acting on his own. There was so much he didn't know.

For instance, he didn't know that one of the many shots he'd gotten to prevent disease was actually a miniature tracking device lodged in his shoulder. Every soldier in the army had one and very few knew it. They kept that knowledge top secret, eyes only.

Torgeson also didn't know that the President's staff had watched the events unfold on the Ravenna field, and then watched as Torgeson followed the Broddin party when they left.

President Santiago sat next to his advisor. "We should have had someone take Torgeson out earlier. We didn't really need him to track them. With that shining armor, their heat signature can be easily tracked from satellite as long as they're not in some cave."

"Yes, sir. But what good has it done us? We can't seem to touch them or anyone they 'commissioned' in that ceremony. Now, there are hundreds of people with that armor. Maybe thousands. We've tried to get it, to confront many of them, but nothing we have can touch them. Worse, every time we've tried to send any kind of force to intercept their party the electronics are shorted out. We've lost a number of choppers that way. If they're somehow transferring power to short them out, we have no idea how it's happening."

"Patience, Gerry. We'll figure it out in time. Have we gotten anywhere with that soldier we caught who glowed like these people? What's his name? Grey. Has he given us any statement?"

"No, sir. Stubborn bastard. We've sent his buddies to Somalia. Let them get the worst of the combat. If they know anything, they're not saying. Maybe putting them in harm's way will convince him. We hoped by doing that, he'd share the technology with us to protect them. He keeps insisting it's not a weapon, but a 'gift.' Still trying, though." Meiring switched back to the first subject. "Sir, should we just drop the whole Broddin thing? We're spending a lot of resources to convince people to try to find him and report him when we know exactly where he is."

Santiago smiled. "No. The search for him galvanized our reporting forces. The reporters are working overtime to find the man, report him and turn him into the authorities. It keeps them motivated. Besides, it pays to give everyone in the cities an enemy to blame. If we have shortages, which eventually we will, we simply blame Broddin and the Clingers. It makes a convenient scapegoat. Keep sending out the messages."

Meiring frowned. "Yes, sir. But what are we going to do about Broddin and Matthews?"

"Nothing."

"Nothing?"

"Not practical. Nothing we can do. And, they seem to be as afraid of us as we are of them. As long as they keep running, we'll just leave them alone."

Meiring nodded. He didn't like it, but the President was right. What could they do if they couldn't get to them? He'd keep the satellite surveillance on them anyway. *"Know your enemy's whereabouts."*

Twenty-nine

In the Rushes. The Day of the Autumn Equinox

Kim Noguchi sat at the fireside with Rachel, the mother of Grace, the woman betrothed to her son. She could not figure out where they were. Grace had only told her that they were "in the rushes." Nor could Grace explain it at all. When asked, she simply shrugged and said, "Here."

Since Kerian was blinded, Grace took on the task of guiding him from tent to fire, to the river where he could wash. The King's hound had taken a special interest in Noguchi. It stayed by him constantly, laying against him at night or sitting at his side during the day. Noguchi came to enjoy its company, petted it and gave it scraps of the food he was given.

Grace left him at another fire, then came to sit by her future mother-in-law. "Ya must find it somewhair in the hairt ta forgive 'im. I've done so."

It had been over a month. Kim still could not bear to even look at her husband, much less speak to him, God forbid forgive him. "Phah! He gives that dog more attention than he ever gave me or Roger!"

"Dogs are easy to love. Paiple, much hairder."

Kim came to love the lilt in Grace's voice and

the deep accent which sounded Welsh or Gaelic, or the way she said, "Rogair." But she could not accept Grace's ease of forgiveness. She looked at the young woman. "How? How can you? How can I forgive? He was going to *kill* my *son!* He's not even sorry."

Grace thought a moment. "Tis interestin', this blindness o' his. Is it na' like the very blindness he's had all his life to the truth o' what Rogair is? Was it no' blindness drove 'im ta the hurt he was doin' ta both o' ya? Hair a month an' he can barely accept tha' this place is real. An' if he was blind, how could he see through to truth? The mahn has so much confusion, he canna' even think abou' the things done and left undone. Sin? He is no' ready to face tha' yet."

"Then let him sit in his blindness. He can keep the dog."

"Ahh, Mather Noguuchi, doona be so harsh. It wears on yair awn soul. Yet, give it time."

In the month since Grace had "rescued" her, Kim had come to love the girl like her own daughter. She listened to the girl's voice, and tried to accept the words. Yet, her mind slipped away, back to six weeks ago.

It was August Eighth. Kerian had come storming into the house, raving about Roger's lies, about some girl who shot him with an arrow. He was filled with rage and shook her. *"**Where is he?** Has he come back? I must find him. If I don't we're all finished! They'll send us to Relief!"*

"What are you talking about? What's happened to Roger?"

"He ran away from me! He took the sword from me! The girl shot me! With an arrow! I don't know where he went!"

"What do you mean, he ran away?"

Kerian Noguchi looked at his wife for a moment. His face became dark and clouded. "Never mind! You wouldn't understand, anyway. You stupid Clingers are all alike! If you hadn't kept that damned armor, maybe none of this would have happened!" He raced back out of the house, across campus.

Kim watched him go. What was he raving about the armor for? She went down to the basement. The back room door was open, the armoire unlocked and empty. *"Roger had the sword? Where's the armor?"* She couldn't fathom what had happened. As she turned and started back up the stairs, the wall in the corner of the basement began to waver and then divide. From within that divide stepped a young woman, tall and lovely. She carried a bow. Kim caught a glimpse of green behind the girl before the wavering closed. She stepped back.

"Doona be afeared, milady Noguuuchi. I'll not hairt ya."

"What…who are you?"

"We doona ha' much time. They will cooom fair ya, soon. Ya must laive this place wi' me. It be too dangerous fair ya to stay."

"Who are you!" This time a statement, a demand.

The girl blushed. "Fairgive me, milady. I am Grace, betrothed to yair son Rogair. I love him beyond all measure o' this wairld." Now her blush turned slightly pale and her eyes looked down. "I must ask yair fairgiveness. 'Tis true, what yair husband said. I shot him, just a while back."

"With an arrow?"

"Yes'm."

"You must have missed. He's fine."

"I dinna miss. I was na' aimin' ta kill. Jus' ta stop 'im hairmin Rogair."

Kim looked at this young woman. She saw a picture in her head: of her husband being shot at by some primitive girl. She burst out laughing, the gaiety in her voice belying even some possibility of Kerian being harmed. "You really shot him?"

"Pinned his arm to a wall."

Kim couldn't stop laughing. She could see what her husband's fury had been about. She didn't understand, yet, how this had happened, but she couldn't get the image of Kerian stuck to the wall, out of her head. Tears began to form and roll down her face.

"Ahh, ah've hairt ya."

"No. No. I just can't…" She broke out laughing again and the girl smiled in return. "But what do you mean, you stopped him from harming Roger? Kerian wouldn't…" And she stopped. The laughter died. "What was he going to do? He said Roger took the sword from him."

Now Grace's expression fell. "He meant ta kill his awn son."

Kim Noguchi stood there, stunned.

The enormity of what she heard did not want to register, to become reality in her head. "It couldn't…"

But she knew. In some way, in the depth of her being, she knew this girl spoke the truth. Her husband would have taken the only value she held in this world from her, her only son. Tears now fell for an entirely different reason. Her knees started to buckle and Grace instantly caught her and lifted her up.

"Ahhh, milady. Ah dinna main ta bring such hairt to ya. Pairhaps, I shoulda left ya in peace, but Rogair will need ta see ya again."

"Where is he?"

"We canno' raich him now. He walks into grave danger, ta battle a daimon along with his good friends. Thair is no help fair him now but our prayers."

"How?"

"Enough, milady. Too many questions fair now. Coom wi' me an' all will be answaired, bu' we must laive." She was rocking from foot to foot, obviously anxious now.

Then, some of the first words Grace had spoken hit. "But, you said you and Roger are betrothed? He loves you? How do you know?"

"We saw and knew the full o' each other. He asked me tha' very moment. He told me tha' he will always love me. Always and all ways."

The reality of what she heard struck Kim's heart with full force. Her energy renewed, she grasped the girl's cloak. "He spoke? It's the miracle I've prayed for so long! Oh, God! *I have to see him!*"

"Ya will. It will be a fair while before we all do, bu' I know ya will see 'im."

They heard noises upstairs: a door banged open; heavy footsteps on the floor. Voices. Grace looked upward. "They're here." She turned, took Kim's hand and started towards the wavering wall.

"Where are we going?"

Grace smiled. "Into the rushes." They both walked through the wavering into a green, cool world.

Now, as she thought back, Kim Noguchi wished she could find the peace these people felt, the simple joy which shone from them. Was it this place, the "rushes?" Or was it something else? The way they easily laughed, the songs they sang of love and forgiveness, of God's grace and redemption. She listened to the children:

"For the beauty of the earth,
For the beauty of the skies,
For the love which from our birth
Over and around us lies,
Lord of all, to thee we raise
This our joyful hymn of praise."

She felt at home…and alienated at the same time. *"What's holding me back? Why can't I be at peace like them? I'd love to be just like they are."*

Thirty

The trail lead them to higher elevations day after day. The air was brisk in the mornings, refreshing compared to the heat they left the month before. Solaris kept the lead, with Torgeson behind and the others following. They had not seen any sign of human habitation for days.

Solaris's senses were heightened. Even without those signs, he sensed movement in the air: a vibration which followed them for a while. There were just slight sounds, out of place from the rest: a swish of branches off to the right. A quiet rustle of leaves to the left. It was never enough to draw focus, but he heard and it kept him on edge.

They were working their way through a dense patch of forest when Solaris sensed a movement up ahead. He stopped, raising his hand in a signal for those behind him and brought his rifle up.

A single wolf walked out on the trail fifty yards ahead, turned to face them and then sat down. It was huge, probably close to one hundred eighty pounds, its fur matted and gray. Solaris's hand signals brought the party up close. "Keep an eye all around. This could be a feint for an attack." He brought his rifle up to aim at the wolf, but it lowered its head and whined. Then it lay on the path and rolled over, looking back up at him. "What the…?"

Broddin stood next to him. "What's it doing?"

"It's giving signs of submission, like it wants to be accepted. It's not showing any aggression at all."

"Why?"

"I don't know." The wolf crawled a few feet towards them then sat up, panting. It looked like it was smiling. Solaris turned. "Torgeson, take my rifle."

"What are you gonna do?"

"I'm not sure. Going to approach it."

"Are you crazy? It'll rip your throat out before we could react."

"I don't think so. Some feeling tells me it's okay. Besides, I have the aura. It can't harm me."

Broddin wasn't sure. "We don't know that they work with animals. Only humans."

"I'll be all right. Torgeson, take my rifle and zero in on the wolf. If it looks like it's going to attack, take it out."

Torgeson looked at him, incredulous. "You're giving me a weapon."

Solaris was exasperated. "You can't use it against us! You know that! Take it!" He thrust the rifle into the soldier's hands, turned and walked slowly towards the wolf.

Torgeson sighted the rifle on the wolf's head. "I'm not waitin' for it to attack. One inch of a wrong move, it's dead."

Solaris walked up to the wolf. It sat low on all fours, relaxed. He could see it was thin, but not famished or sick. It looked healthy enough. "Hey Wolfie, what ya doin'?" He put his hand down towards the wolf and it ducked its head for him to pet it. His whole body tingled with energy. He hadn't noticed, but his aura was blazing. "You have any buddies around?" It rolled over and he petted its stomach. It gave a satisfied huff and stretched, then it sat up and waited.

Solaris stood up and looked around, listening for any telltale signs. He didn't feel a sense of any other creatures out there. He could not feel any vibration. "You should go back to your pack, fella. Shouldn't be out here alone." The wolf whined, then nudged his hand again. "You want to come with us?"

He turned back to the group. "He wants to come with us!"

Torgeson's eye never left the scope, his finger held the trigger. "Solaris you *are* insane."

"Nah, I don't think so. You can put the rifle down."

"Not 'til yer safely away from that monster."

Now Solaris laughed. "Just a few days ago, you were going to shoot me. Now you're protecting me."

"You're mine! I don't want anything else killin' you. That's all."

"Wolfie's fine. We're walking back to you." Solaris began back toward the group and the wolf trotted next to him like a trained dog. Standing, its haunches came up to Solaris's waist. He put a protective hand on the wolf's neck. Both walked back into the group. Torgeson backed away. The rest were nervous. The wolf walked right into the group, then sat and allowed all the group to pet it. "Folks, I think we just domesticated our first pet. Do we have some of the dried deer meat for him?"

Torgeson shook his head. "What kind of people are you? You're on the run. You stop every Sunday for your rituals. Now you're gonna bring a 'pet' along?" He couldn't believe it as the group gathered around a huge wolf, petting and caressing it. He carefully approached, then turned the rifle and handed it back to Solaris. "Jes keep it away from me."

The wolf huffed and turned away from him as if it understood. Broddin looked at Gem. "What do you think?"

She shrugged. "Is this any stranger than the other things we've seen? I can't imagine what it's doing here but let's just go along for now."

Solaris said, "Hear that, Wolfie? You're in the pack! C'mon, you and I'll take point out front." At that, the wolf turned in quick circles and leaped up like a puppy. It walked a few feet down the trail, then stopped to wait for Solaris. Solaris couldn't stop smiling. "Okay. Coming."

Over the next days, the wolf became a part of the group. It slept at Solaris's side, shared in his food when he gave it to him, and rolled over to be petted on its stomach. Solaris kept smiling and shaking his head.

Broddin came up to him three days later. "You keep shaking your head. What are you thinking?"

Solaris chuckled. "I was a Navy Seal, a sniper just like Torgeson. Do you know what my unit called me? 'Wolf.' Looks like my brother wolf came home to spend some time with me."

Thirty-one

They ended up staying for five weeks. The two women became good friends, sharing stories about the old times, "aforetimes" as Rachel said. The night before they were to leave, they held a banquet. The party's hunters had killed a large deer. The town shared breads, potatoes and lettuce. It was the first actual meal for any of them in three months.

"Meat! I near forgot what it tasted like. Niiice. Thanks, Marge."

"No, thank you! This almost seems...normal." Over fifty people sat in a big central barn room at tables set up for the banquet. The warm glow of candles from the chandelier illuminated smiles. Children ran through the barn rafters, dove into haystacks and burrowed through them in some advanced game of hide and seek. "Seems like Thanksgiving."

Renny looked at them around the table. "Ya know, it could be more like this. We each got skills we can share. Y'all could just stay. We'uns talked it out last couple nights. Think it'd be good fer everbody, 'specially the children. They've made some good friends here with ours." Renny turned to

Sirichai. "What ya think, Siri? Y'all've fit in here real nice."

Sirichai took a while to answer. "Let me pray on it tonight, Renny. I'm tempted to say yes right away. We're all tired of roaming like vagabonds. But the decision isn't ours. It must be God's. We were chosen for this. Let me pray tonight."

Renny smirked. "Ya, I know y'all're prayer filled. Grace bafore meals. Nighttime prayers. Ever Sunday havin' a meetin. Singin' hymns. Not fer me. Not too much time roun' here for that lately, but ta each his own. Talk in the mornin." She got up, waved to Margaret and left.

Sirichai left the room, too. He went out to the barn, went into an empty stall and kneeled down. He liked the evening time, evening prayers: a time for reflection on the day. A time to review the triumphs and the many more failings. He felt the pinch of his stitches and chuckled. "*A thorn in my side. Fitting for me.*"

He began the nightly praise to God for bringing them through to this point, for providing the nourishment, for leading them to this place that saved him. It was late into the night when he turned to petitions. He first asked for safety and health and growth for this community which welcomed them in, protected and shared with them. He prayed for each person by name, and thanked God for their strength, their purity of purpose and their joy in life. Then he asked, "Father, I do not see your plan for us. Shall we stay? Is this where we've been called? Or are we called to walk the wilderness longer?" As he prayed, his aura strengthened, deepened, until the stall filled with a warm glow. Afterward, he sat quiet and waited, anticipating nothing. A sign might be given, or not.

The morning came, brisk with frost on the ground, a sunrise golden in its promise. He was given no answer. He rose from his prayers and turned. Renny sat just inside the barn, watching, her dog at her feet. Siri smiled.

"Yer God didn't speak to ya."

"Well, it's not often that He directly speaks. I might say He whispers to us all the time, but we're too busy to hear. Have you been here long?"

"All night. Jes watchin' what this prayin' thing's about. Does everbody who pray do that? Glow?"

Sirichai looked at Renny for a long moment. The barn creaked in the morning sun. "No. It's a special...responsibility given to me. Often, it's a burden. Only a few of us have it like this, but people are the same, and we all pray in the same way."

"So you let this God tell you what to do?"

He smiled. He took a Bible from his backpack. "No, it's not like that. We ask for guidance and there are lots of words in here which help us to find the right way to live. But He doesn't tell us. He gave us the freedom to go our way, to make mistakes — to even reject Him, like our country has done. But as far as we run away from Him, He's still right behind us whenever we turn back."

"That'd be nice, havin' somebody there for ya."

"Renny, don't you feel a longing...for some life

beyond just every day? Are you perfectly happy in life or are you missing something?"

"You mean 'sides a long hot shower? Safety? All the electricity we'd like? Plenty food to eat? My husband back? He's dead by the way. He gone to yer God? Or jes rottin' in the ground?"

Sirichai thought on this, then decided to take a different tack. "A man was once attacked on the road, robbed and left for dead. All the big officials passed him by, wouldn't even stop to help him. Some guy — who didn't even believe like this injured man, who was considered worthless by everyone around him — stopped and saved the man. He brought him to an inn, paid to get him fixed up and fed. He saved his life."

"Look at you. You brought us in. You could have let me die. It wouldn't have been any loss to you, 'no skin off yer backside,' as you'd say. Yet, you put yourself out, put your people in danger. You gave of yourself. You wouldn't look past a stranger on the road and not care. You're like that man."

"Well, that's how my God is. He sees us hurt, dying, sick, sinning...and he cares! He puts himself out for us. For me. For you. He gave of himself so much that He died...for us. Haven't you heard that story?"

Renny shrugged. "Nah. No preachers roun' here. Guess nobody wanted to come out this far from town."

Sirichai smiled. "You sat up with me all night, and you watched, not even knowing or understanding 'this prayer thing' as you call it.. Did you fall asleep?"

"No."

Sirichai nodded. "Your faith is deeper than you know, Renny. Gather your people and mine. My God gave me a sign and that sign is *you*. You are the blessing which saved my life, the watcher who cared, like the man on the road. We'll stay here for as long as you will let us. I warn you, though, we want you to hear some good news. News about a God who watches and who doesn't sleep and who cares."

Renny didn't smile back but said, "I think I'd like ta hear more."

Thirty-two

In the rushes. A cool autumn day.

Kerian Noguchi sat by the fire. He had never felt so helpless as in the last two months. He could do nothing on his own. His blindness made it impossible for him to even walk around. Tree roots were everywhere. He sat alone, in silence. That silence had begun two months ago as morose pouting, as angry rebellion against his fate. At times he thought he'd just throw himself into the fire, get it over with. Only the dog's presence comforted him, kept him from harming himself.

Kim would not help. She wanted nothing to do with him. Most other people avoided him. Day and night were no different to him, but he'd gotten used to the rhythm of the camp, so knew when dawn arrived and night fell. *"What am I doing here? And where is here? Nobody will answer me. They just keep talking in riddles in their strange accents. Will this be what the rest of my life feels like?"*

After two weeks, he found a respite from the strangeness he felt. A man visited him. He could tell when the man approached, because people around him would fall silent. Then, Kerian would feel a warmth which radiated from this person. The man would sit down by him, lay his hands on Noguchi's head and say prayers over him.

At first, Noguchi jerked back. "I don't want your mumbo jumbo!" The man sat back and began to speak. "Your passage has not been easy in this place, Dr. Noguchi." The voice was strong, comforting in its deep tones, the accent a rich British. The words popped into his head, *"This is the King's English."*

Noguchi perked up. "Where is this place?"

"Ahh, I wish I could explain to you, but I do not understand this myself, nor does anyone else. Perhaps my own actions caused this. Nonetheless, it brings us comfort to rest here of a while. This is a place set apart in time from ours and from yours."

"Another dimension?" Noguchi's interest was piqued even more.

"Perhaps, or possibly more like a vehicle. It allows us to move through time, much like you fly in one of your aeroplanes through space. You move from one place to another in much less time than you could do so walking. The Rushes are much the same, like an aeroplane which glides us through time from ours to yours."

The voice was calming, the warmth of the man comforting. The man would come once a day to talk about reality, theory, mathematics, physics, astronomy. He spoke the language of science and mathematics, one Noguchi could understand. Then he began to ask questions: about the probabilities of life, about the contradictions between entropy and evolution, about the nature of man and how he could be perfected, about the theories of genetic therapy.

The last especially irritated Noguchi. "*That's* failed. I know that with certainty! Roger was a complete failure on my part. How could I imagine I could change man, just by manipulating the genetic code?" He shrugged, irritated with his own failure.

"You know that with total certainty?"

"Yes."

"You are wrong."

"What?"

"You did succeed, in a way."

"How would you know that?"

"I have watched your progress, your failures and your success in the last years, with some interest. You failed in that you did nothing to *change* the essential nature of who man is, of who Roger would become. What you succeeded at is correcting a genetic defect bred into man over many generations, one which held a curse on man's ability to think and to understand."

"I don't understand."

The man's laugh was friendly, light. "You see? Roger *would* understand! He did as a small child. Roger sees the implications, the results of logic and illogic. He sees much more clearly than any other man since many generations ago. He is *closer* now to how God made us. Not *as* God made us, mind you. But much closer."

"I don't believe you."

"Really? Why could you not see what was right before you? Think! How did Roger know to follow the very two people who would invent Artificial Intelligence? How did he know to make sure no one else would ever discover their formulae? How could he keep such secrets away from you, from your 'control voice,' Dr. Meiring?" Noguchi started. The voice was gentle now. "We have no secrets, Kerian. God has laid our hearts open. The only thing which holds you back is your own stubborn will." The man left Noguchi with his thoughts confused and broiling.

As weeks went by, the man continued to lay hands on him. The pain in his eyes lessened and he was shocked to realize he was beginning to see at least some light. When the man came again, he sensed a strong color of green wash against his eyes.

"What would you like to talk about today, Doctor?"

"Are you the king people talk about? They grow quiet when you come around. And, your voice..."

The laugh was filled with joy. "That's what you want to talk about? No. I am not the young king. He is occupied at this moment. I am just his advisor. So what do you *really* wish to speak about?"

Noguchi was quiet for a long time. "My son."

"You've done him a grave disservice."

Noguchi grunted and a pained chuckle shook him. "Understatement, there."

"Tell me."

"I was blind to everything about who he was."

"Why?"

A tear formed and fell down Kerian's cheek.

"I never saw him as my son. He was always my 'experiment,' my 'project.' I never stopped to simply *look* at him. He was simply a *commodity!* Some thing for my ego. When he showed signs of autism, I thought he was a *burden*, my failure, to be tossed away, a bother, a waste!" He hesitated. "And, then I heard his voice. He has *my voice!* My voice when I was younger. Clear, strong. He called me father." Noguchi started to cry.

"What would you want of this son, now?"

"I just want…just want to hear his voice again. Once again." His voice broke and he put his head in his hands.

Kim Noguchi stood by, listening. Tears flowed freely down her face. She did not approach her husband, could not bring herself to do so. But she heard.

Emrys — advisor to the King, wizard, healer — had spent his days comforting her husband. Now he rose. His aura blazed green around him, the color of the forest where they were camped. As he passed her, he stopped. His quiet voice pierced her. "There are many forms of blindness. Each is a curse. Each can be healed. Most often, it simply takes love…and forgiveness."

"I don't know how!"

"Our Lord said you must forgive seventy times seven. How do any of us do that? Sometimes, you simply must *act* as if you have forgiven him, and keep acting that way…until your heart catches up to your soul. You know in your heart that you loved him.

You still do, regardless of his actions. Hear what he said and ponder on it." The man turned and walked on.

Thirty-three

Appalachian Trail, North Carolina Border.
October 16: 10 a.m.

As they reached one high peak along the trail, they passed an old stone church, a crucifix on its wall. The wolf stopped at the church door and stayed there as the party passed. Broddin's gaze followed the wolf as he passed. He stopped and contemplated the church for minutes, then shrugged and walked on. The wolf caught up with them a little while later. Solaris patted him and said, "Good boy, Wolfie." A quarter mile ahead, a spring bubbled out from the rock, so they stopped.

Solaris drew Broddin aside. "Wolfie tells me that you and I should walk back down to that church awhile, just us."

"Wolfie tells you? Well, okay then. I always do what wolves bid me do."

As they walked, Solaris spoke. "I could see you looking at the church back there, feel your longing and your need for something. What is it?"

Broddin thought about it. "Not really sure. I...I miss being in church, hearing the homily, feeling...I don't know."

"You miss communion, the Mass, the presence

of Christ."

Broddin started. "Richard, where is He? Why isn't He here? Why are we just struggling on alone? A few months ago, I was a researcher, a teacher, well fed, comfortable. Yeah, I had my demons...literally." Solaris chuckled. "But now we're running from everything and everybody. My work is gone. My life as I knew it is done. All I have is Gem. She's enough. I wouldn't take all my life back if it meant losing her. But there must be more to *our* lives than this. God just wouldn't leave us out here in the wilderness."

"He let the Israelites wander 40 years..."

Broddin looked startled. "Yeah, but..."

"...and remember, He was with them."

"Yeah, but He's not with us now. Sure doesn't feel like it."

Solaris looked at his friend. "You know why you're missing God? He's here, I can tell you that! He's talking, but you haven't listened. He's showing, but you haven't seen."

"Now you sound like a priest."

Solaris smiled. "Remember when we passed through Steubenville, Ohio, the second day out? Remember I took a short side trip when we rested for a bit? I stopped by the seminary, where I taught young students before I was called to the sword. You see, before joining you I was a Catholic Priest for ten years."

"What? Why haven't I seen this before?"

Solaris chuckled. "I don't think you've been looking for that."

"I thought you were a Navy Seal."

"I was for twenty years. I got tired of killing. Got called to a different path. Sure seems like God keeps giving me sharp turns in my life. Now here I am, back in...a type of army." Solaris walked up to the church door, the wolf by his side. "Want to join me for a prayer?" The wolf looked back as if he were questioning too.

Broddin hesitated. "I've never prayed with just two people..."

"Come and see." Solaris turned and walked through where the door had been. Broddin followed him. Solaris walked around the small building, touching the walls. The wolf stayed next to him. A few pews sat in the center. He sat and motioned for Broddin to join him. He kneeled on the stone floor and said some quiet prayers. Then he sat back up. "So, when are you going to ask Gem to marry you?"

The question caught Broddin off guard. "She's too young..."

"Excuse one...."

"...and too much happened with all the..."

"Excuse two...."

"...war and this flight and..."

"...three. When will you stop making excuses?"

Broddin fell silent. "I...I..."

"You're afraid."

"No!" Then, quietly, "Yes. I lost her, once. I don't think I could stand to lose her again like that. It would kill me."

"So you're just going to keep separate from

her? Just withdraw? James, you're pulling back from *everything*, closing yourself down. You can't do it in one place and not have it affect everything else. I see it. The others do. Gem has seen it but keeps still about it."

"I'm pretty busy if you haven't noticed." The voice was irritated.

"Four...."

Broddin got up and stalked away, his back to the priest. "You're not my father confessor."

"I could be."

Broddin stood at an open window and looked out across a green valley, seeing the beauty of nature, the flaming color of the changing leaves. He thought, *"What do I want? I have her back, alive, right here. Right with me every day. Yet I'm holding back. Afraid of ...what?"*

"You're afraid of the very communion you've missed." Solaris had heard the thought. "James, we humans are meant to be in union. *You two* were meant to be in union. I see it; everyone does. You see it, too. Why are you holding back?"

The answer came from deep within him. "I'm not worthy."

"What?"

"Richard, I was responsible for all those deaths!"

"You know better than that. Those men, fourteen thousand of them, refused to accept the power of the vision you offered. They chose to die rather than accept it. The sword magnified your loss and your love, yes. But they did not die by your hand. They chose!"

"What if I can't control this power? What if something happens again, to threaten her...us?"

"I think you already took care of that when you sent the sword back. James, you reject power every time you're given it. You don't seek it. You would empty yourself to save us. I don't know if I would have had the strength to throw away that kind of power. You are the purest person I've ever met."

Broddin laughed at that, then grew serious. I have thoughts.... Thoughts I don't want to share."

And Solaris saw some of them. "Ahhh. I should laugh at you but you're hurting so much. Come here and sit down!" Broddin did as Solaris asked. "You're in church, alone with a priest. Anything you want to say? Never mind, I see them. First, we don't see *every* thought. You didn't know I was a priest. Remember back when you still held the sword? Not every thought was transmitted. Only certain ones and only very strong ones."

"But these *are* strong! And, I just shouldn't be thinking about…"

Now Solaris did laugh. "When will you stop beating yourself up over natural thoughts?"

Broddin looked up at him.

"You love this woman more than anything on earth. And you should. You're going to marry her, and soon if I have my say about it. Of course you want her! Did you forget our Lord's very first commandment? 'Be fruitful and multiply.' What do you think He was talking about?"

"But..."

"James, I've taken a lot of confessions in my day, but this is the first time I've had to tell a man *to accept those thoughts about sex.*" He laughed. "First time for everything. Will you stop worrying about what comes natural?" Now he became serious. "James. Gem loves you beyond all measure. Your love for her is the same. She is waiting for you to ask the most important question of both your lives. Ask. It's time. Don't worry about others 'hearing' your thoughts. Somehow, I think God wants those particular thoughts to be kept sacred, just between husband and wife."

"Now let's get back. And I think it's time we we should begin resting on the sabbath as God commanded and holding services. We all need Christ's presence in a sacrament, a physical form to remind us of the real presence of his love.

Thirty-four

James Island, South Carolina. October 24: Dusk

Night was falling on Charleston Harbor. Across from the James Island shore, the city of Charleston sat empty, its steeples a silent testament to the loss this city had borne.

The new city of New Mount Pleasant lay to the north, its modern skyline lit already in the early evening. The haze of its protective shield traced across the center of the RavNational Bridge then bent down to enclose the empty old city.

Mist stood on the limb of a massive oak on a small bluff and looked across the harbor upon the city which had once been named "holy." He stood well over eight feet tall, his cloak seemingly made of the mist which characterized his name. His mouth moved in a constant, silent prayer in a language no one had heard for a very long time.

He had been here for some time, waiting. He waited for commands to act. He was one of those who came to follow commands. He huffed at the name given them currently: Chameleons. "What do these men know of names, of the power which surrounds such things?"

The forest behind him was alive with sound:

owls and sparrows, nighthawks and bats; mice and coyotes, feral dogs and cats, a lone wolf tracking. He heard the pulse of each one, saw and recognized it.

There were also tribes of the humans named "Ferals" by their peers, as if those who had chosen the forest were somehow inferior.

Some of those "Feral" tribes *had* become less than human. They hunted and killed simply for the thrill. But many, like the tribe who lived within the forest canopy in this area, had adapted to their circumstances and began to live with productive purpose. They turned away from all civilized things, quickly forgot the past and all knowledge, save survival. Yet, within, they found a primitive knowledge. They knew that this place was sacred, knew what "holy" meant, though they could not have spoken the word for it had been banned generations ago.

Mist nodded at the few who ventured close to him. While other men could not see him, he allowed that these Ferals would. *"They need something to believe in."* So he was instructed.

He watched as the evening fell, then climbed down from the oak and entered the cave, his home for these past months. It would soon be dark. He stood at the door and watched the last rays of sunset filter from the sky. He would need to place a protection on the entrance. The night here was not like that once described in a human song: "the dark, sacred night." There was nothing sacred about the night blackness which plagued this world now.

In the midst of his constant words, he spoke other phrases. A pall of force enveloped the whole of the cave's area, protected him from the outside...and the world from him. Here in the protecting arms of the cave, he could release the cloak which held him, could return to his essence.

But as he finished the words to seal the cave, he froze. He should have felt him. Did not understand why he hadn't. Then again, it did not matter. Without turning, Mist said, "Good Eve."

The cave remained silent behind him. Dark.

"Did you come to destroy me too?"

No answer. Then, a breath of foul air escaped from the darkness. Every muscle tense, Mist turned slowly to look back into the cave. He discerned the deeper darkness at the rear of the cave. It was the concentrated essence of the wrongness which pervaded the night outside. Then the darkness took form, molded itself into an image similar to Mist's. Yet, it was a horrible negation of that form, misshapen with hate. A dark being stood at the back of the cave, taller than Mist. No sword stood in its hand, but that meant little. A sword was close.

Mist's heart beat a strong pulse. It had been so long. "Hello, Brother."

Again, no answer. The creature simply stared down at Mist, eyes burning red coals.

"I see you still have no desire to speak. I know you, Brother. Know that you love the darkness of absence. Crave silence and stillness, emptiness. You could not abide constant praise, so you chose silence instead."

The creature opened its mouth, then closed it. Opened it again, as if straining to break some great burden, some yoke which held it back. Then, each word articulated, each painful in its sound, it said, "Raziel, brother. I. Come. For. You."

Fear gripped Mist's heart as he was suddenly transported back in time, back to the times before. Sunlight poured out onto a green world ablaze with glory, with freshness unspoiled. And, the dark creature who had stood in the cave now blazed as wonderfully as the land around him. He was fringed with light, beautiful to behold. He laughed and leaped, filled with mirth. His voice was pure and graceful...and Mist could sit and listen to him for hours. "See, Raziel, I told you that these daughters of Eve were wondrous to behold!" The creature turned Mist around and pointed. "Gaze upon true beauty, my brother!" And Mist looked.

She was fair indeed. Golden red hair fell down to her waist, flowing around her naked form like water from the river of life. She looked up at him just as he turned, and the light in her eyes shone like the rays from the throne.

"You find her fair, don't you!" The voice whispered in his ear, enticing. It sought to plant a seed of desire which Mist did not want to feel. "She is ready. Yours. She desires you, also. How could she not find you fair? How could she not want you, compared to *men!*" The last word fell, cold and derisive, from his lips.

The coldness of that last spoken word seized Mist's consciousness and propelled him back to the present. He ached at the lost vision. Tears flowed from his eyes. He remembered her. "Rachel." He remembered too the pleasant wonder of that voice, now lost in time. He closed his eyes. "You show me that again, now? What do you hope to gain? I chose! I chose so long ago! Do not remind me of what I gave up!"

"I will. Always." Pressure rose around the dark being. The trip back in time seemed to release his voice and he spoke more freely. "I could give her to you. You could hold your heart's deepest wish. I rule this world. I can change history as I please! Imagine what your children would be and do."

Images of children, beautiful and bright, impinged themselves on Mist's mind. Images of the reality he could have grasped, which could still be his now if he chose. Mist focused especially on one young girl. She had her mother's face...and his bright power. The voice whispered again, once again. "You could *love.* Isn't that what you always wanted? To love?"

Mist closed his eyes away from the images. Grief struck at his heart. He turned to his brother. "Those images are *lies.* They hold an element of truth. But to make them real, I'd have to deny who I am. I do love. I love the Lord with all my..."

"*Do not speak that drivel here!* You do His will without question. Unheeding, you just do it. But do you ever ask if that Will is good for you?"

"No. I never do. I know it is." Mist looked at his brother. "What do you want?"

"The man! I want the man. Leave him be. He is *mine!*"

"Really."

"He belongs to me. He gave himself to me long ago. Leave him alone!"

"Really? We'll see."

"You want to see? See what this one man does."

Images of devastation burned into Mist's mind. A future too horrible to grasp. All of mankind struck down. The dark creature leaned in toward his brother. "This is started by the man you want to *save!* Why do you allow them to feed destruction?"

"I have no **choice!**"

The anger in Mist's voice made his brother smile. "Ahhh! There it is! I knew you had a spark of independence in there somewhere." The voice was smooth, mocking. "You *do* have choice! You always have. Choose with me. Choose *me*! Do you not still love me?" The voice dropped to an intimate whisper in Mist's ear. "You loved me once. You looked up to me, little brother. All you need to do now is bow your will to me and everything, *every thing* your heart desires will be yours. Look at me. I worship nothing. I am my own creation."

Mist looked at his brother and the pain of loss was so great. "You ask me to be like you. In the beginning, you chose to shut your mouth to praise...and came to love silence. Bringer of light, you are now darkness. You refuse to praise, yet every fiber of your being cannot help but sing constant praise to the Creator. You are at war with yourself more than with God. I will not choose that."

"Then *die!*" The swords were drawn in an instant, ringing together in the closeness of the cave. Twice, they crossed, then the two stood facing each other. The dark being looked down at his brother. "You cannot kill me, but I can kill you."

"Samael will simply replace me. And you didn't come to kill me." Mist looked at the creature before him, then purposely lowered his sword and turned his back. "I do not choose against the Lord.   Get thee behind me. Leave me."

The strength of the darkness beat at his mind, pressed at him, screamed a piercing cry of fury...and was gone.

Mist stood for a long time at the entrance to the cave and gazed out into the darkened landscape. Tears stood in his eyes. He thought again of his brother, lost so completely to him. He wondered why he had come now, why in this particular time. For what purpose? Just for one man? He added a prayer of preservation to his constant voice and words formed again within the midst of his prayers. "Yes, Brother, I still love you."

He turned back into the cave and released the aching cloak which withheld his true nature. Throughout his body, the essence, held quiet, was transformed. Pulsing fire rushed through him. His body engulfed itself in brilliant white flame. Yet, the fire did not consume him. It was his very being.

He turned his face from the world, opened his chest outward. The cloak enfolding him stretched out, became wings which flexed, then lifted Mist off the floor. The exultation within his body fueled the singing strength of his voice in praise. "Adonai..."

Thirty-five

New Mount Pleasant, South Carolina. October 25: 4 p.m.

David Saul reviewed reports on the various actions around the country. Unlike the reports he gave over the vid feeds to the public, these were highly accurate, factual accounts of what took place in the months after the war.

There was an element of truth in those public reports. Tens of thousands died at the hands of loyal citizens who brought out the leaders of the Clingers and executed them. Thousands more had already been killed by Ferals or in pitched battles with Federal Troops when they tried, in desperation, to attack the cities. Millions died of starvation already.

The reports did not mention the many groups who banded together in cooperation to begin communities throughout the rural areas of the country. This was in direct violation of the Fallow Laws. There were many rural farming communities throughout Kansas, Nebraska, and other western states. Feral groups of mountain men remained in Vermont and New Hampshire, using the dense native forests to hide, living in small communities in remote areas too difficult to reach with mechanized forces.

The difficulty was that there were far too many to be able to expend resources to eliminate them. David figured that the coming severe winter, the radiation from Asia and further warfare between rival groups would help to eliminate many more millions. He felt at least some satisfaction in that. Perhaps there would be few enough after the winter that they could do a final sweep and finish the task.

Most of these communities were very small but a few somehow maintained significant size. For instance, Roxford, Ohio still had a population of close to thirty-thousand. He frowned. *"How are they feeding themselves?"* He wondered if he should direct air strikes against at least the larger communities like Roxford. He was about to key in the recommendation when the windows beside him darkened.

He turned to see an incredible storm rush in from the ocean across the barrier islands and slam into his building. He stood up and went to the windows, transfixed. At one hundred-ten stories above the ground, the penthouse swayed in the wind. He didn't feel any fear; the sway was almost comforting. The best engineers had designed this building to withstand hurricane force winds and a possible earthquake at 8.3 magnitude. The building might sway, but it would stand.

He was impressed, though, as he watched the power of Mother Nature. The storm came so swiftly. Lightning struck down all across the islands, then marched toward the skyline around and below him. He could barely see through the torrents of rain pouring down outside. He watched as mist rose across Sullivan's Island, then saw through the torrents of rain as a bolt of lightning struck at the edge of that mist. A waterspout lifted from the coastal waterway.

For a moment, he could see clearly through the curtains of rain. Four figures stood within the midst of that storm. Even from this distance, he could see that they were very tall. They were wrapped in some kind of cloaks. They looked at one another, then turned and looked up as if right at him. Then they simply disappeared. David blinked and looked again. He *knew* he had seen four men there just now. Where had they gone?

He was still looking intently at the spot where they had been when a bolt of lightning shot from the ground and arced straight toward his window. He leaped back and fell against his bed. He saw the lightning sizzle against the glass, making it crackle. Then it was gone. The glass held, but a lightning pattern had been etched into its face.

David Saul shook his head, trying to clear his eyes. The bright image of the lightning bolt still played in his eyes, seeming to force its way into his brain. He was getting a massive headache. He closed his eyes for a few moments to try to ease it.

When he awoke, night had fallen. He'd been asleep for hours. *"How?"* He remembered the storm but couldn't remember what he'd been doing just before it. The computer security had timed out his session and erased the elements he was working on… a standard protocol. He tried to think back, but just couldn't remember.

Then he did. A particular problem he had grappled with came to him again. It had started with a simple hesitation in the technician's voice at Los Alamos labs when he'd asked about pulse weapons. It was slight, but long enough that his reporter's instincts were piqued.

He had begun some quiet research of his own into the back doors of certain defense department computers. He'd found the documentation for those back door codes when he investigated the cyber war that the AI computer had unleashed on the world. That study gave him knowledge. For some reason, he kept that knowledge to himself rather than reporting the particular breaches to the President.

Now that hesitation came back to him, and nagged at the back of his mind. *"Was the President hiding something? As lead reporter for the government, I have eyes-only security clearance, as high as Meiring's. What is it?"* He opened his private channel into the net and keyed in a special security code which gave him access to those back doors.

He was not happy with what he found. His intuition had been right about the technician's hesitation out at Los Alamos. He read the dry language of a report sent to Santiago.

"We've been able to isolate the propulsion drive and finalize it. Craft will go into production within the next six months."

"The implementation of pulse weapons is improving. We were able to miniaturize the weapon to fit in a pocket. However, the difficulty is our inability to project the force of the weapon any distance against an enemy. Subjects who attempt to use the weapon effectively create a destructive force field in their immediate vicinity. We lost several good soldiers in the testing. At this point, the only effective use of the weapon is a suicidal one, to be used only in dire circumstances: a defensive weapon."

His headache was still there, now for an entirely different reason. *"Why would they hide things from me? I'm Pete's best friend!"*

He memorized the components of the pulse weapon, really so simple, it was elegant. He closed the security channels down. He looked back at the window and saw the lightning pattern etched into the glass. A chill hit him. He walked over to the windows, ran his fingers across the glass and saw that the lightning pattern was etched on the *inside* of the glass. *"Man, what a storm!"* He'd call in the morning for a new window.

Thirty-six

Almost three months had passed since Roger and William had watched the others leave. The months' experience taught them much more than they'd ever wanted to know about the nature of man — both good and evil — and about survival, combat and service.

Roger thought back on that first day, when the others left. William had turned to him. "I know yer gonna wait 'til mid November and I know why. But, what are yer plans in the meantime?"

Roger looked away toward the south and west. "I just can't leave all those people to their fates. Our three hundred and those they guide will be fine. They have Broddin's protection on them and can't easily be defeated, if at all. But the others...." He looked pained. "There's already so much death, so much killing. Starvation will set in soon. None of it necessary. What are they thinking?"

This question was genuine. Roger really did not understand illogic. It was a mystery to him. William could see his confusion. "You really have a high opinion of us, huh?"

"What do you mean?"

William sighed. "I can see it in yer thoughts. You believe man can be good, better than he is. That somehow we could all be rational, do the right thing, with just the right persuasion or the right argument. We're jus' not that way."

"Why not? We have *all* the answers, right in front of us! We *know* what's right. Yet, we don't do it! Why?"

"Why? Go back and read Genesis. Read the Apostle Paul. That's what Father Padrone woulda said."

"But that's not a good answer. We've known it all these years. Lessons from the Bible, from other religions, from our own experience, from the futility of war and combat. What happened a few months ago in Cleveland, that I understand! A demon drove people crazy! But why were they so ready to go there? And why are they busy now killing each other over crumbs rather than helping?"

"You're really a lot like your father — don't give me that sharp look! I read somma his writings. James left 'em one week when yer father first took him on as a student. Couldn't understand much, but I'll tell ya, I didn't like where he was headed. Didn't like at all what he'd wrote about you! Bottom line, he believed he could make the perfect man. Fool's errand there, but *you* and the hell ya went through? *That's* his legacy. Ya gonna take on his beliefs now?"

Roger thought about it. "I just don't understand!"

"Yer never gonna understand. Nobody does.

So what are ya gonna do?"

"Try to save as many as I can. Try to limit the killing. Try to teach. I don't know, try to make some difference!"

"That's somethin' we can do together."

They went out to do what they could. The first weeks were a constant battle, one day with the Ferals, another with Federal Troops. They did not seek these, but constantly ran into the bands of the first and had to defend themselves. Roger insisted that they not kill but only knock their opponents out.

"Why? They're just gonna get mad and come after us later! Or we'll run into 'em again when they wake up. They're really not gonna change. Why not put 'em outta their misery?"

"I made a promise. If I could fight in the center of Crull's army and not kill, I can easily keep from killing these small groups."

"Yeah, but..."

Roger looked at his companion. "What would Father Padrone have said? Who are we to judge how they might change? I don't like killing, not if we can avoid it."

"Wasted efforts."

"So I think man can be good...but you're going to kill him before he gets the chance."

William winced. "Well...didn't thinka it that way." He sighed. "Whatever ya say. We avoid it. But ya know if they shoot at us, the bullet will just reflect back. Aren't we doin' a type a killin' there?"

"Not by our hand!" *"Not by our hand."* He said

his constant, silent prayer. Too many had died in that way already. Would he be judged wanting because of those? He prayed that was not the case.

If someone cared to or could count the deaths in those first weeks after the cities were "cleansed," they would have found millions. This legacy would be forgotten by those in the cities. They did not care. Others witnessed and did care, those who were chosen to remember.

Thirty-seven

The group trudged through an early snow, following slowly in the lead's path. The journey seemed impossibly slow at times, but they made sure to remain unseen. In addition, they had begun holding some kind of service every Sunday. Even the wolf sat in their circle as if listening.

Torgeson sat apart and tried not to hear their mystic mumbo jumbo. He couldn't believe they'd waste valuable time when they were on the run but it suited him fine. Maybe someone would ambush them when they held their Sunday services. He shrugged, disgusted. *"Bunch of half baked weirdos."* Trouble was, they didn't seem crazy. The services were even lead by Solaris. Torgeson respected the man's knowledge and skill, but how could the man be such a good soldier and buy all this religious crap? Couldn't figure it. He'd even tried to escape one Sunday in the middle of their services. Each time he'd tried to run, Solaris simply stepped up and tripped him.

"Dammit, how do you know?"

"Told you. I can read your thoughts. Think about escape, I know it."

"I *am* going to get away. One of these days, you'll be distracted, not thinking, asleep. Sooner or later, your guard will be down. Think I won't kill you before I leave? Think again."

Solaris looked at him and chuckled. "Torgeson, you really don't get it, do you. I *know* you'd kill me if you had the chance. You've never stopped to answer the first question you should have asked: if we really were the people responsible for your buddies' deaths."

"Yeah, I already know!"

"Well, I'll spare you one more death. I keep telling you if you tried to kill me, it would just fall back onto you. You'd be the one who died."

"Better than being a prisoner."

"Hmmm. A prisoner who shares all our food, who we help walk with us, who we've given answers to any questions you asked."

"A prisoner still, if I can't leave."

"You have a point. What would you do if we simply let you go?"

Torgeson thought about that every day. "Head east. Probably try to get down to New Mount Pleasant. That's the closest city. They could get me in touch with the right people. Then, they'll call down airstrikes on your sorry asses."

Solaris laughed. "I like your style, Torgeson." Solaris thought a moment. "I want you to think about something, soldier. I know that they tried to capture us right away on August Ninth. You were there, right with the team. What happened?"

"The damn chopper shorted out. We had to hump it to intercept, but we still missed you. I don't know how, but you guys simply disappeared."

"We can again, if anyone gets too near. But, think about this. While we were fighting the battle before you got there, plenty of people shot at us. Know what happened to them? They died. The guys in the guard unit? Your buddies who were killed? That happened the night before we arrived. We were staying in the same cabin you saw." He liked this soldier, liked his loyalty. "I really don't want to see you or anybody else dead because they attack us. Besides, they already know exactly where we are."

"Bull…"

"If they were going to strike, don't you think they would have already done it? Think, man. Our heat signatures are stronger than normal. Don't you think they could track us easily from the time we left?"

"How you gonna prove that?"

Solaris smiled. "Don't have to. It doesn't matter, because they'll do whatever they want anyway. Tell you what. We thought you might change your mind, but you haven't in all this time. You're free to go. This is as good a place as any. Head southeast. You'll hit New Mount Pleasant in about three hundred miles."

Torgeson looked at Solaris. The others had come up behind him. "He's serious?"

Broddin spoke for them. "Mr. Torgeson, you are free. We won't hold you anymore. We just hope you've listened and gotten to know us."

"Whatever. I have my duty. I'm doin' it." With that, he turned, hesitated as if he were going to be tackled again, then melted into the woods.

Solaris watched as the man left. "Good luck, brother. God speed you in your walk." The wolf looked after Torgeson, huffed as if disgusted, then turned back to follow Solaris on up the trail.

Thirty-eight

Columbus, Ohio. November 11: 7 p.m.

Roger thought back on the groups they'd been able to aid. Often, they would come across those who had banded together to try to defend themselves and to survive. They'd found one tonight. Seeing the two glowing figures approach, those people shrunk back in fear. "Don't come near us! Get away! We don't want any trouble!"

"You have nothing to fear from us."

"But you're those Clingers! The ones who killed all those people in Cleveland."

They patiently explained, tried to convince. They gathered vegetables and fruits from the forests and offered those. Some of the group simply ran away. The people who remained were famished. Hunger overcame fear.

That gave Roger the opportunity to begin to teach. "You're too close to the centers of civilization. You're following the highways. Everybody else came this way, so there's no food left. You need to move away from the well traveled pathways. Head east first, then south and back west. There are untouched fields that way."

In this way, they saved many who would have starved. Those groups continued on until they found places where they felt they could establish small communities out of the way, out of the sight of the National forces, away from the killing by the Ferals.

Roger could see the logic of these small communities play itself out all across the country. They first banded together for protection. They had to learn on their own, to remember planting and harvesting, hunting and fishing. They began to work the land, and turned away from the violence near the cities. The simple things began to take on a value they'd never had before in the noise of the cities. Many would die in the time it took for them to relearn what their great grandparents had taken for granted. Yet, they would learn.

They would begin to see the rhythms of the farm, of sowing and reaping. Some would remember things taught to them by grandparents who had held onto their beliefs in spite of the danger. In time, those people would come to share, would seek out the knowledge they so thirsted for. They would be quietly inspired by gentle whispers on the breeze, by the warmth of the sun on their faces, by lightning's jagged strike upon the darkened plain, by the beauty of the natural world. They would find the Word in books left untouched for generations, now rediscovered. They would learn new life.

Thirty-nine

Washington, DC. November 15: 0300 hours

Gerard Meiring sat in his office in the White House basement. He was reviewing the interrogations of Robert Grey. What a looney! *Had* to be. Angels, demons, visions and nightmares; shining armor, artificial intelligence computers, now missing. *"Trouble is, the guy isn't raving. He sounds 'normal.' All the sensors show he's telling the truth…at least as he understands it. There are even a lot of elements in his story we know are true: the AI computers, the personal shining shields these people had. But demons? Too much."* He looked down at the reports, at the man's descriptions of the battle on the Ravenna field that morning of August Ninth. He read on, following the exchange with the interrogator:

"It was Broddin's army…"

"It was a demon, the Ishar Crull…"

"…that attacked Cleveland…"

"No sir. Crull marched out of Cleveland. Broddin's small band confronted him. The Eden Sword saved them, when Broddin tossed it to Gem Matthews."

"Don't give me that crap."

Meiring looked up. He'd poured over those vids

a hundred times, focusing on Broddin's party, the shining armor and that sword. "What if?...Nah." He flicked on the vid feeds and brought up the satellite images of that day. Now he watched again, but this time focused on the other figure, the dark man who fought Broddin for the sword. The man was huge, close to eight feet tall, dressed in a black robe which almost looked like *darkness* swirling around him.

Meiring tracked the fight until Broddin threw the sword away. The dark figure leaped up to catch it and Meiring froze the image. "Computer, enhance and magnify image." The quantum computer's response was instantaneous. *"AI computer, my ass. I'd rather have this speed."*

He leaned in to look at the image...and stopped, his blood going cold. What leaped for the sword looked up, almost directly into the camera. What stared back at Meiring from the screen was no man; it was a nightmare. Dark wings stretched out. A black face filled with hate and lust and desire. The eyes looked *directly into his.* Meiring's heart began to pound. He backed away from the screen so suddenly his chair almost toppled over. "What the hell is that? It can't be!"

He looked away, thinking. *"It's late at night. I'm alone and that crazy soldier has me seeing things."* He turned and looked back, but the face was still as cold and frightening as before. He punched the button to shut off the screen, got up and went into the war room where all the lights were on. He did not want to admit to himself that he was afraid.

The light of the war room felt familiar, comforting. His heart calmed down. He told himself it had to be an optical illusion. It could not be real! *"Meiring, you're losin' it."* He wouldn't mention this to anyone. But his mind would keep coming back, unheeded, to that image: the image of a nightmare demon.

Forty

Roxford, Ohio. November 15: 8 a.m.

Roger Noguchi and William Broddin stood in a copse of woods at the edge of the city. They watched for movement, waiting to interpret if — or how — the city survived. Akron, Columbus, Dayton sat deserted, their infrastructure beginning to crumble already. Even the Ferals had left by this time. There was no food to find in these cities and no people left to plunder.

Roxford looked different. They could feel it. People were here. Roger did not like the vibrations he was getting. "This is nasty. Dangerous."

"Ya wanna skirt it? Leave 'em alone?"

"No. I have to make sure...that they're not here. I can't feel them, but that might not mean anything."

William Broddin didn't need to ask who. He knew that Roger came back to make sure his parents had not been killed, to try to find them. He really didn't understand. "This is the man who tried ta kill ya, right?"

Roger looked at him. "He's my father. And, my mother might be here, too. We heard that they're both wanted by the authorities, too. Not sure why that would be."

William looked uncomfortable. "I doubt they're here. So, what're we gonna do?"

"No use trying to sneak in. We're just going to walk right in."

"We've never done that before. We've spent three months hiding, avoiding. What're ya doin'?"

"I really don't know. Something is pulling at me. I can't just walk away from Roxford."

"Well, let's go then. Get it over with."

They walked into the center of the campus of University College of Ohio. No one around. Roger thought back on his years here. It was here that he'd acted out his elaborate guise: the idiot, the autistic boy. The boy who'd followed Broddin, then Gem all over campus.

Then, the young man who'd watched Gem forge GemCrys, who'd watched the love between Gem and James blossom. Watched them almost destroy each other. Watched as the demon rose. Finally the man who answered the call. He had been chosen. Chosen to stand with Broddin against the demon. Now, to stand against some other evil which dwelt here.

He turned toward William. "Do you hear it?"

"What? What is that?"

He couldn't believe what he was hearing. "It's a football game! Are these people crazy? Don't they know what's happened? Is football the only thing they live for?" An image flashed through his mind, Shaunte telling him *"Don't go to the game! Don't go."* He dismissed it.

William looked at him. "We need to see this?"

"Yes."

They walked on down toward the stadium. As they did, they could hear the crowd's roar, feel the pulse of the game in the rise and fall of the people's shouts. As they came down the hill, they could see into the stadium and see why no one was in town. The stadium was filled to capacity with screaming fans. Every person of the entire school and town were in the stadium, attending the game.

Now as they neared, they could see the reason for the screaming fans. And Roger knew what had driven him here. They were playing football in the stadium, but a horrifying parody of the game. The two teams wore no protective gear. And every player held a bat, a club, a knife or some other weapon. Dead bodies lay all over the field. As the quarterback called for the snap, the opposing team crashed into the offensive line, slashing with their bats.

The quarterback made a quick pass to the tight end. The end raced toward the goal but a defensive player swung his bat full force, breaking the man's legs. The ball fell loose, but no one grabbed for it. The tight end rolled on the ground and screamed in pain. The players all stopped and looked toward the President's box.

From that box stepped a young man, and Roger caught his breath. The football lineman, the jerk who, years ago, had accosted Broddin, who tried to rape Gem. This filth now stood in the President's box, wrapped in a purple cloak. He was surrounded by a phalanx of guards, men dressed in army fatigues and carrying army issue AR15's. The entire stadium fell silent. The lineman looked down on the playing field, held out his arm, fist at a neutral position, then turned his thumb down. Immediately, the defensive player took his bat and crushed the head of the tight end. The crowd erupted in roars of approval.

The sight blinded Roger. He had never seen pure evil, never known such cold cruelty, never thought it possible. Rage boiled over, an anger beyond any emotion he'd ever felt. He wanted to kill, to wipe every one of them from the face of the earth. He trembled with it, wanted to taste the righteous justice they all deserved. He stalked down toward the field, drawing both swords. No one would leave this place.

"Stop!" William dragged him back. "Roger, stop. I've gone with ya wherever ya've lead me. But this! Ya can't do it! Remember what that kid, Shaunte said? 'Don't go to the game!' He's right. What are ya gonna do?"

"They don't. Deserve. To. Live!"

"Will ya destroy everything ya've worked to build? She's waitin'. Just a few hours more! Ya can't! Ya remember what her mum said! No blood on yer hands."

The voice was filled with cold judgement. "Are you coming with me?"

"Yes, but please..."

The words could not find a hold in his mind. His rage pounded at his soul. He wanted to unleash this holocaust, to give in to the pent up disgust and rage which had been held in check all these months, these years. He was tired of watching men destroy their lives. He could not stand another moment.

Then a breeze arose, gentled down to brush against his face, and whispered the one word which could have reached him. "Grace." Her voice, whispering, reminded him of all that he'd seen that day just six months ago. Grace was his love. But Grace was also love freely given, forgiveness beyond any depth of understanding, an ocean of love covering every sin and every evil.

He turned to look back toward a field near Germantown, twenty miles away. "Grace." He was caught in an impossible dilemma. He could not betray her by killing. He could not let this monstrous thing go on, could not walk away and let them continue in this depth of evil. He turned to William. "What should I do?"

"We go in there, together. We will not kill. I don't even want the guards to fire on us, cuz' we know they'll die. But we have to find some way to stop this, to reach them."

Roger closed his eyes, took a deep breath, prayed. Then he looked at William. "Give me your jacket. It'll act as a cloak. I'm not really sure what I'm going to do, but we have to go in."

Forty-one

They walked into the stadium. Roger had put away his swords and carried only the walking staff. The game had resumed, the teams struggling, hitting against each other, the bats used in a sloppy kind of sword fight, no one gaining ground. Another man went down. The crowd roared, then went silent. Just as the lineman put his hand out, Roger stepped onto the playing field. **"Stop!"**

His shout brought the attention of the entire stadium to him. They turned to see Roger Noguchi, the autistic idiot they'd ridiculed all these years, shuffling into the stadium, followed by a giant of a man. The man seemed as confused as Roger.

The crowd began to laugh. "Look, it's the idiot." "Where's your gay friend, Broddin?" "We'd love to find him and get the reward." "Who's the bear behind you?" "How come you're not following *him*?"

As the derision and ridicule heightened, Roger shuffled up to the fallen ball player and the man who stood above him. He quietly told the player, "You don't need to do this."

The crowd was losing patience. **"Get out of the way! Get on with the game."**

The player shrugged. "If I don't, they'll turn on me and kill me." He looked up to the President's box.

The lineman stood in his purple robes. He'd watched the situation, amused. But, the crowd was turning. His arm shot out, then he turned his thumb down. **"Kill him."**

As the player turned to make his swing, Roger slipped the coat off. He brought his staff up, knocking the bat from the player's hand before he could strike. **"No! No more killing!"** His shout rang throughout the stadium.

The lineman started. He recognized the voice and the figure in leather armor holding the staff which had knocked him out. This was the person who had beat his buddies and embarrassed him. They still laughed at how that little ninja had bested him.

One of his lieutenants, another of the three who Roger had beaten that night, turned to the lineman. "We were beaten by that little kid? By the idiot? I thought you could top anyone." He began to laugh again.

The lineman drew a gun and pointed it. "You better shut up if you know what's good for you." Then he turned to the crowd. **"The wounded player is not useful anymore. He can't entertain us! What shall we do?"**

"Kill him! Kill him."

"And, if anyone stands in our way?"

"Kill them, too!"

Roger stood at the center of the stadium and turned around in a circle, seeing and not believing. The crowds screamed for blood, their faces filled with hate. *"In this world, you will have tribulation."* He knew the meaning of those words. He still did not know how to face this horror. He closed his eyes and prayed. Then, he opened them, set the point of his staff on the ground and began to sing.

"Oh beautiful for spacious skies, for amber waves of grain."

A deep violet color rose within the staff, amplified his voice, carried it throughout the stadium. The entire stadium became quiet.

"For purple mountains, majesty above the fruited plain."

This anthem was banned, forbidden to be sung for well over forty years. None of the younger people here had ever heard it, but deep within them, they recognized it.

"America, America, God shed his grace on thee."

Some older voices in the crowd began to quietly sing with him, tears forming in their eyes.

"And crown thy good with brotherhood, from sea to shining sea."

He turned around, looking at the silent crowd. Then he spoke to them. **"Have you forgotten brotherhood? We were a brotherhood of football, of study, of teacher and student, parent and child. We were men and women who loved learning, loved this school. Have you lost it all?"**

The crowd listened. The song touched a chord within, reaching deep to connect with memories they did not even recognize.

"Oh beautiful, for patriot's dream that sees

beyond the years…"

People now began to raise their voices. They remembered and found a deep emotion within, one which they'd forgotten.

"Thine alabaster cities gleam, undimmed by human tears."

Now many more joined in the chorus.

"America, America, God shed his grace on thee."

Thousands sang, smiles on their faces, the stadium vibrating with the voices.

"And crown thy good with brotherhood from sea to shining sea."

The lineman now saw he was losing the crowd for an entirely different reason. *"No. Not again. That kid isn't going to beat me again."* **"Both teams, kill that kid!"** He ran out of the box and raced down towards the field. "If no one else will rid me of this pain, I will myself."

Forty-two

Without hesitation the teams jumped on Roger and William. The two stood back to back, fending off the strikes. They turned the bats away, knocking the men aside. At each turn, they held back to assure that the men would only be knocked out. Within minutes, the teams lay unconscious on the playing field.

The lineman arrived and was furious. "Who the hell are you? You're those glowing guys with the armor! Why don't you face me without it! C'mon! Fight fair."

The crowd fell silent again. The game no longer was fun. The lineman looked up and yelled. **"Tell him! Fight fair!"**

In unison, they responded to him. They began to chant: **"Fight fair! Fight fair! Fight Fair!"** Then the lineman turned back to Roger. "You gonna fight me fair, kid?"

Roger laid down his staff, motioned for William to back away, then turned back to the lineman. "No. I will not fight you."

"Then I'll fight you!" He picked up the staff to swing it.

Roger raised his hand. "Wait! That won't do. You'll just knock yourself out."

The lineman paused. "What?"

"The auras. Their like armor. Almost any action you take will be returned to you with equal force. Only one thing can kill me." He took the sword from its sheath, turned it and handed it to the lineman, then kneeled down. "Point it right at my heart. Or bring it down on my neck."

The lineman took the sword. "Yer not lying?"

"No."

"Why are you doing this?"

"Because I'm tired of the killing, aren't you? Aren't you bored with it? By the way, if you *are* going to kill me, you better be absolutely certain in your soul that you hate me. That's the only way this'll work."

"What happens if I don't hate you?"

"I don't know. It still might revert back to you, Bill."

The lineman started. "How do you know my name?"

"C'mon, Bill. It's no secret. Bill Lane. Our number one lineman for three years. Nobody got past you. Twenty-eight quarterback sacks. Pretty good numbers. By the way, your mom is still alive. I know that. Don't ask me how. I just do."

The man paused. "No kiddin? She was in Cleveland."

"She still is." Roger saw a quick vision of an older woman sitting in front of a window air conditioner, smiling at the cool breeze "She's cool, Bill. They have AC there, in the city."

The crowd watched the exchange, not hearing

the words. They were already forgetting the anthem they heard just before and were getting impatient. **"Kill. Kill. Kill."**

The lineman held up his hand and they immediately fell silent.

"Do you see the power you have over them? You've lead them to worship death. There's so much more to who you are, to what you can do. Why not lead them to life?"

Bill Lane stood there, looking at this small man who knelt before him. "I can't just let you walk away. What'll they think?"

"They'll think that a great leader knows when to show mercy."

A dark being hovered behind Bill Lane and now screamed at his mind, pushing and probing. *"Kill! Kill killkillkillkill!"*

Lane flinched. Seized by the dark creature's hate, he focused his fury on the small man who knelt before him. "I am *sick and tired* of your stupid words. *This* is all that matters." He raised the sword. **"Bow your head, Noguchi."**

Forty-three

White House War Room: November 15: 0815 hours.

"Mr. Meiring. Sir, look at this. The satellites picked up a bloom from Southwest Ohio. Some color flashed out and then went quiet, but it was definite. Looks similar to the one at the Ravenna battlefield. Take a look."

The tech replayed the feed. A bloom of violet light rose and remained for a moment or so on the screen. Now it was gone, but it was definitely there. "Where is that?"

The tech checked coordinates. "Roxford, Ohio, sir."

Meiring started. Roxford. What connections were working here? "That city should be deserted like every other one. Replay from a few moments before the bloom."

Meiring watched for a moment, and couldn't believe it. "They're playing football! But it's not any kind I've ever seen. Looks like they're beating at each other with bats and clubs! Make sure you capture these images, soldier. Focus in on the coordinates." The cameras turned and focused, bringing a football field into view. "I want full resolution vids on my monitor now! Ground level if you have any sensors at that stadium. They should still be working. I want to know who is there and what they're doing. Also, send a team that way, if there's one close."

"Yes, sir."

Meiring left the room and headed back down to his office. As he got to the door, he hesitated. He did *not* want to go back in, not where that image had been. He stiffened his back, and opened the door. His breath frosted the air. The room was frigid. The vid screen was on and he could clearly see the face peering out. He propped the door open, closed off the AC vents and turned all the lights on. Then turning his head away, he readjusted the vid feed so that he didn't have to look at that image, the one of the "demon."

He dialed up maintenance. "Get somebody down here. The AC is broken. What? No, the room is freezing! It must be stuck on."

He settled into his chair, but he couldn't get comfortable. The image of that *face* kept coming back. "*Hell with it. I have more important things I need to focus on right now.*" He checked the feeds and saw the satellite feed was ready, so he turned the monitors on to watch the events happening in Roxford.

Ground level feeds came from several army issue helmet cams. *"Who is wearing those? We don't have anybody there."* He watched as the confrontation unfolded between some young guy dressed in a purple robe and one of the glowing people.

Now he could see the halting gait of the glowing man as he walked onto the football field. *Noguchi! That's Roger Noguchi. I'd recognize his walk anywhere.*

He saw the two football teams decimated by Noguchi and some big man who glowed yellow. Nobody could touch them, yet they parried the blows so the others were knocked out. *"Why don't they just kill them all? I saw how Broddin did that with one pulse from his sword."*

He saw the guy dressed in purple approach and square off against Noguchi. Then, he watched, in amazement, as Noguchi dropped his staff and kneeled before the other man. Noguchi took out a sword and handed it to the man. It looked like Noguchi was sacrificing himself, allowing this other man to execute him. The man raised the sword.

Forty-four

Wheaton, Kansas. November 15. Early morning

Shaunte Williams was busy milking cows. He chuckled to himself. *"Never even knowed where milk comes from. Never thought I'd be doin' the milkin' myself."* He had come to love this life. It was so different from what he'd known any time in his life. Safety. Real learning. History, math, farm science, writing and Bible learning. Family. Being a part of a real family. Friends. Not clan, scrabbling to survive. Family, loving and safe. Tough life, farming, but it was just work. He could do that.

He turned to the next cow when a vision blasted into his mind. *"Roger had gone to the game! He defeated the teams, but now handed his own sword to some big guy in a purple robe and was kneeling. The guy held the sword over Roger's head!"*

He dropped the milk bucket and ran from the barn, screaming. **"Siri! Siri!"** How long did he have? He didn't know.

Siri came running from the field where he had been with Renny. He saw Shaunte crumple to his knees, keening and moaning. As he ran up, he could hear the boy's voice in a croaking strain. *"Lord. Lord. Save him. Lord!"*

"Shaunte! What is it?"

The boy pulled Siri to his knees with desperate strength and looked into his eyes. *"Pray! Pray!"*

"What for?" But the boy's moans shook him to the core. What could he do? He didn't know *what* to pray for! He simply knelt with the boy, wrapped him in his arms and began a deep, unknown prayer. A golden yellow light blasted out from him, lighting the fields around them and on out across the plains. Shaunte was shaking in his arms. Then a name shot into Siri's mind. "Roger." He, too, began to tremble.

Forty-five

Roxford, Ohio. November 15: 8:20 a.m.

Bill Lane raised the sword. **"Bow your head, Noguchi."** Just as he began to swing the sword down, a shaft of golden light shone into his eyes from the west. It caught his attention, stopped him as the sword was inches from Roger's bowed head. That light reminded him of a sunrise he had seen as a child, a light filled with promise. His mother had taken him out that morning to see the sun rise over the lake. He could see her face as she told him, "Don't ever forget this day, William. This is our day."

A smile crossed his face with that memory. He remembered who he had been…and what he loved. That love transformed him. He turned his face up to the crowd. **"Enough! I tire of this game. I give this man mercy. And, the man who fell!"**

Hesitant cheers rose from some in the crowd. Lane turned back to Roger, reached out his hand and lifted the young man off the ground. Roger held his grasp for a second. "Thank you."

The crowd could see their grasped hands. William Broddin began clapping behind the two and the crowd picked up the rhythmic applause. The applause grew until the stadium vibrated.

The lineman let Roger's hand go. "What now?"

"You have thirty-thousand people to help, a city to rebuild and a college to save. They need a leader. You have been chosen. That leader is you!"

"But, I don't know how!"

"Yes, you do. There's a lot to be done here. If they followed you in this," he gestured at the stadium, "they'll follow you wherever you lead them. Maybe you'll build a new city from the rubble." He smiled, "And, maybe a new *real* football team. But you need to focus on food. Winter is coming."

Bill Lane handed the sword back to Roger, who sheathed it and picked up his staff. Lane turned around to look at the fans. He remembered. This was the glory he'd forgotten, the cheers of the crowd for his accomplishments. He remembered the hard work and effort he put in to become the player he was. He helped to build this team. This school was his second home. **"Let's put this crap away! Who wants to play a *real* game of football?"** The crowd roared its approval. Then he turned back. "I'll need help to do this. Where can I find it?"

"There's an entire library here at the school."

The lineman looked chagrined. "Never been in there."

"Guess it's about time. You'll find everything you need, right there. Appoint some of the bookies to find books on planting, on hunting, on building. They won't be bored...and neither will you. I think you'll find it interesting."

"Yeah, I guess." Bill Lane hesitated. "You two

could stay. We could use the help."

"I'm sorry. We have somewhere else we need to be, a promise I need to keep."

Lane shrugged. "Suit yerselves." He turned in a circle, raising a hand to the stadium crowd. **"These men have my blessing. They are leaving on a quest. Give them our thanks."** The crowd began stomping and the stands vibrated with the sound.

Roger grasped Lane's hand again. He and William turned to walk out of the stadium, then Roger stopped. He turned back and looked up at the man he had once stopped from raping Gem. He wasn't sure if the inner man he'd connected with would remain. Would Lane change back? There were no guarantees and Roger could not discern that future. He could only hope.

He took his staff, the one he'd used to beat this man three years ago. "I would be honored if you accept this gift. It means much to me...and I know you'll use it for good. I think somehow that it may help you focus on what's needed here." He handed it to Bill Lane. The lineman took it and looked at its Japanese carvings. He thought he saw a hint of red pulse from deep within the wood and shook his head. "What do these symbols mean?"

"They represent a journey. You've just begun a new one here, for you and for everyone you lead."

"Thank you. I hope I can use it...as well as you did against me." He smirked.

"You will." Roger and William Broddin turned and walked out of the stadium.

Forty-six

White House. Office of the head of Security.

Meiring watched the exchange between the two men. The helmet cam was too far away to catch the conversation between the two men, but he heard clearly the other man's shout. *"What kind of power does this kid have over people? That other guy was about to kill him, I'm sure. What just happened?"* They desperately needed that armor, or clues to how it worked. It was the only possible explanation. Now it seemed to be able to influence people, change their minds. He called his aide. "Send in another interrogator for that Grey soldier. Step up the pressure. We need this armor. It's the key to everything!"

"Yes, sir."

"Do we have a team near enough to Roxford to get men on the ground to see what's going on? Talk to folks there?"

The aide looked at his force files. "No sir. It'll be early tomorrow at best. Don't we want to disburse those people once we interrogate them? It's illegal for them to be there."

"No, why bother. They're going to run out of food in another month or so. Besides, the football game is amusing. We might institute games like that in the cities, make use of the stadiums. It would be good entertainment for our people. Capture some Ferals or Clingers and just let them beat at each other until they're dead. I like it! Like the way that young man was thinking."

Forty-seven

Roxford, Ohio. November 15: 8:40 a.m.

Roger and William turned and walked out of the stadium, headed further down the hill and away from Roxford. William looked at his friend. "Did you know somehow that he wouldn't do it? That he didn't hate you enough to kill you in cold blood."

"I saw just a spark. Just one bit of humanity left. I hoped I could reach it. Actually, I'm not sure *how* I did, what really changed his mind and heart."

"You took too big a chance."

"No. If he had chosen to kill me, I was ready for that, too."

"Whadya mean?"

Roger stopped and turned to his friend. "If I hadn't reached him…I was prepared to die."

"But he couldn't…'

"Yes he could, with my own sword and his hate. That's how the Ishar Crull could fight against Eden's Sword itself. His hate was so complete he could strike against it and possibly kill the man holding it."

William went white. "Don't ever do that again! If I'd known, I'da stopped ya."

"And if you hadn't?"

The voice was quiet, deadly, frightening. "If

you died, I would have killed every single person in that place."

Roger stopped and turned to his friend. It was no empty threat. An image came to him: a holocaust brought down upon the entire stadium in the form of a wild giant with untouchable power. He trembled, because *he knew* the man would have been able to do it…and he would have done so. "You stopped me from doing the same thing before. What's different?"

"Just that it's you. You're promised. Not supposed to kill. Me? Why not? I'm just one more means ta kill people." His shoulders shrugged in despair. "All the death in the last few months? What's a few more?"

"I'm no different than you. Yes, I have a specific reason for not killing. But you! You have as much a compelling reason as I do."

"What's that?"

"A certain commandment?"

"Oh." William was quiet for a long time. "I have to think about that a while. Seen too much killin' in the last few months. Done my share, too." His voice was quiet, his face fallen.

"Let's leave that aside for now. This isn't the place for a discussion of what's allowed or not in war. You haven't murdered, nor did you kill indiscriminately. I'll argue all that with you later. Meanwhile, let's go on down the hill and check if there's still a ride we might find."

They rounded a bend in the hillside, and Roger reached into some bushes and pushed a button. The entire hillside began to rise, revealing an underground aircraft hanger. A blackhawk helicopter sat inside.

"Ahh, just as I'd hoped. They forgot there were assets hidden away. Would you like a much better mode of transportation than we've had in a while? This hanger was built to withstand an EMP and this should work just fine."

As Roger went through the preliminary checks then climbed into the pilot's seat, he saw the look on William's face. "Must I endure the same thing from you I did from your son a few months ago? Yes, I can fly it. No, we won't die. Get in!"

William laughed. "Whatever! Anyway after what I saw, this wouldn't be a bad day to die. Not at all!"

The chopper lifted, angled out of the hillside and silently slipped across the countryside headed toward Germantown, Ohio. Roger began to talk about Grace, about when they first met.

Forty-eight

Fort Jackson, North Carolina.
November 15:1500 hours.

Robert Yellow sat in his cell. It was cold. The fort was located outside the city zones. It had its own power source, but his captors didn't seem to think it important to provide heat to him. *"At least they've given me books to write in. Some consolation there, though they take them each night to read and review."*

The door opened and his interrogator walked in. Yellow supposed he liked the man well enough, though the man had no imagination whatsoever. He kept repeating the same questions over and over. "Where is the sword? Where is Broddin? Where is the Artificial Intelligence computer? Where is Matthews and her wand? Why won't you give us the armor?" On and on.

They had started with standard interrogation techniques: sleep deprivation, sense deprivation, some truth drugs. They'd raised no response from him aside from the fact that he was called to witness. After a while, they gave up on those and at least put him in a cell with a window. Of course it was sealed, impervious to any attempt to breach it.

Often, a cardinal would perch on the branches

outside the window and sit there, looking in at the man. It watched, turning its head as if it heard some quiet song of its own through the glass.

The Army captors watched and asked and waited. Robert Yellow wrote and answered and prayed. Prayer was the one thing which seemed to infuriate them. They couldn't stand it. He just smiled and kept on doing it.

Forty-nine

New Mount Pleasant, South Carolina
November, 15: 1600 hours

The man showed up at the RavNational Bridge portal. He was dressed in army fatigues, but they were worn threadbare, filthy and hung on him. He was obviously exhausted, starving and near death.

"Who goes there?"

The voice was strained, but the man stood at attention. "Soldier, I am Captain Charles S. Torgeson, Third Brigade, First Marine Corps. Please summon your commander. I have critical news for the good of the nation which must be reported to the highest authorities."

"Pretty far from your unit, bud."

Torgeson stood there. "Listen, shithead. I've run just about three hundred miles to get this news to your superiors. I can't touch you through the screen, but I will get in eventually. And if you don't call your guy in charge *right now,* when I do get in, I'm going to kick your ass from here to China."

Some tone in the voice and the man's demeanor, made the soldier believe him. "Just stay there a minute. I'll call."

"Not moving."

The soldier made the call. Within five minutes an army colonel came walking up. "This better be good." Then he stopped. "Torgeson?"

Torgeson saluted as well as he could. "Colonel Jolie. Good to see you sir. Reporting with critical information."

"Private, open the portal and let this man in."

Torgeson was amazed in the next few moments when they lead him into a room to meet David Saul, who was going to debrief him. He snapped to attention. "Sir. It's an honor to meet you face to face. I've watched many of your reports from the front lines where I fought. Thank you for your straight talk."

Saul waved him off. "No. Thank you, Mr. Torgeson. You're the hero. Meanwhile, we've been expecting you."

"How…?

"Never mind. Mr. Meiring wishes to speak with you as soon as we've chatted. You were right there with the Broddin party for quite a while. Can you tell me more about these shields? Any power source evident? Any way to breach them?"

Torgeson was shocked. "How did you know I was with them? I was going to report this to Washington."

Saul chuckled. "Been tracking your movements since you left. Now, can you help me out?"

"I wish I could sir, but I saw no evidence of power sources at all. Furthermore, they somehow disabled me, paralyzed me." His voice became haunted. "I was taken out by some…chameleon. The *mist* came to life! Some type of soldier who was *completely* invisible! Huge and powerful, too. He simply crushed my rifle into powder. *Transported* me across a valley! They kept me prisoner. They were able to read my thoughts, anticipate any escape attempt. I was, sir, absolutely powerless against them."

"We need to get this info to Mr. Meiring immediately. Hold on, I'll get him on the secure comband. He's waiting."

Torgeson opened the monitor and saw Meiring's face. Torgeson reiterated to Gerard Meiring what he had told Mr. Saul. Meiring nodded as if he already knew what the man would say. "Young man, you've provided a great service to the nation. Thank you for the sacrifice you've made but we can take it from here. Get some R&R, and we'll get you back to your unit when you're better."

"But sir, I'd like to be in on the strike you're planning for these people. I know the general direction they were headed. We can probably pick up their trail without too much effort, round them up and bring them in."

Meiring laughed. "Thanks, soldier, but we know *exactly* where they are. We always have."

"But why didn't you take them out, then?"

"Are you questioning me young man? I don't think you're in a position to question the policy of this office, or of our President, do you? We know where they are. We will act in the nation's interest in our own time, not yours. I suggest you keep your opinions to yourself, do your job and get some rest. If you didn't have so many kills to your credit, if you weren't so valuable, I'd simply relieve you for insubordination." The connection was broken.

Torgeson sat, looking at a blank screen. *"They knew! Solaris said they did and he was right."* He began to wonder about the other things they'd said, wondered what was true, what was real. He really wasn't sure anymore. Could he trust anyone? The country was screwed, his buddies were dead and his superiors let the people who had done it *just walk away!* He couldn't trust anybody anymore.

Fifty

The choppers landed in the middle of a deserted stadium. The commander sent two squads up into the town to see what had happened. They walked into a city blown apart like most others in the last few months. It was early, but people were picking up debris, beginning to clean the streets (as if cars would somehow work again.)

As they walked through people stopped and stared, wide eyed. The soldiers weren't sure whether it was from simple surprise or fear. The commander stopped the first person he saw. "Where is the guy in charge?"

"Who?"

"The guy in the purple robe." He brought his vid up and showed the kid.

"Oh, Bill. He's in the commons, cleaning out the fountain near the quad."

They found Bill Lane in the fountain, lifting a slab of concrete which had to weigh over two hundred pounds. "Hey, you Bill?"

"Yep. Where'd you guys come from?"

"Washington."

"Great! We've been waiting for some help."

"Yeah, we saw the kinda waiting you been doin'. Wanna tell us what the two guys were doing in your 'games' yesterday? And why'd you let them go?"

Bill Lane looked at the two men. They were dressed in all black. Each carried an AR15 down at his side. They looked like they would prefer to use those than ask questions. He shrugged. "Sorry guys. My mistake. We really didn't have a choice. I'd have preferred to kill the little bastard for my own reasons but I couldn't touch 'im. Those aura things. You shoulda seen what they did to my team! Anyway, they decided to leave. Went down the hill, west toward Indiana."

"What kinda game did you have goin' there, kid?"

Bill shrugged. "Just some entertainment. Back to the cleanup today."

"You're not supposed to be here. Either head towards a city and beg to be let in or get your asses out in the wild like everybody else."

Bill Lane bristled. No one *ever* talked to him that way. He stepped out of the fountain, casually picked up the staff and leaned on it. "Buddy, we were told the cities kicked everybody out. If you weren't there, you weren't gettin' in. That's changed? We'll head to Cleveland, then."

The captain stared at him. *"What a dope this kid is."* "You ain't gonna get into the cities. Only option is the wild."

"But those are the Fallow Lands. It's illegal for

us to go there!"

"Are you an idiot? You can't stay here either, any of you. Get out, now!"

Lane stood there. The staff pulsed a red color from within. He felt a power he'd never known, a power exercised in restraint. "Sir, I thank you for that advice. However, I think we'll stay. If you look around on the rooftops, and in high windows, you'll see my men there, guns trained on you."

Men stood up from cover and the soldiers could see they'd wandered into a trap. "You gonna try to kill United States soldiers?"

"No, sir. Not at all. We love our country out here. We don't want any confrontation, just to be left alone. I'm glad to help in any way our military asks. Fact is, we hoped somebody would show up to arrest those traitors. If you head on west, I bet you can get those two. No skin off my back."

As the soldier stood there, his comband buzzed. It was his commander. "Didn't I tell you to leave those assholes alone? Forget those idiots. We've got a heat trail from yesterday. Someone left there in a Blackhawk, headed north. Get back to your unit and follow them."

"Yes, sir." He turned to Lane. "We're going, but heres's some advice for you, fella. If I come back, none of you better be here."

"No problem, Captain. You won't find us."

The soldiers turned and stalked away, back down toward the field. A couple of Lane's guards came up to him. "They're not going to leave us alone, you know that."

Lane thought a moment. "Nah. I think they got bigger fish ta fry. Meanwhile, we should have better perimeter watches than that. We shouldn't have let them simply walk in. Coulda been Ferals for all we knew. Establish a watch. Twenty-four hour. Last few months we've been out raiding. Now we need to start building: tunnels, underground areas, storage. We'll need places to keep outa the cold, to store food besides the underground warehouses we found. We have a town to rebuild."

The scouts watched the soldiers walk back down to the stadium, confer on some vidmaps and take off to the north.

Fifty-one

Germantown, Ohio. November 16: Dawn

They had landed the chopper near a copse of trees at the edge of the field. Roger used a special netting to camouflage it. Then they waited at the edge of the field until the sky turned a violet color on this morning of the new moon's rising.

Roger talked all the way up about his first meeting with Grace, about her beauty, her strength, her hair, her clothes. William rolled his eyes but listened with a smile. This young boy had never uttered a word to anyone. Not until events led him to open up to Gem and to William's son, James. Now, he couldn't stop, especially when the subject was the woman he loved. A dam had burst and the words poured forth in a torrent of joy and love.

The morning mists watered the fields which grew right up to the forest. This was the reason Roger had stayed behind when Broddin's party left. To be at this place, at this time. He was chosen to be here. Knowing the future, he was not sure how long before he would need to continue this ever growing battle. But he knew Grace would be at his side.

As dawn lightened the sky into a violet color heralding the promise of a clear morning sunrise, the trees of the forest wavered, then divided. Rachel, daughter of Revyn and Emrys, walked through that divide toward him from the canopy of pines. With her came an ancient monk, a huge ox of a man dressed in rough robes. He had dark, piercing eyes which took in the breadth and width of all they observed.

Rachel approached and looked at Roger for a long time. He felt a probing in his mind. "Ahhh, good. I see ya've been faithful. I see the loss ya've known, the killin' done roun' ya, but ya dina muhrder. Good lad. Who be this mahn ya've brought with?"

"My friend, William, who stands for me. My best man."

"Ahh. Welcome, Sair William." She smiled. "But, Rogair, ye'll be needin' two more witnesses."

"What? But…"

Rachel turned back toward the wavering veil. From it stepped his mother, who lead his father by the hand. "Mother!" He ran to her, scooped her up in his arms.

She was crying deep sobs. "Roger? Let me hear your voice again! This is a miracle!"

"Mother, I hoped you'd escaped. I hadn't thought that it would be Grace who saved you."

"She's wonderful! Roger…." She pulled him close in her arms, holding him for a long moment.

Kerian Noguchi stood aside. A cloth covered his eyes. They were healing, but he could not bear any kind of light at this point. He held back from his son, afraid to approach.

Roger looked at him. "Father. Why are you

staying back?"

Kerian Noguchi shook his head back and forth. "I shouldn't be here. This is your day. I would have killed…" His head dropped. Tears formed behind the cloth cover.

Roger walked up and took his father's shoulders. "Time and again, you wanted to send me for Relief. You tried to kill me. If not for Grace, you might have." He thought of the demon who had plagued Gem and James, of the thousands who died already in the cruelty unleashed by the blindness of his fellow men, of death and life in a football stadium. And, of "Grace" spoken to him across a distance, a grace which spoke life, not death; love, not hate. He took his father's hands. "The last thing you said to me was that you just wanted to hug me. Is that true?"

"Now it is!"

Roger lifted his father in a great hug. "Welcome home, Dad." He brought them both to stand beside William, then turned to Rachel. They all looked toward the forest. Roger's pulse deepened.

Grace stepped through the veil. She wore the flowing dress he'd seen before, which seemed to capture the essence of a sparkling waterfall, to reflect the light around and contain that light within. She wore the wedding bells woven through her hair. Her radiant smile was all he would ever need to see.

Rachel took Grace's hand and drew her to stand beside Roger. Then she beckoned to the monk. "This mahn is our friend, Brothair Thomas. Nair a wiser mahn ever I have knawn." She turned to the monk.

"Brothair, see now wha' I've shown ya. Will ya say the wairds over them?"

Brother Thomas stepped forward and took both their hands. Again, Roger felt the intense scrutiny reading every secret he ever kept. Then, Thomas nodded his approval. "Ah, bambini! Amore. E essere. Esse."

Rachel touched the brother's arm. "Scuzi Fratello, Inglese."

The monk blushed. "Mi dispiace, Signora." He turned again to face Roger and Grace. "Children. Love. It is the only reality, the essence of all things, the only real being. We are gathered here this day to celebrate the marriage of Roger and Grace..."

Shortly after the ceremony, they heard the distant thrum of the choppers approaching. Roger looked to the Southern sky. "We need to go...into the Rushes. We need time to regroup, to think."

They turned and filed through the veil into green fields. The Homeland Security people would again find no one.

Fifty-two

Appalachian Trail, Georgia, North Carolina border.
November 16: 10:00 a.m.

They made their way carefully through growing forests. Broddin came up to walk beside Gem. He took her hand. "Do you feel it?"

She smiled. "Yes. Roger and Grace. They're married now." She felt an overflowing joy coming from a field in Ohio and marveled at how connected they were across this distance. That joy radiated through her hand as she held Broddin's. She felt a quiet and filling peace, one she had missed for months.

They continued to walk ahead of the party, just enjoying the morning air. Broddin stopped and turned her to him. The joy and confidence he felt was an underlying theme all morning. "It's time. This is what it's like to feel joy. Absolute joy. I was never complete, before I met you. I am now. I've waited so long, waited to ask you." He kneeled in front of her. "Gem Matthews, will you marry me?"

She threw her arms around him. "Yes! James, I've waited too, to hear those words. Yes!"

He had longed for this feeling. It was what he feared he might lose, what he *had* lost, but found again. A part of him worried about feeling that loss again, about what might happen to them. But it was swept away in a flood of joy which filled them both.

They turned and walked on, arm in arm, touching, holding hands, comfortable in a love which nothing would ever conquer.

Gem was looking around at the mountain ridge ahead of her. The area looked so familiar! They had no idea how far they'd hiked, only knew the days because they'd kept a calendar. It seemed so long.

They walked up toward a ridge, and she suddenly knew. *"Chrisair."* It was right over that next ridge. Only a mile away. She *knew* now! *Knew* what and who was waiting there. She started to run.

She'd caught Broddin off guard. "Gem! Stop! Where are you going? Wait for us! Too dangerous!" Broddin raced after her, but she was too far ahead. She ran over the hill before he could catch her.

She stopped at the ridge. The town lay before her, down in the valley. She could see its small buildings, the general store and town hall where the flag still hung. Smoke rose from many chimneys. People were here! Tears came to her eyes. She ran on down toward the town, then jogged left towards their cabin. She could see the roof and the air shimmering as the heat rose from the forge.

"Mom! Dad!"

Estelle burst from the cabin door. "Gem! Gem!" They ran to each other and Gem threw herself into her mother's arms.

Joe Matthews dropped his tools, raced over and

picked them both up in a huge bear hug. "Gem, you're here! Thank God!"

She was crying now with joy. "I prayed you'd be here, that you'd gotten away!"

Her mother now held her at arms length. Gem's aura glowed a brilliant green. "Ahh, to finally see it. I only saw it in visions. It's beautiful, Gem."

The party followed Gem down the path and watched the reunion, smiles on their faces. "Mom, Dad, let me introduce you to my...friends." Her hesitation was short, but her mother knew more than she would let on yet. Broddin stayed back until last and Gem took his hand. "Mom, Dad. This is James…."

Fifty-three

New Mount Pleasant, December 7: 10:00 a.m.

David Saul looked out through the windows which still held the lightning pattern etched into the glass. The technicians told him it would take months to replace the glass. It was a special impact glass only made in Ireland and the "recent unpleasantness" in Asia disrupted many shipments coming out of Europe. Of course, the ships would be vetted for radiation and other issues. Europe had no protective shields like America.

There were extensive diplomatic negotiations after the wars. The European allies were not happy that the technology which protected American cities and all of Israel had not been shared with them. Now, they faced the same kind of increased death rate in their populations which others outside the shields faced.

President Santiago simply shrugged at their protests and reiterated the common understanding. "This can only help the Mother once the radiation issue is mitigated. Meanwhile, you'll have a higher mortality rate which will only help your continued efforts at Relief! Get with the program, guys! You have enough medicine for your Party members to avoid radiation poisoning. Now let's get back to normal trade status as quickly as possible."

David looked at the cloudy haze which lay across the ocean. The nuclear smog hung across Sullivan's Island and stretched to the horizon. He wondered how long this would last, this nightmare haze of nuclear smoke and dust.

Hundreds of nuclear blasts had obliterated all of India, Asia and the Middle East. The resulting nuclear fires still burned, still pumped radioactive dust into the atmosphere, still spread the poison around the globe. How long would it take for the Mother to recover? No one knew. David looked down at the haze, disgusted. *"How did we come to this?"* But he knew how: *"Clingers. Clingers did this."*

He'd watched the vid reports of the devastation, seen how those fundamentalists unleashed the unthinkable. At least, they'd killed off most of their own stupid believers. That's what all the news reports said. David Saul had come to believe them.

He sat down at his desk for the morning's reports.

Fifty-four

Cleveland, Ohio, December 31, Midnight

The Clingers had been gone for four months. The citizens returned to their work, and spent their spare time cleaning up the worst of the city. They quickly realized that the garbage men would only pick up what was in the cans. Citizens worked around that problem by filling the cans with any object they'd find including building debris, rotting food and dead bodies.

Many blocks, mostly on the east side, still sat destroyed because people just didn't feel like cleaning them up. They were having too much fun basking in the heated rooms and eating from the full rations the federals provisioned out to them.

Within the heart of that rubble a building stood, pristine and untouched. No one approached it or even noticed it. As they walked by, their gaze slid past, looking at other things. The sign on its facade was fading but still legible. One could still read the words:

TIME TRAXX
AMERLINZ ENTERPRISES

Within the building a cave sat empty. The cave

had witnessed darkness and desecration, then light and resurrection. Now it stood sealed away, kept from witnessing the events unfolding outside its walls.

The government had provided plenty of food and warm air to reward the citizens for their patriotic cleansing of Cleveland of all Clingers. Cleveland's citizens and those of the other cities looked up at their shining protection and praised President Santiago for his wisdom. The shining promise of the shields not only protected them from any attack the Clingers sent against them but also protected them from the nuclear haze.

The Asia wars which destroyed that continent sent the haze from hot fires across the oceans to cover the land. Gentle winds carried that pollution to rain upon the domes. The radiation fell harmlessly down the dome surfaces to collect at the base, which resulted in highly radioactive moats around each city. Anyone who crossed those zones without using the proper access portals would die within days.

This was just the solution many had dreamed and worked toward. The shields would protect some 100,000 privileged few within each city site: the elite citizens, ones carefully chosen by the authorities. The others, not so fortunate, were simply expendable. Everyone heard it for so long now. "The population grew far beyond the ability of the Mother to support. We must preserve our limited resources. Be a citizen hero. Be **SOME**one. **S**ave **O**ur **M**other **E**arth."

By December rationing had been re-instituted. Reporters roamed the streets and haunted the airways, calling for people to report any citizens who fell back on the old ways. The first they chose were the smokers.

Marta Gibbs, the ABC Cleveland anchor, started the call to report them. "Citizens, our air is now so precious! We see the bright shield which covers our great city and protects us from the nuclear smoke outside. How can we allow those among us who still *cling to their own smoke* to pollute the very air we breathe? These *Clingers of smoking* must be weeded out from us."

The label was enough. To be accused of being a "Clinger" in any form became a death sentence. Smokers were hauled from homes, beaten and driven to the portals. Those chosen as Clingers fought back in vain against the mobs who pushed them through and out to certain death.

This scenario played out in every city, where reporters identified Clingers of every sort to be the next target of the purges. Once rationing began again no one wanted to give up a share of food. The fewer number of people, the more food to claim. They reported one another. First the Clingers of smoke, then the lazy, the retarded, the chronically unemployed, then anyone over forty-seven, then forty-six, forty-five…

No one really cared, as long as they weren't targeted. There was still enough food for those left, and there were plenty of hookons, those times where anyone could join in to share the love and caring of open sex in pairs or groups. That entertainment kept them satiated. Of course, one of the benefits of the years with the lack of enough food was that most people were now attractively thin and looked better than they had in years.

The elites in each city celebrated the continued reduction in population numbers and the corresponding increase in food and other products. They held private hookon parties in penthouse cubes in the top floors of skyscrapers, They shared food, smearing it on each other, reveling in their newfound freedom and plenty. Freedom came in the form of release: in orgies of sharing food and bodies, of open and imaginative sex. Any combination was fine, so long as food was involved. Food became sex and sex, food. And, it was very good.

Fifty-five

Sheol.

The fire of the bitter cold broiled up from deep within the marrow, burning ceaselessly. The eternal form of the Ishar Crull knelt before his master, suffering the burning cold.

"Brother, I could not help it. Our Enemy helped the humans all along the way. At the last moment, *He* took it from me! I could do nothing..." He stopped, for the red pulsing eyes settled their gaze upon him. Pain ripped through him. Now he felt the full force of the power he'd once focused on others: hate in its purest form, pulsing, and coursing through his veins.

"You...will...be...silent." The voice was painful to hear, the gaze filled with scorn. "At least I was defeated by our *Enemy*! I chose *you! You* were the chosen one! You had ten times a thousand years, and could not destroy one stupid human. And at the last, a simple *girl* defeated you." A flick of the master's finger slammed Crull's body against the icy wall, ripping it open to even more pain. "And do not call me 'brother.' I am your **Master!**" The fire of malevolence vibrated within Crull, tore at his being, ate him from within, searing every cell of his body. He thought it might tear him apart, but knew better.

From this pain, there was no release. This would be eternal.

As quickly as the pain began, it ceased. The weight of the voice lightened. "And yet…"

"Yes, bro…Master! Whatever you wish. Let me do something to repay my failure!"

The eyes mercifully moved away from their focus on the Ishar Crull. Crull took the opportunity to glance swiftly at this being who once had been his brother. This being once radiated so bright with the light of the morning star that one could spend eternity looking upon him. The lithe, beautiful form still remained, underneath a shell of cruelty which disformed and twisted until its darkness now mocked the beauty once held.

The voice remained as beautiful and tempting, controlled by a will unmoved by any consideration beyond the creature's own purpose. "There is one. Except for his 'integrity'" — the word was spit out with contempt — "he would be mine already. He already has some…inclinations to cruelty. We must begin…tempting him to deeper things. If we can tempt him to…*betray,* we will have him."

An image came into Crull's mind: a man stood at the window of a tall skyscraper, looking out over the ocean. Crull noticed the haze of nuclear pollution which hung across the earth. *"At least I* was somewhat successful. I helped destroy a great portion of the human cattle and spread this wonderful poison." He felt heartened and proud.

"Enter his dreams. And those of others around

him who are already our servants. We must bring him into our fold, for he holds the key to the destruction of this vermin our Enemy so *loves*." The sneer was palpable in the word. "Go! Leave my presence. I expect success this time."

With that last word the Ishar Crull's form was thrown out of the lowest confines, back to a lesser place; one which still held the piercing, burning cold. He was released from the deepest pain but the burning remained. "I will show you, *Master!*" He spit the last word out with pure hate.

Fifty-six

Chrisair, North Carolina. March 22. Dawn.

The light began to caress the tops of the trees, with the promise of the golden edge of the sun just below the horizon. The sky stretched colors from pinks into golds then the deep violet and blue of the fast receding night.

Gem awoke and stretched. Broddin lay asleep beside her, his face peaceful. She wondered what awakened her, but then knew. She could feel the movement within her belly. They'd been married only a few months, yet she'd become pregnant right away and the baby was growing, already moving. She smiled. "Hey, little baby! Is this the world you've chosen to come into? I don't think so. I wouldn't choose it for you but you're coming anyway."

They wondered about bringing children into this world. The increase in radiation from the nuclear fallout would cause an increase in cancers. It was not readily discernible here in the mountains, but they knew it was ever present. Gangs of Ferals had not ventured out this far from civilization, but the community needed to be on its guard. The Federals knew where they were and left them alone, to their relief; but for how long?

Gem didn't worry about any of those threats. They were controllable. But the world had fallen apart in less than a year. In that time, she'd gone from jetting across the ocean to taking three months to walk a thousand miles. From super computers and high tech labs to a coal fired forge. From the inconvenience of brownouts to no power whatsoever.

Worse was the thought of the demons. She'd always thought of the Ishar Crull as a figment of her nightmares, freakishly frightening but not real. Now she knew they were all too real. She and Broddin had won one battle. They'd had the help of angels and prayer, of Christ's hand upon them and his archangel Michael to help them. Obviously the war was not over. It would be someday, but not now.

As the Chosen, they were called to witness. As such, they would certainly be in the front lines in the war. But who would they witness to if they simply lived in these isolated communities, abandoned the great cities to rot and ruin and their citizens to destruction?

What would the future hold for her children and grandchildren? Was it fair to even consider birth? However, long before they fully considered such things, it seemed that God made the decision for them: she was pregnant. In spite of the worry, she smiled.

She heard her mother up moving around in the kitchen, stoking the fire to warm the cabin for the day, humming to herself. Their days settled into a comfortable pattern. Early prayers, then work. She'd started to help her father in the forge. It felt like the innocent times of her childhood again. But now, she did not need him to guide her hands; they were sure. Along with axes and wheel bearings, they forged weapons from long forgotten lore. Swords of Damascus steel, arrows tipped with tungsten. She hoped that they would never need to use these tools.

Broddin was working on a system to convert the electricity from small waterfalls in the mountains to a type of DC current. They would have some limited power. Enough for emergencies and to power a simple pump to supply water.

Fifty-seven

White House. April 1.

Peter Santiago sat in the oval office, his feet on the desk, smoking a cigar. Gerard Meiring lay on the floor in front of the desk, across the Presidential Seal. He stared at the ceiling. "Mr. President, the winter has been rough. Even with rationing and the purges, we barely had the food to supply our cities. We've had real hunger among the citizens."

"But not our people." Santiago's voice was chipper, almost chuckling.

"Of course not. The party members are well taken care of if only for their loyalty. But, the remaining citizens are becoming restive. We need some entertainment to focus them on something else." He sat up. "I've been thinking about that football game we saw in Roxford. It was genius. The leader had thirty-thousand people eating out of his hand. You could feel a real sense of *solidarity* in the crowd. That's what we need, some feeling to bring them together, to entertain and to forge bonds through that entertainment."

"What are you thinking, Gerry?"

"There are stadiums in every city we've maintained. They're just sitting empty. Most can hold the entire population of the city. What if we bring back football, just like it was played in Roxford?"

Santiago pulled his feet down and ground his cigar out on the desk. "I like that idea! We can capture our 'players' from the ranks of Ferals and of the remaining Clingers out in the Fallow Preserves. Most of them are fairly weak after this winter, but it'll still make for good entertainment. There can be incentives. The team that wins not only gets to live, they get some real food and a clean shower. When the word gets out, the stupid roaches will probably line up at the portal for the chance for one night of satiation. Go ahead and get the plan started."

Meiring smiled. "It's already in place. Just needed your blessing. Best part is, you'll preside at the opening games, give the signal for life or death. Of course, it'll always be death. An additional benefit is that it gets our citizens used to the idea that you alone hold the power of life and death. No one else."

Now Santiago sat up further. "You are a genius. But I have an even better idea. We're going to make examples of some of our Congressional foes. They are truly hated by all the citizens, even those who voted for them. We take a few, put them in the middle of the games. How long do you think they'll last? And, *their* example will help the others fall into line."

The reports went out to the news channels announcing the opening of The National Killball League. Free booze, time off from work and the best entertainment. What more could a citizen want? The first games were scheduled in two weeks.

Fifty-eight

Fort Jackson, North Carolina. April 11

Robert Yellow sat at the desk in his cell looking at the two manuscripts. They were bathed in the rays of a spring morning light and glimmered with a reflection of the purest color from within the light itself.

"The Gem Testament" was the title on the first and "A History of Eden's Sword" on the second. He really wasn't sure if both were necessary, since much of the sword's history was built within the Testament. But he decided to write both.

The Testament spoke of what had happened here in these times. A testament of love and sacrifice, of war in America, spiritual and actual, of artificial intelligence and the reality of visions. He had received this witness directly from Broddin's thoughts.

The history of the sword reached back to the beginnings of time. It was his own research project, born of the love of knowledge the sword had awakened within him. It spoke of the timelessness of those themes: love, sacrifice, war, intelligence, visions. For, just as today, they were there "In the beginning."

It was time to go. The doors to this jail were unlocked, the jailers all asleep on this beautiful April morning. A breeze brushed in through the hermetically sealed windows and ruffled the pages of the books in front of Robert Yellow before it wrapped him in its freshening embrace. It reminded him of a verse: "The Spirit blows where it wills…"

He gathered up the books, walked out of the prison and headed southwest. He knew his destination: Summerville, South Carolina.

Fifty-nine

Wando Ford, South Carolina. May 15

Wando Ford lay at the edge of the shield which protected New Mount Pleasant. This was the location of the pulse power generator, which created the protective shield over the city. It was also the busiest of the many Relief stations dotting the city's edge.

David Saul stood at the construction site overseeing the refitting of the relief stations with pulse power. One effect they discovered when they installed the shields around the cities was that the pulse generators created a powerful localized wave field. Any item passing through that thin field was instantly pulverized, reduced to a molecular level. There was no fire and no waste. A fine dust of carbon or other simple compounds was carried off by fans and released into the air.

The Relief programs, those voluntary euthanasia efforts, had been in place for more than a decade. More people than ever volunteered for Relief, for the release from worldly cares, from burdening the Mother Earth. The rush to Relief placed a burden on the system up to this point, and the factory ovens contributed to the carbon footprint. Pulse power for the stations was the perfect solution.

One of the technicians who ran the station stood looking over the dials, his concentration fully on their readouts. Saul watched the demonstration and was impressed with its efficiency. "How soon can these units be functioning at all our city Relief centers?"

"They are being constructed now in Arizona. We expect to build them in place by the end of summer."

"Superb. Good work. The President is grateful for your dedication."

"Thank you, sir."

"Let me know when you do your inaugural run. I'd like to observe the first thousand "clients' as they 'embark on their final journey.'"

The technician had no inflection in his response at all. "I will, sir." He turned back to his dials.

David Saul stepped on the local tramway back into the city center, headed for his penthouse cube. He had a lot of work to do in the next weeks. He got his daily cup of Starjava, went to the elevator port, and pushed the button. He stood waiting. One minute, then two passed. The elevator did not arrive.

He was getting irritated. He would not excuse this type of wait. They reserved this particular elevator for only the highest floors, for the elites. There wasn't enough traffic to warrant this wait. He opened his comband. "Technician, please."

The computer voice was soft, soothing. "Yes, Mr. Saul."

"Check elevator 98A operation. It should be here but it doesn't seem to be working."

The computer voice answered, "Yes, sir. We apologize for the inconvenience. Allow me to check. Checking. Checking. I found the problem. A mechanical issue with this elevator must be corrected. Please cross the compound, take elevator 102B, then transfer to express C to the north side of your building. We apologize, again."

"This is an inconvenience, having to share the public elevators."

"We will have this issue corrected as quickly as possible. Thank you for your patience."

Saul walked across the compound and waited in line for the public elevators. He made a note to file a complaint. "*Amazing. We control gravitational force, found a clean source of energy, and all the power we'll ever need...and we can't keep an elevator operating properly.*" He shook his head in disgust as he jammed into the elevator with fifty other people.

As he stood there, he could see in the mirrored wall that several young people in the back started a hookon. They started kissing, touching each other, moaning and grabbing. Everyone else on the elevator smirked and shuffled. A few close to the action joined in and were welcomed.

Saul's eyes were drawn to a striking young woman. She was stunningly beautiful, young, very young he thought. He turned away and moved towards the door when the young woman took his hand. Her voice was light. "Come join us. You'd have fun." Her hand — soft, inviting — took his.

"No, thanks. I'm headed to my cube.

"C'mon. Y'all gonna be a dead? They're no fun. Looks like you need some release. You're all tense."

"Again, thanks, but…"

The girl grabbed him and began moving against him, seeking his lips.

"*I said no thank you!*" He shoved her away and turned to the doors.

The girl stepped back, shocked. "How rude! You're not supposed to just reject an open feely like that. You hurt my feelings!"

People around murmured their support for the girl. "Yeah, she wasn't doin' no harm." "Shoulda at least been polite." "Looks like that guy really *does* need a release." Others now joined in the hookon to make the girl feel better.

The elevators came to the floor for him to switch. David Saul stepped out, sighed and turned back to look in. "I apologize for my rude conduct. I did not mean to offend this young girl or any one of you in my actions. I must go." He turned and rushed over to the express elevator. *"Stupid hookies. I don't* care if they hookon in the elevator, but I just don't feel like sex lately. Too much to do."

Saul had experienced his share of hookons in elevators back in the day. Yeah it was fun, but after a while, he'd simply gotten bored with it. His work was much more fulfilling and exciting these days and the hookons just felt…empty.

As the elevator doors closed, the girl was still looking after Saul. She smirked and said, her voice now deep and raspy, "Maybe next time, David."

Then she returned to the action.

The girl did not notice an old Afram man who stood in the back of the elevator. Although Aframs shared the same public elevators, they were shunted aside, ignored. They were quietly given the menial jobs: preparing and serving food, working the docks, supervising the Worker Party members. When space units were assigned, they were all placed in lower ones, clustered together.

Part of the reason the authorities gave for this separation was the Aframs' insistence on having children and raising them on their own, instead of handing them over to the Primary Education Facilities as the more enlightened citizens did.

In only one generation since the Public Service Education Laws were enacted, the separation had solidified until Aframs spoke an older Gullah dialect of English. Other citizens barely understood them. The two races hardly took notice of one another, shared almost nothing.

Scott Thibidault stood on the elevator and turned away so as not to see the sexual activities. He'd been uncomfortable even getting on with this many of the "others." Now he remembered why: the hookons. *"Thank God dey didn't ask me."* He would not have known the way to refuse a hookon invitation without creating an even bigger scene than that man who had left. *"What happenin' to us?"*

Tears formed in his eyes. His mother taught him years ago that just the sight of some things could taint you. Quietly, lest anyone hear, he kept whispering to himself, "Jes will not be. Ain't right."

He realized, then, that he was called to witness this very thing. He was called to watch these deeds and to ward against them. To save the remnant of his people who were chosen to be here. His quiet humming disguised the old spiritual his mother had taught him, a tune no one in this elevator or this city had ever heard.

Sixty

The Rushes. One week after the wedding.

They felt the pull for many days. They honeymooned in the green depth of the forest, near a place called Wyndmoor. They were cradled in its breezes, warmed and comforted. They explored the woods around — and each other, learned the little things which made them laugh, then cry with joy. The time moved too quickly.

On the night before their return to the world, their voices traded quiet thoughts. Grace still worried about the difference in their ages. She knew that Roger had known everything about her from the very first day. He *knew* that she was seven hundred years older than he, though she looked barely thirty. "I'll be gone a long time afore ya, Rogair. I canna know when. 'Twould destroy me twere' it t'other way."

"We cannot know when our time is. What we return to, whatever waits us in the world is far beyond our understanding. I have a great fear. I don't see how we will survive what's already out there, what's coming."

"I've great trust in you, Rogair."

"But it's not up to me, Grace." Their hands entwined. "I prayed time and again for guidance on this. I used every bit of knowledge, looked at every logical outcome. I just can't see…."

"Shhh." She put her finger to his lips. "Ya've not lived lang enough ta lairn ta trust as I do. God will watch over us. 'Ave faith, my love. What cooms will be. We have aeich other. It must be enough fair us."

They lay together on their last night of peace, awake in each others arms, whispering of love and acting on it. Both knew that where they were going would allow little peace.

In the next morning light they walked to the forest's edge. Those they loved gathered around them. William joined them. They were ready. Grace's mother held her close. Roger turned to his parents. "You're staying here?"

They looked at one another. Kerian Noguchi had regained his sight. Since that time, he had not taken his eyes off his wife. He looked back at his son. "Roger, if we could be of use, we would join you. We wouldn't be. Anyway…" Now he took Kim's hand. "… I found a peace I never had. A love I never guessed possible. We will stay here, at least for a time. As long as we are able." Kim nodded her agreement.

Roger took them both in his arms. "Watch over each other. We will try to be back, but I'm not sure how long it will be."

"We'll be here."

Roger and Grace Noguchi turned, joined William Broddin and the three walked through a wavering in the trees and out of sight. Kim Noguchi stood there, tears falling. Kerian put his arms around her. "Have faith, Kim. We'll see them again."

She couldn't help but smile. "*You* telling me to have faith. Now, that's a miracle." They walked back to the campfire, hand in hand.

Sixty-one

Germantown, Ohio. June 1: 6:30 a.m.

The sun crested the horizon. The fields were wet with the cool morning dew. The nuclear winter had extended well into the spring and the temperature hovered just over fifty degrees. This year promised to be cool, if not cold. Large honeybees floated from petal to petal, sluggish in the cold air, drinking in the nectars which were soaked for the last nine months with radioactive rain. Sometimes, one of the honeybees would drop to the ground, twitching in death.

The trees at the end of this field wavered, then divided. Roger, Grace and William stepped through the veil. Roger looked at William. "Something's wrong."

"What?"

"The sun shouldn't be at that angle. The air is cool, but there are flowers everywhere. This is summer. We haven't been gone just a week; it's probably been six or seven months."

Grace laid her hand on his arm. "Sure, ah've nevair seen this happen. Somehow, the rushes ha' slipped and our time ran slower than this."

Roger thought about it. "Perhaps the EMP's

altered time? Can't be. We would have noticed it before. Maybe the gravity of the pulse shields bent time in the vicinity." He was irritated. He wasn't used to not having answers, not understanding. "Let's get going."

William looked around. "Looks like someone found the chopper. It's not where we left it. What now?"

"We'll have to walk, at least back to Roxford." He turned to Grace. "Why couldn't we go through the veil into Roxford…where you did when you shot my father?"

Grace blushed. "I doona know, but the veil seemed to follow you. Pairhaps 'twere a bridge driven by our love. I canna take us through tha' place. No' now."

Roger shrugged. "Sure would've been more convenient. Maybe we can find an old car some place along the way."

William looked at him. "Why an old car?"

"The older cars don't have computers. Much more mechanical. They should still work. We'll need to somehow find some gas, too. There may be some stored at the Roxford underground facility."

They began to make their way south through empty fields. No humans were near. Roger could not understand. Skeletons lay around unburied, the bones bleached from the weather, the only evidence of human life.

Grace was visibly upset. "How can i' be, Rogair? Do mahn today cair so little fair their brathers tha' they leave them to unholy ends? Dinna they no' cair?"

"No. They didn't." He was now silent once again, preoccupied. She had not seen him this distant.

They walked on for several more miles. Roger finally spoke. "They didn't care enough to bury even those they loved. There were too many. Millions…" His voice faded off into a strained silence again.

Grace walked up beside him, and took his hand in hers. Her voice was quiet. "This will no' stand. When we 'ave finished the calling, we will retairn hair, we will bring others. Hair, in this place. Begin to make a sacrament."

Roger walked on in silence. He kept shaking his head, trying to relieve the pressure of this knowledge. "Perhaps it's better that they didn't live. Maybe we should *all* be left to rot without burial. How do we care so little? I *don't know!*" He dropped Grace's hand and walked off.

Grace followed him, catching him. She turned him to her and wrapped her arms around him. "Stop. Rogair, this be no more turrible tha' what ah've seen so many yairs. Do ya forget so soon, the world of wars? Ah've saen it a hundred time. Mahn ha' not changed."

"Then he deserves death!"

"Sure, ya had a better answer in Roxford."

He turned and stalked away. She stood and watched, then began to sing, her voice rising across the field.

"Oh beautiful, for heroes proved...

> *...in liberating strife*
> > *Who more than self their country loved"*

Her voice was clear, resonant.

> > *"...And mercy more than life!"*

Roger stopped, his head bent.

> > *"America, America!*
> > > *May God thy gold refine,*
> > > > *'til all success be nobleness,*
> > > > *and every gain divine!"*

She walked up to him. She could see tears streaming down his face.

"Grace, how could we have let it all go? The beauty and majesty of what we had? America? Why even try to save it? Why not go back to the rushes, live in peace?"

She took his hands. "Sure an' we alway do it. 'Tis in our nature. We fall. Bu' God ha' no' finished wi' us yet. 'Tis no' ours ta judge when He will. Take hairt. We be together in this. Doona let this grief conquer the love ya' have."

"How can you love America? You hardly know this country."

"I lav' hair because you do, Rogair."

Roger Noguchi held Grace tight and cried for the millions who died, for the losses he could never requite, for what had happened and what was to come. They held each other for a while, then he straightened and wiped his eyes. "I wish I had your faith."

"Give yairself a while...pairhaps a hundred years."

He chuckled, then looked at her. "I love you. You give me hope."

"Ahhh, an' I thought tha' it was you givin' me such a thing."

They stood and held each other. They hadn't noticed that William had gone to a barn he saw in the distance. Now they heard an engine start. In a moment, they saw William drive up in a pickup truck. "Whaddya know? We got wheels."

"How old is that truck?"

"Prolly a hundred years old. Simple four stroke engine. The thing still had diesel in it and air in the tires. Amazed it actually works. Some farmer prolly used it around here. Cmon."

"Is it safe?"

William looked at Roger. "You mean safer than you flying the chopper? Yeah."

Roger laughed. "Okay, let's go."

Sixty-two

New Mount Pleasant. June 2: 8 p.m.

David Saul stood at his window and looked out toward the falling evening. His irritation would not go away. He'd come to his express elevator to find a technician working on it. The worker was the usual: medium height, lean, undistinguished, uninteresting. He was looking at the repair manual for the elevator, mumbling. David walked up to him. "What's buzzin'?"

The worker looked up with no expression. "This manual is not the right manual for this elevator panel."

"What do you mean?"

"There are supposed to be only four bolts. I removed the four, yet the panel does not come off."

David couldn't comprehend. "Look in front of you, man. There's a fifth bolt right in the middle, in front of you."

"The manual doesn't say anything about a fifth bolt. I'll have to go back for the correct manual." The voice held no inflection, no anger or bother. It stated a fact.

"Are you crazy? The fifth bolt is right in front of you. Unscrew it."

"It's not in the manual…"

David Saul snatched the power wrench from the worker's hand. He unscrewed the bolt and removed the panel. "There! Now you can fix the elevator."

The worker stood, looking at the extra bolt and at the manual. "Thank you. Have a nice day."

David Saul crossed over to the public elevators. *"Is it any wonder the elevators don't work around here? That's one worker who should report to Relief. Although, the guy who ran the Relief station must be his cousin. They both have an identical personality."*

He would make a report. The elevator should have been repaired two weeks ago, yet it kept breaking down. At least there wasn't a hookon in the public elevators to worry about as he rode up to cross over to his stop.

His mood was foul. A storm rose over the Atlantic, seeming to mirror the way he felt. Lightning pulsed down on the waters. He could see waves crash against the Sullivan's Island shore. The darkness would soon fall. He liked this time of night. He could gather his thoughts, work on some of the reports he'd received.

He had followed some of the pulse research labeled "President's Eyes Only." He was cleared, along with Gerard Meiring, for this research level. Yet when he'd inquired through the normal channel, he'd been refused access. He'd asked the President about it. "Pete, do you have some research going on with the pulse weapons? I should review it for security reporting. Can't seem to get into the system."

"Must be a computer glitch. I'll have Gerry look into it. I think what you're talking about is just some progress reports on the pulse drive. They don't seem to be able to configure it."

"But that's low level stuff. I already saw that. This is for your eyes only."

"Really? Let me check with Gerry. Maybe he's got some other research he hasn't shown me yet. He likes to surprise me sometimes."

No answer was forthcoming, so David Saul decided to look for himself through the back channel. What he found chilled him. Los Alamos had already perfected the pulse drive. Vehicles were being made ready for military use, the first being bombers which would deliver some kind of aerosol weapons. *"What the devil could that be?"*

He was just getting into a sensitive area when someone knocked on the door. He looked up, frustrated. *"Who the hell is bothering me now, and how did they get past security?"* He logged off and went to the door. He looked at the vidscreen and saw the young girl who had tried to draw him into the hookon. He punched the intercom, irritated. "What do you want?"

She looked right into the lens. "Please, Mr. Saul, I really apologize. I didn't mean to embarrass you the other week. I was just *really* into it and...I just lost myself in the heat of the moment."

"Hmm. Well...no problem. You're forgiven."

"But could you just let me in a moment? I brought you your favorite drink." She held up a particular green liqueur in a tiny bottle and now he saw her blush. "I…I researched you. Ya see, I'd like to be a reporter someday…just like you."

It impressed him that she had succeeded in finding out that kind of info and that she'd talked her way past security to get to his door. He chuckled. "Sure, but only for a few minutes. I'm involved in some research of my own." He opened the door.

She walked in, a shy young girl — so different from the aggressive young teen he'd seen two weeks ago. "Thank you so much, sir. Uh, here's the liq… wow! This place is *huge!"*

He smiled. "Now that's a state secret you have to keep. Your first assignment if you're going to become a reporter. The government must be able to trust you to report the goings-on around you and at the same time keep state secrets that are important to the security of the nation."

She walked around the room and he noticed that she glanced sideways at his computer vid. Her mouth gave a cute little downturn and he realized that she hoped to see something of value open on it. "If you keep that up, you *are* going to make a good reporter."

She blushed again and shrugged. "Sorry. Comes with experience, I guess. Since I was very young, I've had to notice *everything* around me just to keep ahead of the games around here. Hey, the glass looks like lightning! Pretty cool!"

He felt chilled even thinking about it. "Not anything I ordered. It'll take a while to get replacements."

She went to stand in the fading light and looked out at the ocean. Her voice was so soft, he had to come close behind her. "I've never seen such beauty. We live on floor two of a back building. I wish everyone could share this."

He came up beside her and saw a tear running down her cheek. She looked so small and vulnerable…and she *was* exceptionally beautiful. He reached out and wiped the tear. Her cheek was warm, inviting. He heard his own voice, distant now, say "What is your name?"

She turned to him and looked up into his eyes, her voice now a whisper. "Diana."

He found his arms around the girl, his lips gently caressing hers. She tasted of strawberries and — impossibly — of his favorite liqueur, which remained unopened across the room.

He had not wanted or intended this. But she seemed lost, so different from the vixen who had attacked him in the elevator. She was trembling like a young first timer, someone inexperienced. His pulse pounded in his head. "Diana! I…I."

She pushed herself into his arms further, giving into whatever he might want, but then she stopped. She pulled back from him and seemed to become even younger. "This isn't right. This isn't what I wanted. I…I have to go!" She started for the door.

"Diana, wait!"

"No, I don't want a job because we sexed! I want to be a reporter because I'm *good* at something *besides* sex! I *really do* want to be like you." She was at the door, her hand on the knob and turned to look at him. Now she smiled, and blushed. "Trouble is I *really do* want your sex, too." She turned and skipped out the door.

He stood and looked at the door for long moments. He started back towards the desk, then turned and went to the window. He stood for hours staring out at the fallen night. His hands restlessly followed the patterns of the lightning on the glass. The black clouds reflected no light except the lightning pulsing down.

He forgot the research, the pulse weapon, everything…except the feel of the young girl in his arms, the taste of her kisses and her pulling away from him. He sighed. "Diana."

Sixty-three

Chrisair, Georgia. August 8: 2 p.m.

Gem wasn't used to the cold air. The temperature never rose above 60 this summer, if you could call it that. It snowed three times…in July…in Georgia. She bundled up near the stove. She could feel her baby moving. The baby was coming and she was afraid. *What if the radiation harmed the baby? What if there were some other issue? What if the birth went wrong?*

Her mother turned from her cooking and came over to her. She'd heard her daughter's busy mind. Estelle Matthews stroked her daughter's hair. "Stop worrying. She'll be fine."

"Mom! How do you know?"

"Faith."

"No. How do you know it's a girl?"

Estelle smiled. "I just know. Have you chosen a name yet?"

"If it's a girl, Mari. If it's a boy, Michael."

"Mari…."

"Stop, you're influencing things."

"Little late for that. Want some tea?"

"Yeah."

Barbara Broddin joined them a few moments

later. She had arrived the month before with a group of people who were lead to Chrisair. She looked at Gem. "Your mother is right. Stop worrying." The wolf had taken to following Barbara around and now huffed his agreement.

Gem laughed. "Ahhh! Is there *no* privacy in this place? The wolf knows too?"

Barbara laughed. "I doubt it, but he can sense you're worried. Any kind of dog or wolf doesn't worry. Not in their nature. Now you want to argue with Wolfie?"

She smiled. "No."

They were sitting near the stove, when Gem felt a strong pulse in her mind. "Roger." She leaped up and ran out the door, even before they heard the sound of the motor. She called back to the other two. "Roger's here!"

Barbara was right behind her. "That means William will be here, too!" They both ran down the path towards the town square. "Are you sure?"

"Oh, yeah! It's about time!"

They reached the square just as the truck pulled into it. Roger got out and started to stretch but Gem grabbed him. Barbara leaped into William's arms. Grace got out of the truck and stood there.

"Roger, God I missed you! What took you so long? Where'd you get the truck? Did you guys have much trouble?"

Roger laughed. "Slow down! Plenty of time for questions. He pulled Grace next to him. "Gem, may I present…"

"Oh, your wife, Grace! Oh, Grace, welcome." Gem threw her arms around the woman.

"I…thank you… I see y'air with child!"

"Yes. She'll arrive any day. (Ahh, Mom, now you have me saying it!) How are you? I can see you've had troubles, felt them all along, but no real danger…"

They were laughing. Roger took her shoulders. "We're here. Calm down. By the way, I have *never* seen a more pregnant woman in my life! As tiny as you are, you're all belly and nothing else!"

As they laughed together, Broddin came up. He and Roger clasped hands, then hugged. "You've given us some worries."

"Stop. No need."

Broddin looked at his parents. They stood, holding each other, looking into each other's eyes. Barbara Broddin was crying tears of joy. William held her close. "There used to be a song. 'Are those your eyes? Is that your smile? I've been looking at you forever, but I've never seen you before.' It's so old, no one remembers where it came from. It's what I feel now. I've never loved you more than I do right now. More in love with you today than the day we married."

"You old romantic." She grinned. "I feel the same." She hesitated. "We lost so much. But I feel like we've found each other again. Like I found my way again, back to you."

William turned to his son. "Cm'ere and give yer old man a hug. I'm proud of what you've done, of who you are, son. Glad we're all here together again."

"Me, too. I worried about you, Dad."

"Nah. Stupid to worry. I had Roger's back. He had mine."

"Yeah, we felt that literally a couple of times."

"Ahh, never mind that. We're here. Can we get some decent food? That Grace is great with a bow, but I'm sick of rabbit and wild boar."

"How about a venison feast tonight?"

"Now yer talkin'."

It was at that moment Gem's water broke. Mari was coming today.

Sixty-four

New Mount Pleasant, SC.   August 8: 4 p.m.

At 46, Scott Thibidault wasn't really old. Yet, his family had passed down ancient memories from generation to generation. As the oldest of the community, he carried authority. And he was filled with a fire which commanded those who listened. He had seen something. He told people of the day when he saved that Worker Party man and then was drowning himself. How the Sun came to give him air, to save him…for a greater purpose.

"I runs'ta'knock dat man oudtdaway from de skid. Fell in'da'watta. Thought I was daid, watta poarin'in'mah'mouf. But da *sun* reach out, downin da'watta, an ketch'*me'up!* Ah afeared somethin' terrible. Like a man do, dat sun spoke to me. Tole me don' be afeared. Tole me things. Tole me Truth."

At first they thought he was crazy. But the truth of what he'd seen rang out and made people listen. As he spoke, more listened, watched and saw truth in what he told them about the things around them they had come to take for granted.

He was speaking to one of the many small groups who began meeting in secret. He chose his words carefully. At this point, he didn't want to be accused of treason. "We see dis hookon culture everwhere roun' us ever single day. Doan know 'bout y'all, but I'm tarred'of'it. My mamma taught me bedder. Taught me respek women, respek my own self mo'den'dat."

"You tell it brother."

"Ain't y'all tarred of it, too? Doan like the sisters bein' made to join dem hookons. Ain't good fer nobody. Things I seed, I cain't unsee. Tried not ta look, but too much goin' all roun'.""

One of the other men spoke up. "So what we gonna do? Leave? Die?"

Thibidault stared at the man. "We ain't gonna die. God be takin' care o' us."

"You say."

"God say, in book o' Dan. Three men go into dat fire. Three men come out. God watch over dem? He watch over us."

"You talkin' treason, Fro!

"No! We ain't startin' that talk, chere me? Ain't no bad talk any more. No bad works, neither. We gonna prepare. Prepare our own selves fo' what He want us do."

The man spoke up again. "You talkin' faith, you talkin' Chrishin stuff. That treason!"

"Nah. I ain't talkin' faith. Talkin' fack. Don' take no faith ta see what goin' on roun here and that it ain't goin' ta no good. Now you gonna report dat?"

The woman sitting next to the instigator nudged him in the ribs. "You shut it, Tebby. You know you ain't gonna go talkin' to nobody. Jes makin' troubles."

"Yes'm."

Scott Thibidault smiled within. If you got the women behind you, the men followed. And, the women were fed up with just about everything going on here. "We gonna leave this place and soon. Dey won' care. Mo' fo' them, dey think."

Sixty-five

The knock came at the door — soft, seeking. David Saul sighed. He knew who it was. He knew he would let her in. He knew they would sex…again. He never thought he'd be addicted like the hookies, wanting it all the time. Diana had invaded his mind, his dreams, his heart. All day, he could barely work, distracted by the thought that she would be in his arms that night.

He thought back on the last two months with desire and trepidation. He told himself it began innocently, that he was tutoring her. He had called up the screen recognition program the morning after that first night and it identified the girl as Diana Tauck. He'd sent her a text that day inviting her to join him for a report at the local station. She watched his reporting, attentive. When they went to lunch afterward, she pelted him with question after question. He looked at her. "You want to be a reporter?"

"Yes."

"You're already on your way. I like your spirit. Follow me around a few days. I want to see what you pick up, if you see violations which need to be reported, people who aren't doing their duties. If you pick up the things I see, I'll take you on as an apprentice."

She leaped up and gave him a hug. "Thank you."

He hadn't been wrong in his first impression of her. She would be a good reporter, probably a *great* reporter. The thought hit him. *"I wonder if she's reporting me! And who is she reporting to?"* He chuckled. It wasn't as if they were doing anything wrong. She'd reached consentage four years ago. So the sex they enjoyed in his cube was not only legal, but encouraged. He brought her here in the evenings to show her how to research on the computer, how to scan the security vids to watch for signs of insurrection. Over the next month they became more comfortable. He'd not touched her since that first night, but it remained in both their thoughts. His touch. Her words.

In the month, that comfortable feeling progressed. She would lean into him, touch his arm, look up into his eyes as he spoke, smile, laugh at a joke. Then, on July Fourth, she came to him dressed in a soft chiffon cloak, clinging and shimmering. "Do you know what today is?"

"Your birthday. Happy one."

She blushed and walked over to the window. In the bright evening light, he could see her body right through the dress. She spoke quietly again and he came up to stand beside her. "What?"

Another tear fell down her cheek. "I'm sorry."

He reached out and brushed it away again. "Why?"

"I can't help it. I still want to sex you." She turned and his lips found themselves kissing her again. The taste of the liqueur and strawberries once again assaulted his senses. This time, she did not pull back but leaned in, building an urgent need. He picked her up and carried her to his bed.

Since then, every night, they shared every imaginative way to enjoy each other. She was creative, and more experienced than he wanted to think about. But his thoughts became fogged when they lay on the bed together.

Some emotion deep inside gnawed at the edges of his mind. A part of him, unthought within, wished things were different. It hadn't even started out as "just sexing." Something deeper, more tender, fought against him every time he took her to bed. The image of that first night plagued his mind: Diana at his windows, looking out at the ocean view, *crying;* of his first touch of the tear on her cheek. That act was not motivated by sex at all. He'd only felt a tender care for this young childlike girl. He only wanted to comfort her. Then, suddenly he was overwhelmed, his whole being taken away.

He found he wanted to sex her less and less, to just lay and hold her in his arms. Not to use her, but to protect her. *"What's happening to me? What would I protect her from? She's probably more dangerous than I am!"* He chuckled. "C'mon in, Diana."

She unlocked the door. "Just wanted to make

sure you weren't busy with 'eyes only' stuff before I came in." Her tone was sweet, but a little petulant.

"I will *not* show you any research that could compromise me…or you. Some of this stuff is too sensitive. You would be sent to Relief immediately if you don't have the right clearance. Anyway, you need to learn *patience.*" He smiled. "Come here. I want to show you some things you can see."

She danced over, excited. "Show me!"

He opened the screen and began to show her some of the history of the party's founding, of the sacrifices great leaders made to bring their nation to the forefront in the war to save The Mother. He showed her the original, raw footage of the dedication video, where the great ones from Hollywood and Washington dedicated their Relief to the good of Mother Earth.

She sat, transfixed, and watched the vids, asking questions about each person, wanting to know more. "How old was he when he gave himself for Relief? How about her? What did she do? How many have gone for Relief? By the way, how's the new program going out on Wando Ford? You said it's moving along well?"

"Yes, the…particular mechanism we're using should be ready any day. I'm going to watch the first thousand go through their Relief. It's very moving. Do you want to come with me to see it? The neat part is that this new method is so quick and clean! No pain, no cries, no mess for us to worry about, no pollution of the Mother's resources. It's amazing."

"What drives the station?" The question was casual and timed for him to answer it easily.

"Pulse…Hey you! I told you not to ask certain questions. Now forget the word I just spoke! You're not cleared for it."

"What word?"

"Good girl."

She started touching him, her voice soft, her lips turned up toward his face. "Am I cleared for this?"

Two hours later, she left him sleeping and let herself out. She walked to the express elevator and took it down to the first floor. As she stepped out, she passed a shadow in the recesses. Without looking aside, she said, "Pulse something. It has to do with powering the new method for Relief." She continued on towards her own cube.

Sixty-six

Chrisair, Georgia. September 22: Night

The party went on late into the evening. The townsfolk gathered to celebrate the birth of Gem's daughter, Mari. The joy they felt was reflected in each face, written in each heart. They could know and feel the deep longing and love James and Gem felt for this child, and the joy at her arrival.

At one month, Mari was smiling and bright eyed. An aura of deep rose glowed about her when she smiled…and sometimes when she cried too. Now she lay in Gem's arms and their auras flowed into and through each other, changed and moved with the love shining between them.

James Broddin watched them. Everyone else was partying around them, but he really only wanted to be with his 'two ladies' and relax at home. Their parents were all there, and Roger and Grace.

The community had grown considerably. Throughout the summer people began to show up, seeking refuge from the wilds, from Ferals or Federals. They could not figure how the people found them, but those who came specifically sought out Gem and James Broddin. "We'd heard rumors that you came this way."

"Who from?"

"Don't know, really. It just seemed like we would hear a voice out of the mist. It would say, 'Go here.' Or, 'not that way.' Really can't explain it."

Broddin thought back on Torgeson's comments, and Solaris's. *"It's like the mist came alive."*

After the last of the party grew quiet, they lay in bed together, Mari cuddled between them. Broddin lay awake for a long time, staring up at the wooden rafters. He turned and saw that Gem lay awake. "You feel it, too, don't you."

She sighed. "Yes. We can't stay here. We have to move towards the coast."

"It's safe here."

"It is, but we're not chosen to be safe. I've thought a lot about it, about why God brought us here if we're to witness and how we'd do it. I don't think I found an answer, but I think He's given me a conviction."

"Me, too. I keep thinking of one word. It keeps rising in my mind from out of the mist."

She nodded. "Summerville."

"Yes."

"Just us?"

"No. Everybody. We're all going. Our community stays together."

"What if the townsfolk don't want to go?"

James Broddin smiled, now. "I think they'll all go. None of them would want to be that far away from Mari."

"Do you think they all really love her as much

as we do?"

"Can't you feel it in their hearts?"

Now she smiled, too. "Yeah. They'll come, but…what are we leading them into?"

"I don't know. We just have to trust."

"We'll be awfully close to one of the cities. New Mount Pleasant is only a few miles away. Aren't the Federals going to bother us?"

Broddin thought a moment. "I think they know they can't touch us or anyone who is under our care. They may not like it that we're there, but they'll leave us alone."

"But why are we going? What's our purpose there?"

"To witness. You said yourself that we can't do much of that here, isolated as we are. We've had it fairly easy, compared to the millions who faced death in so many ways. We were 'protected.' That's not an illusion, nor is it without purpose. Our time is coming, for trials."

She trembled and he took her into his arms to provide what comfort he could.

Sixty-seven

New Mount Pleasant. September 24. 8 a.m.

The soldier stood at the portal at the base of the RavNational Bridge, on lookout against any intruders. He heard a commotion behind him and turned. A multitude of people were walking down Central Avenue right toward him; hundreds, maybe a thousand or more. He punched his comband. "Sir, I need reinforcements *right now!"*

A bored voice answered the call. "What's going on, Jackson? Someone else at the portal want to come in?"

"No sir. There's a thousand people coming this way. Lead by a very big Afram guy. Not sure what they want, but they're carrying all kinds of stuff."

Colonel Jolie sighed. *"What now?"* He opened a vid feed looking up Central Avenue and sat up in his chair quick. He punched his comband. "Sergeant, get a squad up on the bridge, *now!* Armed and ready. I mean *now!"* He opened a channel to David Saul. "Mr. Saul, there's some activity going on down here at the Bridge. Take a look at the vid feed of Central Avenue."

"Colonel, what's that crowd? Where are they headed?"

"Not sure. Towards the bridge. Look pretty angry if you ask me."

David Saul closed his research and took the elevator down to the ground. People streamed past him, carrying what they could on their backs, pulling makeshift carts behind them. They sang some song about "Moses gone down from Egypt." He shook his head, and pulled one of them aside. "Where are you people going?"

The man looked at him. "Don' know jes yet, sah. Be goin' oudaheah. All I knows."

"What? You'll die out there!"

"Be dyin' in heah."

David cut back around the buildings to work his way toward the bridge. The crowd did not rush. They simply marched along, singing their songs. He ran ahead and arrived at the bridge just as the squad got there. "Status, soldier."

"We've set up a platoon and cordoned the area off. Not sure what's going on."

At that moment, the crowd stopped about a hundred fifty yards away. A huge Afram man stepped forward, waving a white handkerchief. "Hey, boss. Can I come on up deah and jab some?"

"Who are you?"

The man stood taller. "You kin call me Elijah."

David Saul turned to the colonel. "Face recognition. What do you have?"

The colonel looked at his com. "Scott Elijah Thibidault. Dock supervisor. Never in any trouble in his life. Forty-six. Relief due in six months. Probably has these people worked up to try to get out of it."

David shrugged. "Let's see what he has to say. **Elijah, approach.**"

The man walked up to within twenty feet. The soldiers trained their guns on him. He was huge, his muscles rippling, his chest and shoulders far larger than any man Saul knew. "You be dat David Saul. I knowed you from dem news repotes. I trus' you. You tell dese soldiers heayah we don' wan' no fights. Got no thing wit y'all. Jes want to leave."

David had a hard time catching the man's language. It sounded foreign. He knew that the Aframs lived separated for half a century, sharing the same elevators, same rations...but not the same culture. The two races grew completely apart; lived together but ignored each other with a practiced purpose. The language changed, too, but after a moment his mind understood the words. He was surprised. He looked back at the crowd. "How many are you?"

"Guess 'roun twelve hunnert of us."

He figured this was about Relief. "Look, Scott..."

"Elijah, sah..."

"Okay, Elijah. I know Relief is coming up for you soon. Know you might be afraid of it, but you know it's for the best. You said you trust me...."

Elijah shook his head back and forth. "Nosah, dats not it. Not 'fraid o' no Relief. We jes tarred o' bein' here's all. Don' like wat go on wit' da hookons. Tarred o' dese stupid Worker Party idjits. Tarred o' your kind tellin' us when, how, what. Tarred o' havin' ours made ta jine in dem hookons."

"Ahh, your daughter's reached consentage."

"Nosah. She way beyond dat now. But she don' want keep hookin." He reached his hand out toward David and David was startled to see how close the man's reach brought him. "Don' you see, Mr. Saul? I don' wanna says any words again what y'all do. Not mah bidness. But, we'uns, we jes wanna live our own lives. We not doin' much work heah anymore, anyways. Let us go. Jes be mo' food fo' y'all. We taken some little fo' da road, but not much."

David Saul looked at the man. "Don't you realize that when you walk out that portal you'll all die anyway? There's radiation out there. Not a pretty death. Long and painful. You want to die, why don't you all just report to Relief. It's a lot quicker. More humane."

Elijah shook his head again. "Fogive me, Mr. Saul, but we ain't gonna die. I jes know. Now I knows you don' wanna let us out to dat Fallowland you call it. We don' wanna fights, but too many o' us an' we gonna be leavin'. If'n we have to rush dis gate, some of us be killed. An' all o' you. If we really be daid from dat readyation, then not yo' worry, right?"

The colonel stood next to David Saul. He said, quietly, "We have enough firepower to stop some, but most of our guns are trained on the outside. If you delay them a little more, we can retrain them, take this bunch out completely."

David Saul looked at the man called Elijah.

"You know Colonel, last year we were expelling Clingers from this very gate at the rate of thousands per day. What's another twelve hundred? They want to go out there and die? Let them."

The colonel shook his head, but he was not going to cross the President's friend. "I don't agree with you on this, sir. We allow this, what other kind of independent action will people take?"

"Don't worry. I'll take the responsibility."

The colonel shrugged. "Your call." He turned back to the troops. "Stand down. Private, open that portal and let these crazies through."

The man called Elijah came up to stand beside David Saul and motioned for the multitudes to begin. They marched out, singing that strange song about Moses come down from Egypt. Elijah was the last man to cross the portal. He turned and waved. "Bless you, sah."

The colonel still shook his head. "*That* was treason! Christian talk. How dare he! We should go teach that man a lesson."

David Saul smiled. "Nah. C'mon. If they really are Clingers, we would do the same thing: force them out! They saved us the trouble of an expensive investigation, reporting and forced expulsion." He turned his back and walked away.

Elijah, the leader of this multitude, stood and watched David Saul go. "You be a good man under dat face yo' put up. Ole Pharaoh, he had a stone heart. Gawd brought de plague on his folk, to let His people go. You be smart'n dat." He turned his face away from the city of New Mount Pleasant, walked through with his people and lead them west, into the forests which now grew all around. The green under the canopy felt cool. Elijah smiled.

*   *   *

In every city throughout the nation, similar events unfolded. Many grew tired of the hookons, of boredom, of the Killball games, of the empty entertainment. In each city, a leader was chosen. Creatures of Lightning, Wind, Rain, or Mist would visit and inspire. Creatures who judged and who called those men. In each city, a host of people heard the calling from these leaders…and responded. They went out to seek some deeper vision.

Sixty-eight

New Mount Pleasant. September 30. 5 a.m.

Diana left earlier in the night, and David finally had the cube to himself again. He turned on his computer feed and quickly keyed in the sequence to get into the back doors. He had come across an obscure reference in an email from one researcher to the President which caught his interest. *"Charon is ready. Boat rides almost ready. Once released, no survivors."*

"Charon? Boat ride? What could that be?"

He returned to the study of genetic research he'd followed in the last month, searching for any references to Charon. He'd been careful since the CDC had their own trace and antivirus programs in place. They'd been compromised a year ago and were desperate that it not happen again. They never considered that their own security protocols were used against them, that the very codes securing the heart of their systems were the ones compromised.

He finally found the research: genetic links the CDC used to create a most unusual virus. It was a genetic nano-virus, which would effectively destroy every single human being on earth. No antivirus or defense against it existed. Only two scientists were working on the virus. They had already weaponized it. The virus would be delivered across the world by simultaneous direct release from the new pulse-drive bombers he'd found in his earlier hacking of the research systems. He knew the pulse bombers would be undetectable by any current defense systems.

He continued to read the reports on the nano-virus. *"The time between infection and complete incapacitation is calculated at less than three hours. No enemy or ally will have the time to react before their end."*

David Saul was suspended between chilled horror and fascination. *"They've finally done it: the ultimate solution. No more mankind to pollute, to destroy, to harm the Mother."* The horror lay in his realization that the virus killed everyone, including him. He was seeing his death right in front of him.

He was also incensed. *"Why haven't they told me? I'm Pete's best friend! Didn't he think he could trust me?"*

He called over to the airport. "Mac. Rev up the hyper-shuttle. I need to get to DC."

"Yes, sir. Have it ready when ya get here."

Sixty-nine

Wheaten, Kansas, September 30: 6 a.m.

Siri Charoenkul sat up in bed. He'd been awakened again by the vibration. He knew what it was. The high speed rail passed some fifteen miles from Wheaton. The trains carried troops and mid-level government executives. Sometimes worthy citizens were given a reward trip for reporting illegal activity to the authorities — or to a reporter, which amounted to the same thing.

No horns sounded from these trains. God forbid anyone get in the way of them. At two hundred miles per hour, they would obliterate anything standing in their pathway. Their rate of speed set up a vibration in the earth. In the quiet of the early morning, Siri could feel the vibration and could just hear the distant rush of wheels on rail as the train passed the nearest point to their town. The sound brought no comfort.

Something else awakened him. An urgent voice called upon the breeze drifting in the open window. *"Baptize."* He rose immediately, kneeled on the floor in the stall he'd made his home and began to pray. "Lord, I don't know if these people are ready. Don't know if *I'm* ready to pastor some flock, to lead them. I don't know if I have the words. What if…"

The word came again upon the breeze, quiet yet urgent. *"Baptize."*

Siri prayed for a while longer, accepted the word, and sought strength and wisdom. He asked for the words; the right words to help these people see. He knew that Renny was ready. They talked long hours every night. She could not read, but he read passages from each covenant, explaining, seeking to show her the truth. Would the rest of them follow her? He prayed they would.

He didn't understand the urgency of the word, why it was so important that he do this now. He recognized what had been growing for months: an underlying pull drew at his heart, and now called more clearly until the word came audibly in the breeze. "Baptize."

He could feel the stitches where Renny repaired his hernia. They pulled whenever he first got up, since they didn't stretch like the rest of his stomach muscles would. He could smell coffee brewing in the cookhouse (or what they claimed was coffee). He put on his clothes and went out for a cup, then to find the leader of this small town. He found her driving a pair of oxen, plowing the field to prepare for winter crops. He stood and watched her for a while, admiring the her finesse with the animals.

After she finished one section of the field, she stopped. He held up a cup of the brew for her and she came over to him. "Hey, Preach. What brings ya outchere so early?"

He smiled at her. "My Lord once said that we're

a lot like that team of oxen you have there. Except, we're weak and he's strong enough to pull the load for both. Unless, as Paul says, we 'kick against the goads."

Now Renny laughed. "Them people know 'bout the goads? They's a lot smart'n most today. Chu know 'bout goads?"

"Only from the Bible story about it. Show me."

"Really?" She brought the team of oxen around to face him. They were huge animals up close. "See here?" She pointed to a cross bar at the level of the oxen's legs. "Thisheer's the goads. Keeps 'em from striden' too far, from runnin' 'way from ya.   Helps keep 'em in line. That there Paul guy knew his oxes."

"Today is the first time I actually saw real goads in action. Wish I'd come out here before this."

"I sher wish ya had, too. Coulda used some hep wit' them oxes last week." She looked at Siri, and grinned. "Come ta think of it, guess ya wouldn't'a been too much hep at that. So what's doing?"

Siri sat on a fencepost. "Renny, I have a feeling. A bad one and maybe a good one at the same time."

"Huh?"

"My God spoke to me this morning."

"Thought you said he don't do that kinda thing."

"Not often, but today He did. He said I have to baptize you and all your people. As soon as I can. That means that we commit to you to guide you in your faith. And it means that all the adults in your town commit to that faith."

She turned and walked away a few paces, her back to him, looking in the direction of the town. She fell silent for a number of minutes. The breeze blew the golden hair away from her forehead. Without looking back she said, "Not sure if'n *I'm* ready, much less other folks 'round here. What's so rush? Why'nt wait fer a bit?"

Siri walked to stand beside her. He followed her gaze across the field at the town which had become his home. "I honestly don't know, Renny. See that town there? You're their leader. They look up to you. You would give your life to protect them, to keep them safe. Our leader, my God Jesus, already did that for me…and for you. Now he's asked me to do something I think will help protect us all."

"Don't see your God. Didn't hear him speak."

Siri took Renny's arm and turned her back to the field. "You plowed under this field today. You're going to plant seed here tomorrow. You can't see what those seeds will do under the earth, but you *know* that they'll come up in a couple of weeks, that they'll grow and that under this earth, potatoes will grow for us to eat through the winter. You don't see them grow, but you know it's happening."

She shrugged, but he continued. "My God is the same way. He's plowed the field. He'll water us and feed us. The ground is fertile. We're much like those potatoes. We're buried under a load of dirt, but we grow. Now, I'm not sure what's coming, but it feels like some kind of pestilence, some disease which would kill the crop before it could take hold in the soil. He wants me to help strengthen the plants — you — against it. Will you help me?"

She turned back to look at the town. A number of children played in one of the yards. She could see Jeb out working on some plowshare. Shaunte hung around Jeb, watching him closely. The two had formed a friendship. The morning sun filtered down to shine on them. "I'll ask 'em."

"But will *you* agree to be baptized? Do you want to be?"

She looked at him now. "I'm afeared a' this. All my life, heard nothin' but bad came from thisheer faith stuff. Now I seen ya here a'most a year. Don' look so scary, but sayin' yes sher makes my bones shake."

Siri sighed. "Renny, you don't know how wise you are. If the rest of us approached 'thisheer faith stuff' as you call it with that kind of fear, it might change the world."

Seventy

New Mount Pleasant. September 30: 8 a.m.

The hyper-jet was on the runway when he got there. David Saul sat, impatient, waiting for the time to pass. He thought about the pulse drive ships. The time to travel from here to Washington, DC. would be almost instantaneous. He wasn't sure he'd even want to move that fast, even if he didn't feel anything. He shook his head.

When he arrived at the White House, Peter Santiago was in the oval office, feet up on the desk, smoking. David saw reports on the exodus in front of him. "Hey, Pete. Snappin?"

"You're so old fashioned. That expression went out years ago, just about..." and the President smirked, "...the time your new girlfriend was born."

David was irked, but didn't show it. *"Should've known they would track that. Hope it covers for some of the other things I'm doing."* He changed the subject. "I see you're looking at those reports. The only city it didn't happen in is right here. Can't figure that out."

"Yeah, who cares? So what brings you up here? You like it so much down in the boons."

"Question for you. Who or what is Charon?

What have you heard about that?"

The President sat up. "Nobody's supposed to know about this, Dave. Who told you?"

David laughed. "C'mon, Pete. I have my sources! So when you gonna clue me in? I'm supposed to be your best friend and closest advisor, save for Meiring."

Peter Santiago looked at him. "Okay, Davey. But this is *only* for you…not that girlfriend. The only people who know about it are me, Gerry and the two researchers doing the work. I wanted to surprise you for your birthday, but you beat me to it. Actually, Meiring probably shaded you on it, but I know he'll deny it."

Santiago turned on a white noise filter to interfere. David realized then how critical this might become. He'd never seen the President do that in the fifteen years he'd been in office.

"As I'm sure you know, all our programs for Relief are very effective. Now even more so since we've applied the pulse system to our 'centers.' Nationwide, we're Relieving thousands every hour. However, everywhere else in the world, in those primitive areas of Europe, Asia, Africa, and South America they just keep having babies. No matter how rapidly we relieve our people, the Mother becomes more populated every year."

"Aside from the danger to the Mother, we have a practical defense consideration. It's certainly not as important, but we still must think about it. As our population voluntarily reduces itself, we'll have fewer soldiers to stand against the barbarians who keep getting more numerous. In twenty years, we'll be unable to raise an army for defense. David, you see all the defensive wars we're fighting all over the Earth now. How can we continue that with fewer people?"

"For certain...reasons, we can't rely on the police or other worker forces. They're great at following orders, but they just don't have the *oomph* to make it in the armed forces. That's why we never recruited any of the Worker Party members for the services."

"It's time, Dave. Time for us to take an aggressive stance. This will protect our freedom, relieve the Mother and free us to use resources which we haven't had access to before."

David frowned. "What are you talking about, Pete?"

Santiago leaned back. "Do you know who Charon was?"

"Some mythological figure, right?"

"He was the boatman who carried the dead across the River Styx to Hades. The agent who delivered all people to their deaths. We thought that name would be apropos for our virus."

David looked directly at his friend. "What is Charon?"

"The ultimate solution to rid our Mother Earth of the virus which plagued her for so long: from grasping, warring, destructive mankind."

"So my source was accurate. The genetic virus

will do that. A world without any human beings." He could not believe he so calmly spoke about his own death, about the death of all mankind. "Fascinating. The great thing is, it won't harm the environment at all, right? Not like all out nuclear war would. Will the virus do its job? Get everyone?"

Santiago grinned. "Pete, I knew you'd be on top of it. All the industrialized centers will be covered in the same time frame. There will be pockets of primitives deep in places like the rain forest. The nano-virus is airborne and does not degrade in intensity since it's at the genetic level. Sooner or later, those primitives will go too. It'll all be finished in less than two months." Santiago gave a satisfied sigh.

Seventy-one

New Mount Pleasant. September 30: 8 a.m.

David Saul's cube was bright with a rare clear sunrise shining through the windows. Diana Tauck let herself into the cube. She'd seen David leave and saw the destination he keyed in. He was headed to the airport, so she knew he wouldn't be back for a while. She went to the computer and keyed it on. She had installed a simple keystroke recognition program, one so old that no one remembered they even existed. She watched as the keystrokes followed David's original path. Her pulse quickened as she saw where those strokes took her…into the heart of the CDC in Atlanta. *"What's he into?"*

As Diana read, she kept shaking her head. She saw the research on this virus called "Charon." Now, she could not believe what she saw. She'd known, as everyone else did, that the programs for Relief were necessary to save the Mother, to limit mankind's growth. She approved of that. No one had the right to live so long that they taxed the resources the Mother gifted to them. But this! This would destroy everyone and right away. She looked up, staring out the window. *"Are there no other options? Are humans that bad, that we couldn't find the way to live properly on this earth?"*

She saw the lightning pattern reflecting the glowing sunrise. It looked as if the lightning were alive, striking a frozen bolt across the glass. She went to the window. Her fingers traced the lightning pattern down the glass.

What did it mean, all of this? What was life for, if everything they'd done would simply disappear in a matter of hours? If everyone, everywhere died? And David was actively working towards that purpose.

"He doesn't care at all." A tear fell down her cheek. This time it was not a false one laced with pheromones, meant to entrap. She hadn't intended it at all. This time, the tear was real.

Seventy-two

Washington. September 30: 10:00 a.m.

David Saul sat back and looked at Peter Santiago. "Here you and I are talking about our own deaths. We're so calm. Don't you have any… regrets?"

Now Santiago burst out laughing. "Oh, Davey, that's what I love about you! You are so naive. Do you really think I wouldn't protect *us*?"

"What do you mean?"

"Davey, we're not going to die. There *is* an antivirus…or you might call it that. We will institute a program of inoculation soon, to be administered to only a very few select of our leaders in Hollywood, New York, Washington and other cities. Once it's finished, we will release the virus."

"I've seen the data. It's essentially fatal for everyone."

"Yep."

"What about the animals? It's not going to harm them?"

Santiago smiled. That's the concern he wanted to hear, the care for those who deserved to live with them in this new natural paradise. "They'll all be fine. This is specifically targeted to human DNA. We finally rid ourselves of this pestilence called 'Man,' of all these huge populations."

"But won't the people left over eventually have offspring and repopulate the Mother?"

Santiago laughed. "That's the beauty of this. Let's just say for now that the 'vaccine' is going to radically alter *everything!* It'll protect you from the virus…because in many ways, you're no longer going to be 'human' at all. That's the golden ticket. We rid Mother Earth of every human being…and we survive…as a new species."

"I haven't heard about this part. What do you mean, a new species?"

"Do you remember the genetic experiments that Dr. Kerian Noguchi did on his own son, trying to create a new genetically improved human being?"

"Yeah. He failed. The kid was fundamentally autistic. Never spoke a word to anyone."

"Well, he thought he failed…and we let everyone else think so, too. With an autistic kid like that, I'm not sure why he didn't have it immediately relieved. Actually, we're glad that he didn't since there were other…developments which arose that he wasn't aware of. The upshot was, Noguchi got so discouraged, he dropped all of his research. *We* picked up where he left off. Let's just say we were…" and Santiago smiled. "…a little more successful than our good doctor."

"So we're able to change our own genetic makeup, even after birth?"

"Ahh, Davey, you're a natural reporter. You ask

too many questions. Don't worry. I've got it figured. Yeah, we'll be new men...and don't worry about dying. You won't."

"What?"

"Enough for today. Now you tell no one! Not even that pretty little thing you found in the elevator."

"You can be sure of that! This is explosive. By the way, will she get the vaccine?"

The President's voice was soft, teasing. "Oh, you really *have* grown fond of your little playmate." He looked at his friend, serious. "Now, Davey, you *know* she's not our kind. She's cute and fun and, yes, I've heard she's smart. But, c'mon! She's not really one of *us!* She's from *down there!* Looks like she's part Afram. The vaccine is *only* for the elites, for us, the purest Americans. You don't have a problem with that, do you?"

David Saul smiled. "Nah. Course not. It's just that she *is* so entertaining, as you say. Guess we all have to make some sacrifices." He smirked.

Santiago smiled. "Don't worry. You'll still have your fill of...'entertainment.' Promise, and they'll be even more fresh than she is. In fact, stay tonight! We can buzz it, have a great time, enjoy a hookon with the best from Hollywood."

David hesitated as if tempted. "Nah, I better get back before I'm missed. At this sensitive time, I don't want to raise any questions. ...You know, I can't wait for this! We finally get rid of all our concerns with one stroke. Genius! Okay, Pete. I'm on board. Whatever you need, let me know. Gotta go."

"Suit yourself."

David waved, smiled and left the oval office. He kept the smile on all the way through the various checkpoints and out until he had some privacy on the jet ride home. He could always read his friend. He did not like the answers. And the idea that Diana wouldn't get the vaccine was simply…unthinkable. He could understand the need for it, all the reasons behind such a solution. It *was* the perfect answer to save the Mother. Yet…why not save Diana too.

Seventy-three

New Mount Pleasant. October 6: 10 p.m.

The knock came at David's door, soft, seeking. He ignored it. He'd been back a week, and stayed away from Diana. Each night she'd come to knock on the door, would wait for a few minutes, then would leave. Now she continued. The knocking grew louder, then she was shouting. "I know you're in there, David! What's going on?" He could hear the tears in her voice. "Have I done something? Tell me!" He opened a one-way vid channel so he could see her one more time. Tears streamed down her face. If he didn't know better he would swear she was looking directly into his eyes. "David...please! Let me in." She leaned her forehead against the vid screen. Now her voice was a whisper. "Please..." After a long moment, her shoulders slumped. She turned and walked, defeated, to the elevator.

David Saul made himself stay still. Within the depth of his bones, he wanted to leap to his feet, to catch her before the elevator reached the floor, bring her in and hold her. Maybe if the elevators were slow or stuck, like they'd been so many times in the last months. But the elevator doors opened. Diana looked back as she entered and gave a small wave. The doors closed. "Goodbye, Diana."

He spent the week arguing with himself, debating, trying to find solace in the understanding he had of his friend's words. *"She's not really one of us! She's from down there!"*

He knew it was true. Knew she wasn't worthy of the elite status he enjoyed, which he'd taken for granted all his life. Those words didn't bring any comfort, nor did the knowledge of their different stations. All he could think of were those soft words, —so final, so easily stated by his best friend: *"The vaccine is only for the elites: for us, the purest Americans. You don't have a problem with that, do you?"*

Of course, he didn't. He had acted on those words a million times. How many did he sent to Relief with that same thought? *"They're not really like us."*

He didn't really care about those others. When he'd come back, he'd spent two full days watching as the crowded rows marched to the relief stations. They walked with joy or with resolve. Some trembled as they approached their Relief. Watching brought no satisfaction. What he saw only added to his dilemma, created more conflict. He did not like what these days revealed to him.

He had no concern about the nano-virus which loomed in everybody's future. The entire population of men, women and children could all die and go to hell for all he cared. Except one. There was just one he wanted to save. His voice was a strained whisper, and his eyes filled with tears. "Diana."

*   *   *

The elevator hit the first floor level. Diana Tauck walked out past the shadow which always waited. She knew it waited for her report; knew that, in her next words, the fate she sealed was her own. She stopped, turned to look toward the blackness which never revealed itself. *"You. Go. To. Hell."* She turned and stalked away. She could not understand why, in the midst of the pain and loss she felt, and the stabbing ache of missing David Saul, she suddenly felt better than she had for months.

*   *   *

The shadow which hid in that alcove seemed to tremble. No bodily form, no substance caused the trembling. Yet, the wavering of that shadow continued. The spirit which was once the Ishar Crull looked out from the depth of that shadow and despaired. He had failed...once again. He did not want to consider the pain of the eternal damnation awaiting him from his master. Before he *did* return to the place Diana had mentioned, he would try again. There *had* to be some other way to touch this human vermin of a man, to bend him and direct him back towards the purposes they all sought.

Seventy-four

David awoke from the nightmare, almost screaming. *He saw himself: dark with black hatred, filled with cruel lust. In his dream he was sexing Diana, but it was not the tender sharing they'd come to know. He'd been raping her, forcing her, beating at her, choking her until her face was blue. He could feel his hands around her throat, feel himself filled with absolute glee as the last breath left her body, as he convulsed.*

He sat straight up in bed, his eyes wide open in panic. His heart pounded, and a shout screamed out: **"NO!"**

David Saul looked around. Diana wasn't there. He couldn't get his heart to slow, couldn't get his bearings. He lurched up in the darkness. His breath was ragged. A pulse of lightning traced the distant sky. He stumbled to the window, placed his hand on the lightning pattern in the glass, and looked out. His hand felt the pattern as he traced it again, as he had so many nights in the past months. As it always did, the feel of the pattern beneath his fingers calmed him, helped slow his racing mind.

He could not get the last image out of his mind:

that of Diana's body — convulsed, blue, dead. *"Is this what I'll do to her? This?"* The nightmare, directed to fuel his lust for death, drove him to the opposite shore. He had made his decision. He spoke one word, now certain. "No."

Night after night, he woke screaming. The nightmare's vision plagued him, beat at his mind. It desperately sought a hold, sought to soil the resolve he found, to remind him of sexing, of using Diana's body. Words kept drumming at him. *"She's not really one of us! One of us. One of us."*

Seventy-five

New Mount Pleasant. December 24: 3:00 a.m.

She took up the shadowed place and waited —
just like the being who once directed her had waited.
The place still felt chilled, as if it could not hold heat
against the thing which once occupied this corner.
She paid no attention.

She did not know why she had come tonight. A
voice spoke to her from within her heart. It had been
months. She'd given up trying to make David see her.
He steadfastly refused, would not even speak through
the shield of his cubescreen. She'd been locked out,
the elevators locked against her codes. Tonight was
different. She knew he would come. Somehow.

The elevator doors opened and a cloaked figure
walked past her. She paused a moment, then stepped
out to follow. She walked softly. She did not want
him to know she was even here.

David Saul followed on a path he knew well;
one he'd taken many nights at this deep hour; one
which took him to a shadowed place he'd made his
own. He stood there, looking up intently at a dark
window in the second floor of a back building.

Diana saw, now, where he had come. Her breath
caught in her throat. He stood looking up at *her* room.

He stood still for long moments and watched. She saw his shoulders slump. He turned to start back toward his cube, his face clear in the light.   Tears streamed down it. He saw her and stopped.

She walked up to him, reached up and wiped the tears from his face. "I love you, David Saul. I am not sure what's driven you from me, but I will not allow you to tear yourself apart like this. Before I met you, I didn't know what love was. Now, finally I do. Let me in. Let me love you."

He stood, frozen. Seeing her, he could not make the transition from the sorrow he felt at the ending he knew would come and the joy he felt in her touch. The tears coursed down his face and his voice strained to keep back sobs. "Diana….Diana. I can't…"

She took him in her arms, held him. She felt him resist, then felt his arms close around her. His body shook against her. She stroked his hair. "It's all right. I know. I don't care, as long as I can hold you, be with you for whatever days are left. Please don't keep me away."

He held her body tight to his. This was not the way he'd felt in the nightmare that plagued him. Not the way he'd felt sexing this woman in his room. This was the fulfillment of what he'd felt that very first night, when he saw the tear running down her cheek, and reached out to her. He did not want to lose her. He wanted nothing else on earth but to hold her for all the days remaining. He trembled, now, because he knew what he would do. He would protect her.

"Diana. Come home. I need to hold you."

"No. We're here. I want you to come up to my place."

"Why?"

"I want you to meet my father."

He blanched. "I don't…."

She laughed. "Calm down. He's okay. He knows about us. And he knows how I feel about you. Besides, this place is probably a lot less bugged than yours."

Seventy-six

Summerville, South Carolina.
December 24. 6:30 p.m.

They entered the town, a train of people, horses and cattle, dogs and cats…and one wolf. There were wagons, some drawn by horses, some by a new solar power system James had created. Much of the approach to town was overgrown, choked by weeds and kudzu fueled by the GenArbor growth factor. But the roads remained, the broken concrete still held back the forest growth.

At a center point of the town, a square remained remarkably clear. Signs at the crossroads pointed towards churches. James Broddin turned to Gem. "Do you know what day it is?"

"No. What?"

"It's Christmas Eve. Let's go open up one of these churches and celebrate."

As they walked towards the churches, they heard singing from within. They looked at one another. "It can't be! People living here, worshiping this close to a major city?"

Broddin listened. "I know that music. It's a Christmas Carol by John Rutter. I've always loved his music, this one especially. Let's go up and join them."

They could hear children's voices raised in quiet joy. Instruments accompanied them. The sound drifted out through broken windows.

> *"What sweeter music can we bring,*
> *Than a carol, for to sing*
> *The birth of this our heavenly King?*
> *Awake the voice! Awake the string!"*

James Broddin's voice raised in answer with the men inside.

> *"Dark and dull night, fly hence away,*
> *And give the honor to this day*
> *That sees December turned to May.*
> *That sees December turned to May."*

The church grew silent within. Then, the young voices continued.

> *"The darling of the world is come,*
> *And fit it is, we find a room*
> *To welcome him, to welcome him."*

Broddin answered again as they walked to the doors.

> *"The nobler part of all the house here, is the heart,*
> *Which we will give him; and bequeath*
> *This holly, and this ivy wreath,*
> *To do him honor, who's our king.*
> *And Lord of all this reveling."*

Now they entered the church to see it brightly lit with hundreds of candles. A choir stood facing outward, but seeing Broddin's group enter they stopped singing. Their voices carried out through windows shattered by vandals and Ferals. A huge Afram man sat on the other side of the alter, looking at them in amazement. Then a smile came to his face. "Brothers. Welcome. We somehow knowed ya'll be comin.' Welcome to de celebration o' de Lord. You kin call me Elijah!"

Broddin opened his arms. "We come to share this place with you on this Christmas Eve. May we join you?"

"Come in, come in!" The man turned to the choir. "Chillen, sing! Sing dat song finish while our friends sit."

Broddin joined in finishing the carol.

"What sweeter music can we bring,
  Than a carol, for to sing
    The birth of this our heavenly King.
      The birth of this our heavenly King."

Seventy-seven

Washington, December 25. 9 a.m.

Gerard Meiring sat next to President Santiago. They watched the security vids, which showed David Saul leaving his cube earlier that morning. They saw the girl follow him, saw them embrace.

Meiring turned, triumphant. "You see? I told you something was off! I haven't trusted David Saul for a long time, but you wouldn't listen."

"Gerry, he's my friend."

"And look! Your *friend* is sneaking around at night, meeting this waste of a hookie, crying over her like a little boy! Is this the friend you told all about our plans?"

"Knock it, Gerry. He already knew, since you'd told him!"

"I didn't breath a word to him! I tell you, he's either gotten to one of those two idiots who are doing the research or he's somehow hacked the system! I don't know how he did it, but I'll get it out of him!"

"Gerry, calm down. Do nothing! Our plans are in place. All we have to do is give the word. What's he gonna do? He can't stop it. He can't change anything now."

"I don't like it sir."

"Gerry, you worry too much. It will only be a few more weeks for all the inoculations to be completed. Then we launch and…all our worries are over. You and I were the first to have the changes. Don't you feel it?"

Meiring smiled. "Yeah, I do. This new body is stronger. Never felt better."

"Then quit worrying over details."

Seventy-eight

New Mount Pleasant, South Carolina.
                    January 1. 12:01 a.m.

They lay together in the low light of candles, and whispered small, tender words. The light of bursting fireworks flashed across the ceiling from below, illuming their faces, their smiles with its joyful wash. "Are you sure you don't want to go out and join some hookon celebrations?"

She chuckled, but it felt almost painful. "I never want to do that again. It's only you that I want to sex, even though we're waiting. Only you I want to hold. Only you. No one else, ever again. I just wish…"

"What?"

"That I had never done those things, never knew sexing or hookons or gropes or all those other empty shades. That I'd saved it so you were my preemie. I don't know why…" Her tone was soft, wistful. She looked up at him and smiled.

He took her face in his hands. "I understand. I did it all, too. We all did. We were missing something all the time. It's why I pushed you away. I hated the hookons long before then. What I pushed against…" Now he smiled, too. "…was that when I looked in that mirrored elevator, I saw you…and I wanted nothing more at that moment than to join in, to sex you. But something pushed back against that. Now I'm glad it did. I wouldn't want that to be our first memory."

She snuggled into him. "Do you remember that very first night I came here?"

"Yes."

Now she sat up and looked at him. "I was trapping you. I had pheromones. The tears were planned, set to overwhelm you. I was supposed to sex you right then, use you. But I couldn't. When I pulled away, it was the hardest thing I'd ever done…because for the first time in my life I did something for someone else."

"Diana…"

"Can you forgive me?"

"Shh. Yes. We were lost. Now…we're found." He looked into her eyes. "Before you, I feel like I was never really alive. Before you were here, I was just… empty."

She lay back down in his arms. "We're still missing something. I'm glad we're waiting to sex 'til later, but there's some other part to this we've missed. I just don't know what it is!"

"I understand! It's like it's right in front of us, some secret waiting to be seen with the light." He looked at the window, seeing the lightning pattern upon the glass. "I only know that I love you."

"I love you, too."

Seventy-nine

Summerville, South Carolina. January 1: 12:01 a.m.

They lay together, quietly seeking the joy they'd shared in the discovery of each other. Here, soft darkness was lit by the gentle glow of the candles. No light filtered in through the thick forest. In the distance, they could hear reports. It wasn't thunder. It wasn't the sound of fighting, but of celebration.

James Broddin looked at his wife. "Fireworks. I can't imagine they would allow them. They cause so much smoke." He shrugged. "Remember fireworks? July Fourth? New Years? I never really paid them much attention. Now I wish I had."

Gem snuggled into his arms. "We were so focused. We missed so much right in front of us." She sat up and looked at him. "I'm sorry. I wish we could have seen earlier, found our way to one another. Three years lost."

He took her face in his hands. "Not lost. We had so much to work through. I'm just glad we saved the most important things…for the right time."

She chuckled, but it felt almost painful. "Do you think we could have avoided all the death and destruction if we'd listened earlier? If we'd allowed ourselves to love?"

He smiled now. "You know better than I do. Crull's hatred plagued us both. For reasons only God knows, we had to await the time's fullness, had to stand against Crull in that field outside of Cleveland. We would not have avoided that, no matter whether I accepted your love earlier than I did." He looked out of the window to see the North Star shining through branches in the dark night. "I just wish I'd known, wish I hadn't been so afraid."

"Shh. We were lost. We found each other. And, we found the source, the..." She looked out the window too. "...the North Star of our lives; our guide, our Lord who completes all that we are, who gave us Mari."

She lay back down in his arms, quiet for a while. Then she said, "Do you feel them?"

"Yes. They're close, not far at all. I'm not sure who they are, what they're doing. But they've found each other. Their love is radiant, calling out across this distance. Pray they find the rest of what their purpose is for each other."

"Will they come here?"

He took a long time to answer. "I'm not sure. I can't see." He lay back down, cuddling his wife in his arms. His heart ached for this other couple. He felt forces closing in upon them. He fell asleep, praying peace for them.

Eighty

Summerville. January 6. 5 a.m.

Roger Noguchi lay awake. The darkness of this winter morn and of the canopy high over their heads kept any light away. He was focused inward anyway, seeing patterns of logic and illogic, of being and nothingness, of the call of this community and the danger of battle.

Broddin and Gem were chosen to be here. They would stand as witness against some coming force, to protect those who made this forest and this town their own.

He did not see that calling for Grace and for him. He tried to discern some way to stay here, to live in peace. They were at peace with each other back in the Rushes. They'd had peace for an entire year in Chrisair. No one came to challenge them.

The Feds knew where they were, of that he was certain. They could not be touched and the Federal forces had learned that lesson at great cost. He also knew they would not allow this to remain, allow the existence of these people of faith to become known, or to last. He knew they were seeking a means to destroy them. He could not discern through any logic what they might be planning.

He sat up in bed, watching Grace sleep beside him. This bothered him, too. He'd brought her here and put her into the gravest danger. Was he just being selfish? All he wanted was to be with her, but a constant calling deep within held him. He shook his head. The calling was for them both. Again, he could not understand why. He just knew.

He kneeled down beside the bed. "Lord, I am not used to this: not knowing. I praise you for all you've brought into my life: for Grace, for the restoration of my family, for the gifts you've given..." He continued on for a while, then said, "Tell me, Lord Christ. What am I supposed to do? I don't know."

As he spoke, light rose from the darkness in the corner. It grew in strength until it coalesced into the form of a man and woman. "Hello, Roger."

He whispered. "Adam. Eve. Shh. Grace is..."

"I am awake, husband."

Roger smiled. "Grace. I wasn't sure if we'd have this chance." He stood and pulled her up beside him. "Grace, this is Adam and Eve, our former Artificial Intelligence computers." He gestured towards Grace. "This is my wife."

She curtsied to the forms. "Ah see yaair not as us. Ya be the created beings of this computering Rogair ha' spoken of. Now y'air like the angels. 'Tis my blessing ta meet the both o' ya."

The forms bowed back to her and spoke in unison. "You are old. You have wisdom and the love of our friend. We welcome you into Roger's life."

Roger watched the exchange. He saw that neither Grace nor the two intelligence forms smiled. "You've come to give us knowledge."

"Yes. You are almost as quick and logical as we are. The Lord instructs us to tasks. It is wonderful... and fearful. We do not see, in logic, the conclusion of what we must tell you."

"It's not good news. Tell." Grace took his hand. She took up her bow and twirled it as she stood there, an unconscious habit when she was worried.

The two forms looked at one another, then turned back. "The leader of your nation will unleash the Fourth Horseman within a short time. It will mark the end for all of your kind. The end of all goodness, of all that is worthy in this creation. From this plague there is no release. The name of this Horseman is 'Charon.'"

Roger felt a deep dread. "The Fourth?"

"The first three Horsemen — Conquest, War, Famine — have already been given free rein by mankind. These were released by your nation and others. The Fourth Horseman, Charon, the bringer of death, stands waiting."

The dread took form. He wished he could have grabbed the cloaks which shone around these beings. "Has everything we've done been for nothing? Why are you here?"

They held their hands up in unison. "Fear not, Roger. This plague may not come to pass."

Roger's hand gripped Grace's tighter. He knew, now, the pull he felt, the calling for which they were chosen. "We must stop this plague, Grace and I."

"Yes. You must go from here, to a place where they prepare the Horseman. Atlanta. A place called CDC. We know the research they have done. The Horseman is ready. Nothing can prevent or escape it once released. It cannot be destroyed except by one means. We will show you."

A virtual screen appeared next to them. "See the formulae they developed for this weapon. It is not complicated. In fact, so basic that we find it... elegant."

Roger winced. They were talking about a destructive force unmatched by any weapon ever fashioned. And they called it elegant. "Adam, why don't you simply let us do it? Let us destroy ourselves. Do we deserve to live?"

Adam looked at his friend, his mentor, the companion who first spoke with him all those years ago. An expression crossed his face which filled Roger with absolute horror. It was one of ruthless judgement; judgement not tempered by mercy. Absolute, complete. The eyes of this being of energy blazed with fire. "My love, Eve, and I debated this very issue many times. If one were to consider only what man does, then my answer must be... 'No.' Your kind does not deserve to live."

"Then why? Why not let us destroy ourselves?"

Both forms answered in unison. "The weak form of this argument uses reason as its base. If it is evil for man to kill one another, to lay waste the earth, then the answer to that evil cannot be the complete destruction of mankind. That answers evil with evil. That is the argument your fellow men make at this moment."

"What is the strong argument?"

Adam and Eve turned to look at one another and smiled. "The full answer is what we learned from your friend James when he grasped 'Lehat Chereb,' the Sword of Eden. Through that sword we came to *know* that which man takes for granted." They turned back. "Grace. You love your husband beyond all things?"

Her heart filled with joy. "Yes. Beyond all things save for our God."

"Of course. God is the source of your love. Roger, you love your wife?"

"Yes, you know that I do."

"You will sacrifice, give anything for one another?"

They answered, together. "Yes."

The two forms held hands. The light which formed them began to fade and disburse. From within that fading light came a whispered answer. "Love. That was the gift your kind gave to us, Roger. It is the reason that the answer to your question is tempered. Not that man deserves to live, nor has he since Eden's fall. But that he is *loved* by God…and he *loves*."

Tears filled Grace's eyes as she watched the light of the forms recede. The room was again dark. Dawn was still a half hour away. "Coom to bed, husband. I need to hold you. It will na' be laing befair the trials begin. This last morning o' peace, tha' is what I desire."

They lay back down in each other's arms. Roger focused on his wife: on her strength, her beauty. Yet, a part of his mind worked the logic of what he'd learned now. He knew where they needed to go; what they had to do. It filled him with fear.

Eighty-one

Summerville. February 6. 11 a.m.

Roger and Grace Noguchi stood in the center of Hutchison Square. Roger spent the last month at the foundry, working with Broddin and with Gem's father, Joe Matthews. He shared the plans for the pulse weapon with them and they fashioned it. Broddin wired the mechanisms and shaped the elements which created the break in the gravitational field.

While they worked on the weapon, Roger spent hours standing next to a wall, tossing a ball against its base. He memorized this muscle movement so that it was perfect...every time.

When the weapon was ready, Broddin said, "We really don't know if it will work, or how large the force field will be if it does. There's only a one-second delay built into the thing. Are you sure this is the only way?"

Roger looked back, serious. "I am. Adam would have told me if there were any other way to stop it."

"I don't like it."

Roger shrugged. "Some are chosen to witness. Some for...other callings. We are chosen...for this."

"But not you two!"

"Yes. We have always known that we were chosen. Both of us are...different. We see things, even more so than the sharing you have all gained through the auras. I cannot see our end...but I know we were chosen for this."

Now the entire population of Summerville stood around them. Broddin and Gem stood in front. "No one wants you to leave. Your home is here now."

Roger shook his head. "Yes, this is our home. But, this is a task that only we can take on." He saw William's thought. "And no, William. No. This is not for you. Grace will be my back."

"But…"

His voice was soft, but now spoke a command. "No."

Grace took an arrow, notched it and drew. The arrow flew straight to imbed itself in one of the elms, two feet above the ground. She looked around her at all the people who had become her family, who she loved and loved her. "I doona know tha' what we do will ha' success. Canna see it. Nay can Rogair. I tell everyone o' ya. Keep hope and pray. Should the day coom when Mari's head raiches that arrow, ya are ta take it out, fair we will no' return. We will ha' been taken to our God's rest."

They walked out of the town, headed west, just two. They turned at the edge of the forest, and looked back to where Gem and James stood. Roger raised his hand in benediction. Then they disappeared into the depth of the forests, the swamps and rivers of the lowcountry.

Gem Matthews watched, tears in her eyes. "I'm always losing him. Will we ever have peace? Will we ever?"

James Broddin wrapped his arms around his wife. "I wish I had that answer. Wish I knew where they were going, what they're facing. Can't even pray for something we know to pray for! They wouldn't tell us anything."

She felt his arms around her, but for the first time in memory they brought no comfort.

Eighty-two

David Saul sat at the computer showing Diana the back doors he had found. The artificial intelligence computer had opened those doors. He used those openings to gain knowledge, to track what his friends were doing. He'd motioned for her silence. She tracked every stroke. He showed her the progress on the pulse bombers, almost ready, and the referents to the Charon virus. The weaponized virus was stored at the CDC vaults in Atlanta. President Santiago ordered it to be held there until the bombers were fully functional. It was too valuable and too dangerous to be unguarded.

Diana read the reports on the effectiveness of the virus and paled. She started to speak, but he put his finger to her lips, stopped her, shaking his head. "Tell me about your thoughts on the Worker Party members. You said you'd been doing some research on them?"

"Yeah. They're just *weird*, ya know. Like I said before, they just don't respond like anyone else does. Go about their jobs, whether it's dockers, cleaners, repair or police work. I've watched vids of them over and over. Different workers, but they perform the same jobs with *exactly* the same motions, in the same time. They don't ever drink or play games. Never do hookons. In fact, no one asks them into a hookon either."

"Any conclusions?"

She took over the vid, cleared out of the private security feed and logged into the regular feed where they would be tracked. "I've researched back some forty years. There *was* no Worker Party at all…and no Worker Party members. You know we're all tracked from birth with our monitor code, but there are no codes related to the WP members."

"What? Let me see that!"

"See? I've tracked into the birth logs and monitor logs from the last forty years. We're all identified at birth, all given our 'marks' so we can eat, go to school, get job placement. Just part of the system." She unconsciously touched the mark on her forehead.

"This really caught my attention. Not only doesn't anyone not invite WP members to hookon. No one *ever* even looks at them closely. We just take them for granted. Well, *I looked.* They have no mark."

"That's impossible! Everyone's been given a mark."

"None of them do."

"How could that be? They're probably, what, a good fifteen percent of the population? Our leaders wouldn't allow them not to be marked. That's how everything is distributed. Like you said, it's even how we get the rations to eat."

She looked at him with a triumphant smile. "They don't eat."

"C'mon! That's crazy!"

"I've followed them. They live underground. There are sealed cubicles. They receive some kind of nourishment, but they're not eating. Couldn't get close enough. Gave me the creeps."

David looked through earlier records. The population figure was 15% lower than it should have been in every city. "Diana, any ideas?"

"I checked some much earlier records of scientific research." She looked at David, hesitated, then said, "I think they're clones. I think we've been cloning Worker Party members for forty-two years. It must be. Only thing that makes sense."

"Can't be. At one time, they'd outlawed it, but that wasn't even necessary. We could never get a human clone to be functional. The brain functions just didn't spark. The clones they made in China and Malaysia had some response function, but were never able to…." Now he stopped speaking. He thought back to the interactions with the WP members. In each case, he realized that he *never* looked directly at them, nor did they ever look at him. Further, his interactions with them were characterized by *a failure to fully function.* He'd often wondered how stupid some of them could be. He began to see an insidious logic at work in them.

"You see it, too, don't you. They don't interact, because they're *not really human.* I wonder what would happen if we killed one and examined it.

Would it even have…" She blushed.   "…the right body parts? Maybe nobody asks them to hook because there's nothing to hookon with! And, have you actually *ever* seen a female Worker Party member?"

He shook his head. "No, not that I can remember." Then a thought hit him. Now he knew how Santiago planned to keep the elite from dying.

Eighty-three

Washington, D.C. The Oval Office
                    February 6: 1600 hours.

Gerard Meiring sat in President Santiago's chair, behind the Resolute desk. Santiago lay on the floor, sprawled across the President's seal. He ground his cigar out on the carpet. "Gerry, you're sure you didn't drop a hint about Charon to Davey by mistake? He pretty much knew it all."

"Mr. President, I don't make mistakes. Especially ones like that. And, I can assure you that neither one of those assholes who developed Charon told him either." He smiled. "They absolutely swore, right to their deaths, that they never spoke to him."

Santiago raised his eyebrows. "That wise? Killing them? They were brilliant."

Meiring shrugged. "Scientists are a dime a dozen. Anyway, we've got the product ready to deliver. And the formula, though we won't need it anymore. Once Charon's released then, "No More Worries!" The Aussie accent made Santiago laugh.

"So how did he know?"

"Working on that. He has to have some deep cover access. Did he look over your shoulder when you coded in access to our files?"

"Nope. You know better. I never go into those files unless I'm alone. Don't want to slip."

"Yet, he has them. I'm gonna put a trace program to notify us if he goes into the channel." Meiring sat up and looked at his friend. "I'm sorry, Mr. President. I know David Saul is your friend, but I have to conclude that he's treasonous. Why else would he still be seeing that Tauck girl?"

Santiago looked serious. "He hasn't said anything to her about this, right?"

"No, and we've been monitoring his every word, night and day. She must have pheromoned him, cuz he's completely besotted. Doesn't even sex anymore. We can hear them laying there, just talking about how much they 'love each other.' Puke."

"What does he see in her? She's not half as sweet as some of our Hollywoodies or even some of the babes up here."

Meiring chuckled. "She *is* smart, I'll tell you that. I didn't think anyone would ever be observant enough to figure out the cloning program, but she did. In fact, I expect we'll be getting a visit from our treasonous friend soon. Listen to this." They listened to the exchange between David and Diana from earlier in the day.

"What were they doing before this?"

"Just laying there, I guess. No activity on the vids. But, you see he's letting her use his research vid. See where she keyed in to show him the programs." Meiring had to admire the girl. "Smart. Damn smart."

Eighty-four

The Fallow Lands. West of Summerville.
February 8: 9 a.m.

"Run or die!" Roger and Grace ran. They were both winded, but they didn't dare stop. They had learned things they did not want to know. Roger was nursing a gunshot wound to his shoulder. The auras were not working anymore.

A party of Ferals had attacked them as they approached the upper Edisto River near a place once known as Orangeburg. They heard no sound as the Ferals closed in. Roger felt a sense of unease, snatches of primitive thought, which he couldn't seem to catch before it was swept away in one emotion: rage.

They were making their way through a clearing. He kept looking around him, but did not see anything until the Ferals were suddenly in front of them, brandishing knives and swords. One aimed an old hunting rifle at him. Roger had not seen any humans as dark and filthy as this group since he had marched into the middle of Crull's army. Grace's arrow was notched and ready instantly and Roger drew his swords.

"Y'all kin putcher stuff down. We mightn' not

eat y'all if'n ya'll do."

"We don't want any trouble. Just passing through. We have some venison to trade."

They laughed, then attacked. Grace's arrows brought down three with leg wounds, then the force of the party was on them. Roger could feel the hate. He parried thrusts from pikes and makeshift swords, danced away from blows. He was using every bit of the Kendo craft he had learned years ago. Yet, as soon as he knocked some out, more took their place. They were being overwhelmed.

"Grace! Run!"

"Ah, cain't. There be no way!"

"Follow me." He began to run toward the western edge of the clearing, knocking the Ferals aside, the swords flashing in a constant swirl as he ran. He could see more Ferals drop from the trees and he knew why he hadn't caught any movement. They were up above, hunting from the canopy.

They almost reached the edge when he felt a sharp pain in his shoulder, and heard the shot. He stumbled, but kept going. He did not see Grace turn. She drew her arrow, ready to kill the gunman. She saw him aim his rifle at her. Then, from the forest, a wolf lunged, knocking the man to the ground. It turned and tore at his arm. Other wolves joined it, attacking the band of Ferals from behind. "Wolfie! Thank ya."

She pulled Roger up and helped him as they ran. They could hear the movement in trees above them, were afraid of what might drop on them. They kept running. "Wolfie is taking care o' some back, but we ha' ta run! Many be still coomin."

The pain was intense, but Roger ignored it. *"Run or die."* He did not know how the auras had failed. Then he realized. *"Hate. But, how could they even know me enough to hate like that?"*

They reached the river's edge and plunged down into the water as a hail of spears and arrows sailed over their heads. The swift current carried them downstream as the Ferals screamed their anger at the lost prey. They swam for the opposite shore and pulled themselves up on the bank.

The Feral party continued screaming its frustration across the river. They knew that they would be punished for losing this prey. The dark shapes which crept around the edges of their vision did not warrant failure. Those forms fed this Feral party with lust for eating flesh, for killing, for every abomination. Those forms now came into sight all around the Feral party. The pain intensified within their heads until the Feral party was screaming for an entirely different reason. "No masters! We will do better! We will go after them!"

The whispered voices became screaming commands in their heads until they all plunged into the river, trying to cross. Most drowned, unable to control their movements with the searing pain which radiated from their souls. A few made it and were driven to the chase. The whispers kept lashing. *"They must be stopped! Be stopped...be stopped...be stopped."*

Eighty-five

David and Diana stood on the edge of the pier, and looked across the harbor. The sun just peaked over the New Mount Pleasant skyline. It was peaceful. No people, no electronics allowed since this was a protected enclave. They leaned on the rotting wood of the pier.

"We can talk here with some security. Nowhere else."

She looked up at him, touched his face, but she couldn't smile. "What are we going to do about it? I approve of the Relief programs. They're needed to control our resources. But this virus will destroy everyone!"

"I don't know. Nine months ago, I really wouldn't have cared." He winced. "To be honest, if they included you as one of us scheduled to get the vaccine, to be reborn into the 'new man,' I might have been okay with that. But then they simply dismissed you, wrote you off. I started thinking."

She smiled at him now. "Back in the fall, I thought you didn't care! I knew about their plans." She blushed. "I hacked your computer. Read what you read. I thought you just dismissed me. That you *had* written me off."

He took her in his arms. "I could never do that! That's what stopped me. I loved you. That they could care so little about *you!* I couldn't live with that. It shattered my world. If they were wrong to just dismiss you, to sentence you to death with no care… well, wasn't I doing the same thing to all those people we so casually send to Relief?"

"But it's not the same…"

"Yes, it *is!* It is the same thing! I went out to the Relief Stations days on end, supposedly to watch the implementation of the pulse fields, to calculate their efficiency. I watched people walk to the stations. They were from every background. Some as old as forty-eight. Some younger. Even some children, those kids who were deformed, or didn't have enough intelligence to work their fair share. You know what I saw?"

"What?"

He looked into her eyes. "I saw *you* in every one of them. Your hair color. The way you walked. A look. A hand to help someone who stumbled. They reached out to one another, even at the end." His voice became quiet. "They were beautiful. Like you."

Her voice was strained. "Not me. I don't have the purity, the beauty within that you're talking about. It's someone else. I don't know who, but someone whose beauty rests in every one of them, of us. It's like we're all made in some image, some reflection of…something? Someone? If I only knew…"

He turned and looked out across the harbor toward a hill which glowed in the sun rising from the east. "We have to stop them. To stop it all. Stop the Relief Stations, stop the killing. We can't let them release the virus. Simply killing them isn't the answer either. Someone else will just take their place, find the same virus, and eventually we'll be right back here again."

"So back to my original question? What do we do?"

He was not happy with the only answer he could think of. He'd been over it a hundred times and had no other solution. Yet, in some way, this solution fired him, made his blood race, gave him hope. "We become what we were designed to be: reporters."

He outlined his plan in detail. She did not like how he laid it out. "We need to go together, to find a way to reach them. To convince them."

"They won't be convinced. They're as blind as I was. I *know* how blind that is. They will not change, and they don't care about any of the people."

"But, it's too dangerous for you! How will they react?"

"How can they? Once the vidfeed is out, once the people see the President, Meiring and the rest for who they really are — that they care nothing for any of us — they'll be lucky to escape alive. Prison would be too good for them, but it'll have to be. I don't even want to send *them* to Relief. Not after I've seen…" He shook his head and walked away down the pier.

She followed him. He looked across the harbor.

"If only I could *see!* There's some truth that we've all missed. I can feel it, sense it almost as if it's watching, waiting for me to turn away, to turn toward...some other path."

He looked up toward his penthouse across the harbor in New Mount Pleasant. A trick of the sun's angle showed the lightning pattern on the window pane. From this angle, the sun formed the shape of a cross upon that glass. A deep thirst within his heart resonated, yearned to understand.

Eighty-six

Fallow Lands, 100 miles west of Summerville.
Sunset. February 8.

Roger and Grace finally outran the remaining ferals. Periodically, they would hear growls and screams behind them. The wolf and his pack worked a rear action, protecting them. They stopped to rest for the night after making sure they hid their trail. Grace tended his wound with some salve she made from local tree roots. "This doona look too bad. The wound be clean. This salve helps in the healin'." She frowned. "Ah doona understand how ya could be harmed!"

Roger looked at his hand. The violet color swirled around his fingers, bright and pulsing. "I've thought a lot about the auras. When we battled the Ishar Crull and his army, a few blows with swords or other things got through. We had to actually defend against those, knock them aside, maim those people. I think *those* people especially hated us, were driven to such pure hate that it gave them the power to pierce the shield of the aura. I felt the same thing when I confronted Bill Lane at Roxford. I was pretty sure he didn't hate me enough to kill me."

Grace thought back. "Ah've seen many a battle

through our times. Ah've ne'er seen but one or two auras strong as yours — the King's an' 'o course tha' of Emrys. They could na' be touched."

"I don't have an answer. You felt the hate of that tribe. They were *driven.*"

"Ya." A chill went through her. "Ah doona know what could drive men ta such hate."

Roger looked back toward where they had been, but was seeing all of man's history. "It doesn't take much. We're inclined to murder! Yet, there are other forces, ones like Crull who feed our hate, tempt us with all kinds of things. There are forces just outside of my vision or understanding. Call them powers, principalities. That's what an apostle called them. In today's world, we've lost our belief in them."

"How could mahn no' believe? Those craitures be a part o' history jus' as Emrys or Arthur, as Patrick or the Holy Fathers or the many kings o' this earth. They be in every legend, every place. They be a part o' their awn dairkness. E'en children sense them and be afeared. How has mahn becoom so blind?"

Roger shrugged, then winced with the sharp pain in his wounded shoulder. "They have eyes, but do not see. Let's get some rest before we move on." They lay down in the dense undergrowth where they had made a hiding place.

The wolf who had followed and guarded them crawled in beside them. It was bloodied, panting and exhausted. "Wolfie! We thank ya fair the help ya brought us. We be vairry grace filled tha' ya chose us as your pack. Ah see ya ha' foun' othairs."

The wolf huffed and laid down next to them, facing the west. He waited, still guarding.

As they fell asleep, golden rays from the setting sun filtered in through the dense forest and warmed them. Those rays concentrated into a blazing light. That brilliant light formed into fourteen shapes, tall and powerful winged creatures, unheeded by man. They took up positions to defend these sleeping charges against the screaming darkness which roamed, seeking and searching.

The wolf saw, and sat up on his haunches. His eyes blazed a golden yellow, the same color as the creatures which surrounded him. He bowed his head in recognition. A low purr came from his throat. Then he lay back down among those guardians and fell fast asleep.

Eighty-seven

Washington. February 22: 11 a.m.

David Saul knocked, then walked into Peter Santiago's office. Gerard Meiring sat at the desk, watching him. Pete was laying on the floor. "Hey, Gerry. Pete. Buzzin."

"Hey old man, what brings you up here?"

David smiled and sat down on the opposite side of the desk from Meiring. "Guess you can be here, too, Gerry, since you're in on it."

"What's that, *Davey?*" Meiring did not like this man and he wasn't going to take much more.

Saul walked over to the security panel and turned on the white noise filter, then turned to Peter Santiago. "I wondered what you were talking about a couple months ago when we discussed the virus and the 'vaccine.' You were so smug. What's more, you guys both look *really* healthy lately! Probably ten years younger, each of you."

Peter Santiago smiled. "What are you saying, Davey?"

David Saul leaned back. "Just that I figured it out. I didn't want to say anything until I was sure. Been using that cute little bitch you sent after me for some work of my own."

Santiago laughed. "C'mon, Davey. We didn't send her. If I want to get you hopped up, I'll just send the best from H'wood."

"Whatever. I've been playing her. Took me quite a while. I knew she had tricks up her sleeve. Figured that she pheromoned me. Sure enough. Now we're all just 'hugs and kisses.' Anyway, you know what she's found? Your secret…and now mine! You got it. I want it."

"What's that?"

"The 'vaccine'? It's not a vaccine. You've perfected cloning! The Worker Party members? They're clones! I feel stupid that I didn't see it before this! Diana had to show me!"

"What's more, you've used some of that clone DNA to re-clone yourselves. You do it using some of the genetic material from the Worker Party members. So you're not really human anymore. That's how you'll survive the virus! I'm right aren't I? C'mon! When do I get my treatment?"

"Davey! I never could keep you in the dark for long! Yeah, we've passed the 'singularity' as they used to say. Who needs the rest of mankind, all these stupid idiots taking up oxygen? The Mother was made for *us!* For a race that deserves her. A race that will surpass anything that *man* ever accomplished! All man ever did is pollute and destroy the Mother, kill each other off and make this beautiful planet a wasteland."

"Now we will live…while all of mankind, every single man, woman and kid of that cursed race will die! And us? Finally, free! Elite. Enlightened. Immortal. And there will only be a few thousand of the elite. Who needs more? We'll have everything we need. And with all the time and resources taken care of, we can focus on peaceful coexistence, on research and fun. We'll do anything we want!"

"Pete, it's brilliant! I can't believe you kept me in the dark. It sure would have been exciting to see the first results. How's it feel? Different?"

"You bet. I wouldn't recommend you try to arm wrestle me. You say that little nothing found this?"

"Yeah. She may be just a boonie, but she's brilliant! Don't know how her path wasn't laid out for reporting rather than for hooking, but whatever. We're entitled to some errors, I suppose. So, when am I scheduled for treatments? When do I get the cloning?"

Meiring sat back. "You want to tell him, Pete? Or should I?"

Peter Santiago looked up at the ceiling, yellowed with cigar smoke and said quietly, "I suppose you should, Gerry. You get a much greater charge from this."

Gerard Meiring sat up and pulled a Ruger from his pocket. "Sorry, *Davey!* You're not getting the treatment. I'm not sure how you found out about the Charon virus, but you violated every security protocol! We can't trust you anymore."

David looked at the President. "Pete! I'm your friend! I'm the lead reporter for this nation! I have all the clearances I'd ever need! What's he talking about?"

Peter Santiago sighed. "C'mon Davey. No whining. We only had so much time for the cloning to be finished. And you were never around. If only a few thousand of us are left after we kill off the rest of mankind…well, we've had to be *really* picky. No need for reporters anymore, anyway. Sorry."

David Saul stood up and looked at both of them. "You must be stopped. Relief was one thing. That was for the Mother's benefit. But this? This is just Peter Santiago and Gerard Meiring making the world over in their image! No one will stand for that!"

"Who's gonna tell them, Davey? You?"

"Yes." David Saul reached for his comband, for the public channel. Gerard Meiring shot him in the heart. "That's for calling me Gerry." He then pulled out a second gun and shot President Peter Santiago. "Sorry, Pete. Looks like our friend killed you before I was able to stop him."

Eighty-eight

Washington, Los Angeles, Cleveland, Miami, New
Mount Pleasant
February 22: 11:15 a.m.

Everyone in the nation stood frozen, watching.
On every vid, every channel, they saw the exchange
going on in the Oval Office. David Saul had brought
a simple transfer device which unscrambled the white
noise filter and reissued it on the public emergency
channel. Vid and voice testified. The people saw and
heard with clarity.

They began with amazement that they could see
what was going on. Amazement quickly changed to
anger as they heard the exchanges, heard the
President's plans for them. Then shock when Meiring
shot David Saul and the President. The shots were
like physical blows to each person watching. The
President, dead? Was this fiction? Entertainment?

The scene faded to a reporter, a pretty young
girl. She was crying openly, and struggled to control
her voice. Her words and manner convinced the
people that what she told them was true. "Diana
Tauck reporting. What you witnessed today is the
greatest betrayal of our nation and the Mother. We
have all heard with our own ears the treasonous

plans of Gerard Meiring, who must have influenced our great President Santiago…and has now killed him along with our lead reporter" — Now her face twisted in agony. — "David Saul. Bring him to justice! Stop Gerard Meiring! Stop these people who call themselves the Elites! Stop the cloning! Save mankind!"

The people responded. They did not need to guess who were the "few thousand" selected to be saved. They knew. An impulse rose within them, a revulsion against those they admired as special, as above them. Those people were rounded up, killed, or forced out of the portals. Some were marched right to the Relief Stations, protesting all the way.

*   *   *

Gerard Meiring locked the door to the Oval Office, then opened a channel to the CDC in Atlanta. "Get me the head of security." Several minutes passed before the man came on line.

"Took you long enough."

"Sir, we are under attack. Two persons have breached the unit and are making their way down toward the vault. We can't seem to stop them! We're trying! I'm in the vault now, protecting it."

"Release the virus. We hoped to release in a coordinated manner, but that's now become impossible. We need to stop these madmen. Release the Charon virus and get the hell out of there as soon as you do! You'll be okay."

"Yes, sir." The man was trained to follow orders without question. He'd been given this special duty as a reward for serving the nation with distinction. He called his buddies in the unit. "Get out of here now." He hung up the phone and made his way down toward the high security vault.

Gerard Meiring smiled and hung up the phone. "Well, that takes care of that. Might take a little longer, but we'll shift blame to the CDC, call it an accident. More than one way…" He walked out of the Oval Office. A detail of the President's Secret Service stood there, guns drawn on him.

"Put the gun down, sir."

"Soldier, get in here, quick! The President's been shot! I think he might be dead."

"Sir, put down the gun! We saw you shoot Mr. Santiago."

He could not register what he heard. Gerard Meiring looked around the room now, and saw monitors, saw the interior of the office he had just walked out of. He saw the stupid little Tauck woman standing at the microphone in that stupid backwater city of New Mount Pleasant. Saw the tears running down her face.

Meiring heard her tell what a great man David Saul was to sacrifice his life for his nation. He brought the gun up to shoot himself. A volley of shots from the Secret Service did the job for him.

Eighty-nine

Atlanta. CDC. February 22: 11:15 a.m.

They raced down the stairs. The elevators were blocked, the emergency defense measures working. They fought the soldiers at ground level and disabled them. Roger was shocked the stairwell doors were actually open.

They kept going down and down. The vaults were ten stories below ground. Not enough if the virus were released. *"Release! Relief!"* He would be overjoyed if he never heard those words again.

Roger kept moving, Grace behind him. No soldiers guarded the landings. There should have been men here. They reached the final landing and burst through the door. The door to the inner vault was propped open. They could see a soldier standing at the controls. He had coded the venting to reverse, to flush all the virus out of the room instead of keeping it in. His back was to them.

"Stop!"

The soldier turned, his finger on a red button. It was Torgeson, the man James Broddin had released a year before. He smiled. "More of you shining people? I'm sick of you all! Of everyone. I told that Solaris I'd kill you all eventually! This'll be the best way!"

"Wait!" Roger stopped at the vault's entrance. Torgeson paused. "Just listen a minute."

"Why? We're damned. Cursed anyway!"

"Don't you love anything?"

Torgeson's face twisted in rage. "Loved my country. They lied to me! Used me! Screwed me over! Let my buddies be killed by *you!* Now that bastard Santiago wants to kill everybody! Maybe he's right. Do the job for him." He turned and punched the button.

As the virus was disbursed, a passive door system, designed to prevent any such release, began to descend.

The pulse weapon had been simple to fashion. It was just as "elegant" as the genetic nano-virus which would destroy everyone. Effective and clean. Trouble was, it destroyed everything within its radius. Everything. And no one knew how wide its radius would be. If the radius were wider than the vault, Roger would never know. He and Grace would simply cease to exist within a nanosecond. He had been praying all the way down the stairs.

Roger activated the weapon and bounced it into the vault just as the falling door slammed shut. He took a deep breath. There was no sound, no thump, no explosion. Only a slight vibration. He could not hear Torgeson's scream through the walls.

Death's Door, the vault which held all of the world's deadliest viruses, including Charon, the Fourth Horseman, simply winked from existence. The structure surrounding it began to yaw, to collapse upon itself. Roger turned to Grace. "Run!"

They raced back up the flights of stairs, feeling the walls begin to shake as the floors above began flowing into the void. The stairs gave way, and they felt themselves being sucked down toward the abyss.

Ninety

New Mount Pleasant. Five years later.

Diana Tauck stood at the portal which opened out onto the RavNational Bridge. There were cameras all around her, shooting vid. Crowds gathered around her to hear what she said. Well-wishers threw her garlands of flowers. She looked at the throngs of people and wished that David Saul could have been here to see. These people were hungry for truth. They had been manipulated, lied to for so long that truth rang bell-like to them. They heard it and clamored for more.

She stood, looking at the cameras on this cool, clear spring morning. "I do not know if my quest will find the others, if they'll be friendly or violent, civilized or brutal. Don't know for sure how much radiation is left, if it's deadly or not. I only know that we need to see, to understand who is left. If there is anyone, how we might aid them and them, us. I'm going out to find the truth. I will report back to you, the people — because *you* were made to lead our nation."

As she turned, the cheers of the crowd flowed out and across the river. She walked through the portal and across the bridge. Her comband showed no extreme levels of radiation. The first hurdle passed, she turned and gave a thumbs up to the crowd.

No crew followed to film her. She simply carried her comvid camera to mark her journey. "You'll see what I see. Follow me on my vids. We're explorers in a New World." She walked on across the bridge, down to its end, then turned west toward Summerville. They had heard that a thriving community lived there. "This is for you, David."

Ninety-one

Summerville, South Carolina, United States of America

James and Gem Broddin lay together swinging in a hammock, as the summer sun filtered through the trees. Children ran in and out. Many of those children glowed with auras of every color, brilliant with joy. They sang as they played. James Broddin thought of an old folk tune which told of a city where children played: *"Conquering, singing, laughter ringing, voices raised in the song."*

He remembered this scene. He had seen this day in his first real dream. He did not know how long the peace would last. He could only hold onto it, pray that it did.

Tomorrow was Sunday. Father Thibidault, newly ordained by Richard Solaris into the priesthood, would celebrate his first Mass. They would have riotous singing, old spirituals and new, traditional carols and joyful songs, clapping and dancing. They would again thank God for all His blessings upon their community. They would keep the Sabbath, rest and commune with one another, sharing in all they produced.

Robert Yellow sat at a picnic table, talking to

Scott Thibidault about his writing. He worked to make copies of his Testaments, that others might learn the truth of the events regarding Gem Matthews, James Broddin and Roger Noguchi in the last decade.

The day he finished the first copy, a young boy, Shaunte Williams, appeared and asked to take one to his small farming community in Kansas. "Father Siri told me some of this, but I want to read it for myself and share it with the others." Many more copies were carefully made by hand.

Before he left, Shaunte asked for Roger, his face betraying a deep worry. "Is he here? I can't really feel him."

Robert Yellow's face fell. "No. No one knows what happened. We've heard nothing. We can't feel him either, or his wife. I'm sorry."

Richard Solaris sat at a table near James and Gem. Wolfie sat at his feet. The wolf had returned to Summerville a few weeks after he had followed Roger and Grace towards Atlanta. From the day he returned, the wolf would not leave Solaris's side. The two hunted together and defended the community.

Occasionally, Solaris would look across the square to the tree where an arrow was still embedded in the bark, two feet above the ground. Mari had grown ten inches beyond that mark, but no one would remove the arrow. They still hoped and prayed.

Scouts still kept guard for the community against some of the evil Feral tribes. Those Ferals would try to raid near the community, to pick up anyone alone, kill them. A constant battle of small skirmishes went on, but most had given up long ago and gone away. They had seen no attacks in months

Other Ferals found a peaceful life within the Fallow-Land canopy. They visited and traded fruits for meat and vegetables. These tribes ceased to speak years ago, preferring the safety of silence in order to avoid the electronic listening of the satellites. However, they sent their children to learn from the two priests and from Robert Yellow. To learn history and science and faith. Often, they would come to the Sunday Mass and sit, signing the forms and prayers.

As the sun peeked through the trees, the community heard the scout's whistle. Someone was approaching, but it wasn't deemed dangerous. Gem and Broddin, Yellow, Solaris and Thibidault, looked at each other. "Who could that be?"

They walked toward the edge of town. As they arrived, they saw a young woman approach. She was alone, but she seemed to be talking to herself. "… coming near to this town. I'm not sure what reception I'll get. David would have loved to see this, to experience this kind of reporting, to let our citizens, our nation learn the truth of who they are, of who we are. About to make contact."

Gem Broddin stood in front of the group, her aura blazing green, the color of the forest surrounding them. She smiled. She could not feel any bit of guile or of falseness in the woman.

Her smile faded, though, as she saw deeper to the loss, the grief held within. Tears came to her eyes, and she walked out to greet the woman. "I welcome you, Diana Tauck. I know your loss and nothing I say now would be a salve for it. Yet, come in. Find peace. I think you'll find what you've sought all your life."

The nation watched as Diana Tauck walked into the town of Summerville, seeking the truth. She found Him there and she found peace.

Epilogue

The man sat on a stool with the forest as a backdrop. The morning sun lighted his face for the comvid camera unit which they used to record him. He wore his faded Army Ranger fatigues with the insignia and name tag on the front. He looked directly at the vid as Diana Tauck silently gave him the count, then he spoke.

"My name is Robert Yellow, born Robert Grey. I am an historian. I speak to you today to testify to the history of the last decade, which I recorded in this Testament of The Chosen and in The Gem Testament. I was a direct witness to much of what happened throughout this nation and the world. Or, if I did not directly witness, I have recorded the testimony of hundreds who did witness to the truth of this history."

"The National Authorities either deny that these events happened, or have created explanations for them that do not reflect the true causes and reasons for the things to which I testify."

"This testimony is being recorded in all media to be published throughout the Digital Underground. It is to be hoped that some form of these words will remain for future generations to hear."

"I speak about these events as any historian

does, in the hope that those in the future who hear me will understand the history and the errors which lead us to our nation's current crisis. I also hope that those who hear this may find the faith and the trust to rebuild, to rediscover what we lost."

Robert Yellow sat straighter. "I also testify and openly confess to you today that I copied these Testaments on paper. Further, I have personally distributed those paper copies to numerous communities throughout this nation. I realize that these actions are in direct violation of recent Federal Regulations against the use and distribution of paper products and fully confess my guilt of these violations without duress."

"I testify that I alone did the copying and distribution and that no other persons or organizations assisted me in this action in any way. I will not reveal either the communities where I distributed the paper copies, nor will I reveal the names of those to whom I presented them."

"I have taken this action in case all forms of electronic communication cease to function, so that a form of these Testaments will be preserved."

"This is the record regarding Gem Matthews Broddin and James Broddin, Roger Noguchi, Richard Solaris and others. I am Robert Yellow and I am chosen to witness."

"He that hath ears to hear, let him hear."

About the Author

Joseph Stringer writes and speaks on Christian issues in the current culture. His prayer is that all who read his works might see through them to the One who has chosen us for life.

Stringer's other works include: *The Ten Commandments for Business, Alien Nation*, a children's illustrated book, and the first book of the trilogy: *The Gem Testament*. His works have been published in various venues and are available on Amazon.

The U-Pick Farm, published in early 2014, is a delight for children from ages 2 to 12. Read it to them and they'll insist you take them picking.

These novels are set in America in the near future. Stringer is not sure if these books, first envisioned in the 1980s, are fantasy or prophesy.

Watch for upcoming releases:

The Fallowers: Where will Gem and Broddin's calling take them? Peace will not come to a world torn apart by hate and rebellion.

The Ten Commandments for Life: A reflection on how the Ten Commandments direct us to lives filled with grace and love.

God Came Down. A meditation on the reality of Jesus Christ in this life and in our own lives.

Contact the author at: **www.chosen4life.org**
May God the Father, Son and Holy Spirit, bless us and remain with us all the days of our lives.